A Rocky Recovery

A Rocky Rollins Mystery

by Gioya McRae

Mocha Mind Communications

I0629767

Publisher's Note

ISBN 979-8-9903264-0-8 (Paperback)

ISBN 979-8-9903264-1-5 (E-book)

Book Cover Art by Bia Shuja

For information address:

Mocha Mind Communications

Montclair, NJ 07042

https://gioyamcrae.com

info@gioyamcrae.com

Published by Mocha Mind Communications

DEDICATION

This book is dedicated to the angels who helped me in this journey, my mentor Valerie Wilson Wesley, my ever-supportive sister Giselle Montague, and my friend of half a century Adrienne Glover.

ONE

I sat on the front porch in my cheap wicker rocker and leaned my chin on my bony knuckles. I stared at my quiet Newark, New Jersey street through tear-filled eyes. I lived on a tree-lined street in the neighborhood of Paradise. We sat comfortably sandwiched between the Fairmount and University Heights sections of Newark.

Many condemn Newark based on news reports of robberies, murder, and other chaos. Truth be told, Newark, like any other big city, has some good, some bad with many miles of ordinary between. I rarely hear sirens in my neighborhood and never gunshots.

Except for a few sullen teens, my neighbors seemed friendly. We knew each other by face, if not name, and waved our greetings. We lived quiet lives in modest well-kept homes. The smell of barbecues fills the air in the summer. Both kids and adults engage in snowball fights on frosty days. From time to time, a family will throw a party but they either keep the music low, or turn it up and invite the neighbors. All in all, Paradise was my haven.

Since my divorce from Holy the junk man, I did temp work, babysat, mowed lawns, and took odd jobs. So far, I managed to squeak by on my bills. But my last temp job ended two months ago, and all the other work seemed to dry up at the same time.

Today, I returned home from an unsuccessful day of job hunting. I threw my mail on the table and started toward the kitchen for a comforting snack, but something caught my eye. I shuffled through the envelopes of junk mail and bills and stopped at a yellow envelope. There's something about bad news mail that stands out. Sure enough, the envelope displayed my bank's return address. I debated on enjoying a glass of soy milk, and an Oreo, before I opened the envelope, but decided to face the bad news. I dropped my handbag on the floor and tore open the envelope. Big, bold lettering declared I had seven days to pay three months of back mortgage, or my cat Murphy and I are out. I dropped the envelope on the floor and forgot about my snack. If I don't get some money soon, I will lose the one thing that allowed me to keep my dignity and independence.

The letter was signed by Mr. Hartness. Mr. Hartness and I had had many discussions, some heated, some humble, about my late payments. I had nicknamed him Heartless. He had no empathy about the rising cost of cat nuggets or Corolla repairs. His one focus was collecting that mortgage. In the past, I had begged, cajoled, yelled, and cried through our tête-à-têtes. Nothing moved Hartness except cash.

I had met Hartness in person only once. I hand-delivered a mortgage payment to prevent him from evicting me the next day. That day I raced into the bank seconds before closing time. The startled guard, who was locking up, pointed out Mr. Hartness. Hartness' appearance astonished me. He had intimidated and berated me on the phone, sounding like an ogre. In truth, he stood at 5'7", 150 pounds. Fluorescent lights bounced off his balding head and wire-rimmed glasses. I couldn't reconcile my mental image of him with his actual appearance and almost laughed in his face. That meeting lessened my fear of him but the dread of losing my house remained. Since then, we danced a financial two-step of pay up and fall behind.

I craved money. I dreamt of opening an abandoned suitcase and cash spilling into my lap. I wanted to know how it felt to live in abundance, debt-free. I didn't have big dreams of traveling to Bora Bora or owning wild, exotic animals. I just wanted peace in my heart and home.

My home was everything to me. Secure and comfy, Murphy and I have settled into our lives. If I lose my home, I'll lose everything I've fought for in my divorce from Holy the junk man. My independence would vanish, along with the little dignity I had left.

A lone tear rolled down my cheek and cleared my vision long enough to spy my neighbor wobbling up my path. I sighed. I didn't think it possible to make my day worse until now.

I had met my neighbor Elustria "Lusty" Magoo when I married and moved into Holy's house. In fact, Holy had purchased the house on her recommendation. I never knew how they connected before becoming neighbors, but I have my suspicions. I liked Lusty. I just needed to be alone with my thoughts.

I never saw much of Lusty during my marriage. But after the divorce, Lusty would sway her 5'6", 300 pounds over to my house to check on me. At fifty years old, she wore big hot pink sunglasses and thick blotches of makeup on her pale white cheeks. And no matter what the weather, she topped her dyed red hair with bright turbans.

I opened the door and invited Lusty in. We settled at the kitchen table, and I shared my pain. "I've been searching all day, but nobody's hiring a woman with a high school diploma whose only job was in a junkyard. I can't even use Holy as a reference. He'd like to see me out of work. He thinks I'd crawl back to him for help." I opened a bag of Oreos.

Lusty took a cookie and said, "I know how you could make some quick money on the side."

I gave her a sideways glance and raised an eyebrow.

Lusty rolled her eyes and said, "Not working with me."

Lusty was a phone sex operator. That's right. She backed up her voluminous body with the sexiest female voice this side of the Rockies. Even I'd get tingly listening to it.

Lusty said, "I heard through the grapevine there's a lady in town who needs someone to find some items." She snagged a napkin from the holder and laid more cookies on it.

"Do I look like a detective to you?" I said.

Lusty's grapevine stemmed from her clients' other needs. She would recommend anything from porn movies to local mechanics. Lusty gave good all-round customer service. She'd say, "My referrals add to the overall experience, and I don't even charge extra for them."

Lusty folded her ham hock arms over her chest and said, "You don't have to be Sherlock. You sound like you need money now."

I shook my head. "I wouldn't know the first thing about finding stuff."

Lusty said, "It's a repo business. What you need to know?"

I said, "Doesn't repo mean you steal cars from poor people?"

Lusty put her head in her hands and shook it. She looked into my eyes and said, "Get your head out of the box."

I screwed my eyebrows together, as I tend to do when I think, and said, "Do you mean 'think outside of the box'?"

Lusty groaned. "Whatever. She needs someone to retrieve rare items. Her late husband sold them and never got his money. So, she wants them back."

I thought for a moment and shook my head. "I don't know anything about the repo business."

Lusty waved a dragon-nailed hand at me. "How hard can it be? My friend used to repo stuff. He gave me three steps. Find the person who stole the goods; bring the merchandise back; and get paid."

"But how do I know who the item belongs to?"

Lusty rolled her eyes. "Do I have to tell you everything? Get a bill of sale or something."

I furrowed my eyebrows to the point of pain this time. "I guess that makes sense."

"What kind of items are you talking about?"

Lusty smiled. She said, "I believe she said some antique phones. Someone bought them from her late husband, but never paid for them. She wants them back."

"I don't think so, Lusty. Thanks anyway."

Lusty huffed. "I don't know why you're looking for work. You have entrepreneurial chops like me. Think about it. The only long-term job you've had was working with your ex at his junkyard."

I shrugged. "That's work experience."

"Really? You hauled boxes and did whatever he told you. He's didn't teach you any skills you could use in the outside world."

I said, "We both thought we'd have that life forever. I didn't realize how hard getting work could be."

Lusty waggled her finger at me. "You've been fired from or quit every job you've had since. You're not meant to work for anyone else."

She had a point there.

Lusty said, "Remember that customer service job you had at the wig factory? What happened there?"

I said, "I told a lady she'd look better if she shaved her head."

Lusty said, "And you got fired. What about when you worked at the car wash?"

I said, "The guys kept pushing me in the water, so I'd have a wet tee shirt."

Lusty said, "The owner had to call the police to break up the fight. You're lucky you didn't put out that guy's eye with the Armor All."

I said, "I worked pretty well at the pet shop."

Lusty said, "You quit that one."

I said, "I had no choice. A lizard crawled into my pocket and scared the crap out of me. The owner accused me of stealing, like I'd want that creepy creature. I quit before he could fire me. I had to think of my reputation." I sank back into my chair. "You're right. I'm pretty useless."

Lusty raised an eyebrow and smiled. "You're looking at your situation all wrong. My point is you have the spirit of a business owner. Start your own enterprise."

I couldn't hold my head up. I sat in silence staring at my coffee mug.

Lusty gave a sly smile. "You could sell some of your shoes."

I sucked in air. Lusty had hit me in my heart.

My mom had worn stilettos every Sunday to church. She'd slip on her fancy heels as her last act before we left the house.

My dad would say, "You shouldn't wear party shoes to church."

Mom would ignore his grimace, click clack to the car and stand there, arms folded, until he opened her door.

It amazed me how she could defy the man who controlled my every move. I vowed that one day I would stand up to him, too.

When Mom died, I stole as many pairs of her stilettos as I could and hid them in my room. In his grief, Dad didn't miss them. Manolo Blahniks, Jimmy Choos, Pradas...you name it, I had them. I kept those shoes and when I grew old enough, began building my collection around them. I'd never be a glamazon like Mom. But when I slipped on a pair of Louboutins or Ferragamos, I absorbed my mom's fierce independence. In stilettos, I stood, shoulders back, head held high. I need them to survive.

Lusty wiped her mouth and pushed her way out of the chair. At the front door, she said, "Or you could go crawling back to Holy for money. I'm sure he'd enjoy that." She started down the steps. Her slow pace allowed me to catch her.

I ran down the steps and said, "Wait."

Lusty smiled, displaying dazzling white dentures between grinning red lips. Visions of circus clowns danced in my head. She said, "That's what I thought."

The next morning, I drove through the stately oasis of the Forest Hill section of Newark. I admired the well preserved, quiet neighborhood filled with historic homes and landmarks. The luxurious landscaping amid the quiet, dignified atmosphere exuded money. Even the birds chirped in perfect harmony. I came to the right place.

I swiped my forehead with the back of my hand and hoped I didn't sweat through my blazer before meeting the client. The morning sun beamed streaks of killer heat. I parked in front of Mrs. Depew's Victorian home, wishing I had washed my dusty car. Maybe she wouldn't peep out the window. I clicked my Stuart Weitzmans up the stone path, rehearsing my introduction.

The white lace curtains fluttered as someone peeped out of the bay windows.

Before I could ring the bell, the door swung open. I craned my neck to peer into the face of a hulking man. I flashed a bright smile and stuck out my hand. "Hi I'm..."

He jerked his head toward the foyer which I took to mean "Come in."

I trailed "Lurch" down the hall, taking two steps for each of his long strides. Following his 6'5" frame reminded me of driving behind a tractor trailer. You can't see the signs or traffic lights. You drive by faith, hoping to reach the right destination.

As we walked down the long hallway, I glanced to each side to glean pieces of my client's personality. Flowers and lace thrived in abundance here. Elaborate, gilded frames displayed oil paintings of flowers and other still lifes. White doilies covered gleaming mahogany side tables that smelled of lemon oil. Ivory statuettes posed atop the doilies awaiting admiration. I examined the mauve and gray oriental carpet, and slammed into Lurch's solid back. Without a word, he stepped aside. There sat my client.

"Hello. I'm Lilac Depew," she said.

A minuscule woman, Mrs. Depew, sat suspended delicately in a motorized wheelchair. An oscillating fan fluttered her gray curls. Her tiny, sneakered feet barely reached the footrests. Even in this stifling heat, she covered her legs with a pink and white crocheted throw. She wore a white cotton blouse with a high ruffled neck and an exquisite ivory dolphin necklace. She seemed to be the kind of woman who had always taken great care with her appearance.

Mrs. Depew said, "Welcome to my home. My husband spent most of his time in this sitting room." She tugged at the ruffled cuff of her blouse. "I see you've met my nephew, Ernest."

I glanced up at him but couldn't tell if anyone was home behind those hooded eyes.

Mrs. Depew gestured toward a wingback chair. I sat and Ernest hovered behind me.

I decided to start out on the right foot. "That's a lovely necklace Mrs. Depew."

She touched it with a delicate hand and said, "Thank you. Perry gave this to me on our first wedding anniversary. We had honeymooned in Senegal. While there, we went on a boating excursion and watched wild dolphins in the ocean. Their beauty touched us. He bought the necklace as a remembrance of that trip. In return, I gave him a cane with a dolphin handle. But I'm sure you'd like to get to business, Dear. My late husband, Perry collected rare items." As she spoke, she turned and smiled at a huge portrait of a scowling, fat man sitting in an antique throne-like chair. His hands perched on the cane she had described.

Her eyes misted as she clasped her hands to her heart. She gazed so long, I expected to hear harps and trumpets, and see angels float down on sunbeams.

I cleared my throat. "Mrs. Depew, I understand you want me to retrieve some rare phones?"

Mrs. Depew frowned at me. "Oh no, dear. What I want are rare bones."

I gulped. "Bones?" My body chilled at the memory...

The first few years with Holy had been fun. Life with him floated from bed to his junkyard and back to bed. I worked with him in the junk business he inherited from his father. Under his direction, I helped customers, answered phones and moved crates.

I had a lot of fun until the day we found the skeleton. Often at junk yards, people unload their crap in the middle of the night. They think we won't notice it among the other garbage. One morning we rolled in and found an old, locked trunk in front of our gate. Holy broke the lock revealing a black garbage bag. He ripped the bag exposing a human skeleton.

Holy took the situation in stride.

I, on the other hand, lost my mind. I had never seen a human skeleton, except in a museum or a book. Alarm bells rang in my brain. "What the hell is that?"

Holy shrugged and said, "Bones."

"It's more than bones; it's a flipping skeleton," I said.

He reached in, cracked off a foot and grinned. He turned to me with slitted eyes, resembling a Cheshire cat. I backed away. I had seen that expression, always before he did something annoying or embarrassing to me.

I said, "Now, Holy..."

Holy crept around the trunk.

I kept my distance. We circled the trunk as if performing a ritual to bring the skeleton to life. My boot caught on something, and I fell into the dirt.

Holy raced to me and danced the skeletal foot on my chest.

I threw up. My blood turned to ice making me shiver, and I threw up again.

After that incident, I approached boxes with caution. The skeleton had taken the fun out of the job, but Holy took it as a bonus. He sold it to a couple of college kids who thought it would be a great dorm mascot. Go figure.

I shook off the recollection and stood to escape. "I don't think I'm the person for this job." A meaty hand clamped down on my shoulder and pushed me back into my seat. My eyebrows ground together as if in battle. Since Ernest stood behind me, I panted and searched the room for another exit.

Mrs. Depew said, "You misunderstand, Dear."

"I must be going now." I stood again and stepped away from the chair before Ernest could touch me, but he stepped in front of my path.

Mrs. Depew pointed a delicate finger at me. "I want you for this job. Mrs. Depew pointed a delicate finger at me. "I want you for this job. A dear friend of Perry's recommended you."

Had Lusty serviced every man in town?

Mrs. Depew said, "Please forgive me. I cannot recall the name of your business. Do you have a card?"

I made a quick note to rectify that situation. "Rocky Recoveries, Ma'am. That's what I'll call this...I mean that's the name of my business." I rifled around in my handbag, hoping they couldn't see through my charade. "I'm sorry. I gave out my last card yesterday." I felt crappy, lying to a little old lady like that. "Mrs. Depew, why don't I find someone else to help you?" For a flash, that seemed like a great business idea. I could earn a fee finding jobs for other people. A second later, I realized I couldn't find a job for myself, let alone others. *Back to reality.*

"I will pay you handsomely. I must insist you take the job." She gestured toward a roll top desk.

Ernest moved toward the desk, clearing a path to the exit, and I took it.

I click-clacked down the hallway to the front door and onto the porch with Ernest close on my heels. I held onto the iron railing as I descended the steps so I wouldn't trip and fall like a bimbo in a horror movie. I jumped in my old Corolla and sped down the street, leaving Ernest standing on the sidewalk.

TWO

I rounded the corner and swung to the curb. I tugged my blazer off my sweaty arms with relief. The Corolla's air conditioning had been on the fritz but the breeze from open windows cooled my arms. As I drove, I thought of excuses to give Lusty for turning down the job.

I could say I had a better offer but that would lead to an interrogation. Where did you get another job? What will you be doing? Would you get more money? I could say I wasn't feeling well. Lusty would slap her hand on my forehead and declare me healthy. Would I even be able to look her in the eye? I'm not the best liar. I turned onto my street with no solutions.

In truth, I needed cash, even though we never discussed my fee. I hadn't given any thought to how much Mrs. Depew would pay me. She appeared to have lots of money but that didn't mean she would part with it. I read that rich people stayed rich by holding on to their cash. I should have waited to hear how much she would pay. She might have insulted me with a paltry amount. Then, I could have refused the job with dignity. Instead, I darted out of there like my ass was on fire.

I arrived home to see Lusty waiting for me on my porch, meaty hands sitting atop round hips. I inched up to the curb in front of my house. My mind spun trying to weave together words that didn't sound like excuses. I pulled my blazer from the back seat where I'd thrown it during my drive. I slowed my steps to delay the confrontation. If I had seen Lusty sooner, I would have driven past my own house. My eyes darted left and right, seeking escape. My shoulders sagged as I accepted my fate.

She said, "Have you lost your mind?"

I gave her my most innocent smile and said, "What you mean?"

Lusty held up a rhinestone encrusted cell phone. "Mrs. Depew called me. She said you burned a hole in her rug, racing out of her house. What the hell is wrong with you?"

Adrenaline still quivered through my body from my fright. I lowered myself into my wicker chair and said, "She wanted me to find bones. Can you believe it, bones?"

Lusty rolled her eyes. "Not bones, you idiot. Statuettes, ivory statuettes. Sometimes people call ivory bone."

My mouth hung open as I stared at Lusty. "That's not what she said."

Lusty said, "You didn't give her a chance to explain. My reputation is at stake here."

My eyebrows started up again. *Her reputation? Is she kidding?* "This isn't about you. This is my job."

Lusty tilted her head and raised an eyebrow. "Oh, so now it's your job. Does that mean I can call Mrs. Depew and let her know you'll be returning?"

I looked at my feet. "No. I don't have the heart for this kind of business. I need to rest. I'm sorry, Lusty."

Lusty shook her head and sighed. "I'm trying to help you. Let me tell you something. If you had the heart to put up with Holy all these years, you can run this errand."

When I didn't respond, she took me by the shoulders and said, "I have more faith in you than you do. I know what it's like to doubt yourself. You have to make the life you want. Once you realize you deserve the best, you'll fight for it."

What could I say? I didn't have the chutzpah to make it on my own.

Lusty released me and lumbered down the walk. She glanced back at me with disappointment in her eyes.

I shook my head and rose to go inside. I needed a nap and a pound of chocolate. A bright orange sticker pasted to my front door stopped me in my tracks. It read "Three day notice to quit these premises." My throat went dry, and I forgot to breathe. My seven-day grace period had shrunk to three. Lusty had time to plod all the way back to her house before I could react. I turned and said, "Hey, Lusty."

I waited in Lusty's living room while she called Mrs. Depew to promise my return. As soon as she hung up, her cell jingled. From the kitchen, I heard Lusty "Uh huh, uh huh. Sure. I have just the person for that."

Lusty returned to the living room, grinning. "Guess what? I've got you a second job. It's a quick pick up and delivery nearby. Do you want it?" She ran down the details.

I stopped home to freshen up before venturing out. Murphy watched me refresh my melted makeup and change my long-sleeved blouse to a tank top.

I shared my thoughts with him. "I'm going to do the latest job Lusty gave me. Then, I'm going to cancel the bone job with Mrs. Depew."

Most people have a good angel and bad angel that stand on their shoulders and battle their instincts. Hopefully, the good angel wins, and you do the right thing. I, on the other hand, have a Shitty Kitty. She usually comes out when I want to do something mischievous, and I don't want any interference. Sometimes she gets me in trouble, but she backs me up when no one else will.

Murphy approved of my plan. He rubbed against my leg, leaving comfort and orange hair. I grabbed my lint brush and swiped my pants leg. I said, "After all, if I do the second job well, Lusty will forgive me for not doing the first job. Don't you agree? I know it's a little sneaky, but this should work. I want Lusty to keep sending me referrals." I looked down. Murphy had disappeared.

The new referral took me to University Heights, a neighborhood dominated by colleges. A goth girl wearing thick black eyeliner and matching lipstick waved me down in front of her dorm. She held a cake box tied with red cord.

I hopped out of the Corolla and said, "Are you waiting for Rocky Recoveries?"

Goth girl snapped her bubble gum and nodded.

Her sullen expression meant I had wasted my enthusiasm. I took the box and popped it into the trunk. I said, "Thanks for the job. I had another offer, but yours appealed to me more."

She blinked at me, showing her first signs of life. She said, "Do you mean you skipped another job for me?"

I smiled and said, "I sure did." This should impress her, right?

The girl put her hands out and said, "Give me back my box."

I thought I heard wrong. "What? Why?" I handed her the box and closed my trunk.

She said, "You passed over some downtrodden person for a more lucrative job. I suppose you would do the same to me given the chance. What a capitalist move."

I opened my mouth to explain but didn't know what to say. I had taken her job to avoid another. How could I explain a fear I couldn't truly identify?

Before I could manage a response, Goth Girl started calling up to her dorm and waving students down. Goths streamed from the building and gathered around us. The girl said, "Down with capitalists; down with greed." The others joined in, chanting her protest. They loomed closer. I jumped into the Corolla and drove off, leaving the growing protest behind.

I now had no choice but to take the Depew job. I hoped Lusty wouldn't mention the campus job to me.

Mrs. Depew smiled at my return. We sat in the elaborate sitting room. "My late husband invested in antiques. On our honeymoon, Perry fell in love with the ivory carvings displayed in Senegal. That's where he acquired a large shipment of rare ivory pieces. He sold a collection of these pieces to one of his clients."

I said, "I see. But if your late husband sold the items, they no longer belong to you." I squirmed in the wingback chair.

The oscillating fan blew gusts of lemon-scented hot air through the room.

Mrs. Depew wrung her tiny hands. "The customer received the shipment but never paid for the items. That's not fair. Wouldn't you agree?"

I nodded. I had no idea what questions to ask so I winged it. I said, "Do you have proof the customer didn't pay?"

Mrs. Depew gestured towards Ernest who grabbed a sheaf of papers from the roll top desk. He handed them to her. Mrs. Depew shuffled through the papers, settled on one and handed it to me.

I squinted at a faded handwritten invoice for $300,000 for a collection of ivory statuettes.

Mrs. Depew said, "Perry tried to reach the buyer numerous times."

I could see dates and times scribbled on the invoice.

Mrs. Depew nodded at Ernest. He shoved more papers in my face, the original bill of sale and certificates of authenticity. That satisfied me.

I said, "I can't make out the customer's name."

Mrs. Depew said, "I can't read it either, Dear, but I do believe the invoice says Charles something."

I cleared my throat, hoping to sound business-like. "Mrs. Depew, why aren't you taking a legal route like suing for the items' return?"

Mrs. Depew looked down and shook her head. She reached under her throw, pulled out a lace hanky and dabbed her eyes. "We tried, Dear. The police didn't have enough evidence to catch up with him. I've never seen him in person, so I couldn't even give them a description. The house at the address on the invoice is abandoned. We're at our wits' end." She waved a hand towards Ernest.

I glanced up at Ernest, uncertain if he had any wits.

He stood immobile.

I said, "What about your nephew? Could he help me?"

Mrs. Depew began to wring her hands again. I thought she might rub them raw. She said, "I need Ernest by my side night and day. He's the only one I trust to take care of me."

Ernest showed no reaction to a conversation about himself.

I glanced from one to the other.

I said, "Do you remember the name of the detective on your theft case?"

Mrs. Depew's shook her head, and her lower lip began to quiver.

I blinked rapidly and averted my gaze. "Okay, I'll do the job." I wanted to give her a reassuring hug but that would have been unprofessional.

Mrs. Depew said, "Are you sure Dear? Your help would be a blessing." She tucked her hanky back under the throw, her eyes now dry.

I wanted to promise I would return her statuettes or her money. I wanted to champion her.

Mrs. Depew handed me a slip of paper bearing Ernest's cell number. "You can text any questions or updates to Ernest. I don't have one of those fancy phones."

I cleared my throat. "Mrs. Depew, we haven't discussed my fee." I assumed she would toss me a number. I hoped the money would pay at least one month's mortgage, but I would take any amount she offered. I held my breath and waited.

We sat in uncomfortable silence a few moments.

Mrs. Depew splayed her hands. "Well, Dear, speak up."

My eyes darted about, scanning the expensive furniture, carpet, and drapes. The artwork looked valuable, but I was no connoisseur. I didn't want to bid too high and price myself out of the job. A lowball estimate could reveal my inexperience. I clenched my hands and gave her a number. We agreed on the price for my services (which I totally guessed at).

I rose to leave when Mrs. Depew said, "When will you return with our merchandise?"

I blinked. I had no idea, but I hoped I could find it quickly. I had only three days to pay my mortgage. That meant I needed to find the statuettes, get paid, and pay the bank in that time frame. My ego wanted me to say "tomorrow" but I didn't want to start my business with false claims. In some strange way, I wanted Mrs. Depew to be proud of me. Who knew what future work would come from this job? I said, "In a day or two." That would satisfy both our needs. I went on my way.

On my way home, I called Lusty. I recounted my experience. "I wanted you to know I'm on the job. Thanks for the referral."

Lusty said, "You said you found her nephew intimidating?"

I said, "Yeah. Even though Mrs. Depew did all the talking, Ernest stood nearby listening to every word. He's a scary guy, kind of threatening. He never leaves Mrs. Depew's side like he's controlling her."

Lusty said, "How could he control her if she did the negotiating?"

"I don't know. He could have told her what to say before I got there. Also, he was the one who kept me from leaving during my first visit."

Lusty said, "But you left anyway, right?"

I said, "It was more of an escape. There's one more thing. Mrs. Depew gave me Ernest's cell number to text updates. He must be the man in charge."

"Some older folks don't have cell phones. That's not unusual."

I scratched my head. "But what I don't understand is why Ernest didn't contact you himself, not that I've ever heard him speak."

Lusty splayed her hands. "Because Mrs. Depew knew me through her husband. I didn't even know she had a nephew. You're making something out of nothing."

I said, "She knew you serviced her husband?"

Lusty said, "Of course not. She thought Perry and I were friends. That's all."

I heard a phone ring in the background.

Lusty said, "I've got work to do."

I disconnected with questions rattling in my brain. I put my crazy thoughts behind me and started forming a plan of action. The sooner I got the job done, the quicker I'd save my house.

I'd have to build my nerve to track down thieves and steal back merchandise. I should have started a mattress testing business. I would have made a great professional donut taster. But those jobs are scarce. What have I gotten myself into? I've made such a fuss about being independent. Now I have to find a way to do that.

THREE

I thought I would go home and put together a statue stealing outfit. Oops, did I say stealing, I meant retrieving. I would start my investigation at the abandoned house. Maybe the thief had stashed the statuettes there. I could search unchecked crevices and knock on walls to find hidden rooms. I shivered. That sounded like something out of a murder mystery.

Half a block from my house I got a sinking feeling. Yes, there sat Holy's red truck. I thought about turning around and making good my escape, but Holy could hang out for hours waiting for me. He reminded me of an unwanted plant you tried to kill by withholding water for months. Then you give it a test drop of water and it perks right up. I braced myself and pulled up behind his truck.

Holy had hunkered down on my porch. He jumped out of my rocking chair and ran down the steps to greet me. He gave me a big hug.

I squirmed away and crossed my arms. "What's up Holy?"

Holy grinned. "I brought you something special, something you can't live without."

I mouthed the words 'you can't live without' as he said them. Every time he brought me a piece of junk from the yard he said the same thing. I said, "What is it this time? I'm really tired."

Holy gave me his sad puppy eyes that I had long become immune to. I told him a million times to stop bringing me crap. It did no good. In fact, he'd use any excuse to be a part of my life. Holy's actions invoked feelings of pity, sweetness...and annoyance. He said, "Why do you have tape on your door?"

I spun around in horror only to remember I had snatched off the eviction notice. In my traumatized state, I had left bits of tape. I said, "I let some kids advertise their yard sale."

Holy's presence reminded me how I had gotten into this predicament. Holy had controlled our finances, so when I divorced him, I had no money for a lawyer. He got the business, the bank accounts, our new truck and the junk. I thought he felt sorry for me when he surrendered our little house to me. Then the letter arrived.

Soon after the divorce, I opened the mail to find an overdue notice from the mortgage company. Without my knowledge, Holy had mortgaged the house to buy his shiny red truck. I have been playing catch up ever since. I'd pay up, then fall behind, pay up, fall behind. A never-ending pattern that still existed.

Now, I hurried him along. "What did you bring me?"

Holy said, "Can I come in? I haven't seen Murphy in months."

I refolded my arms across my chest. "You hate Murphy. You've always hated Murphy."

Holy tilted his head and batted his baby blues. "But now I miss him."

I said, "Not a chance. Let's see what you have in the bag." We sat on the wicker loveseat. Holy opened a wrinkled paper bag and pulled out a cell phone.

"I have a cell phone, Holy." I started to rise.

Holy pulled me back into the seat and said, "This is special. It's not a cell phone, it's a stun gun."

I peered closer. It sure looked like a cell phone. Based on Holy's past gifts, I had no faith this would work. I snatched the phone from Holy, held it to his arm and pressed a button. I awoke on my living room sofa to Murphy licking my face.

My vision cleared to the sight of Holy sleeping in my favorite armchair. His dirty boots rested on my coffee table. I got up, tottered over to Holy and kicked his feet off my table. I overestimated my strength. My knees wobbled and I fell to the floor.

Holy shook off his sleep, picked me up and sat me back on the couch. He leaned in and said, "Are you okay?"

I slapped the crap out of him. Satisfied with the loud crack of my hand on Holy's cheek, I dozed off with a dreamy smile on my lips. I re-awoke alone. The stun gun lay on my table with a note that said, "You were holding the gun backwards."

I shut my eyes and plunked back onto the sofa, exasperated. I awoke to a dark house. I pushed up on my elbows and wiped my crusty eyes. My aching muscles creaked to a standing position. I shuffled toward the kitchen in the hopes of finding chocolate ice cream. Armed with that and shoe magazines I could fortify myself for the night's venture. Let the pity party begin. As I approached the kitchen, I wrinkled my nose. A stench like spoiled eggs hit me in the face. I shook my head. *Not again.*

I stumbled into the kitchen. Murphy, the fattest orange cat in Newark, lay prone on the floor in front of my open refrigerator door. How he could nap, surrounded by torn food packages and spilled soy milk amazed me.

I had adopted Murphy a year before my divorce from Holy. I had stepped on a tiny ball of orange fluff in our backyard that turned out to be Murphy. He's been retaliating for the last three years.

Holy had spent the last year of our marriage swatting at Murphy and pushing him out of the house, saying he ran away. Many mornings I would open the front door to find Murphy waiting for his breakfast.

In six months, we noticed something unusual. Murphy gained weight whether I fed him or not. After long days at the junkyard, we'd arrived home to find Murphy's food bowl still full of cat nuggets. Yet Murphy grew rounder every day. At first, we couldn't figure out this mystery. Then one day we returned home to find Murphy ravaging the refrigerator. He had managed to open the door and grab my leftover salmon steak. The fish lay on the linoleum. Even in my anger, my mouth salivated for that salmon. Murphy shut the refrigerator door with his fuzzy butt. He licked his lips, picked up my salmon and dragged it down the hall to eat in privacy.

Holy said, "See? I told you I didn't eat your cheesecake."

After our discovery, Murphy didn't bother to hide his travels into the refrigerator. He would leave the refrigerator door wide open. I used to believe he was thumbing his nose at Holy, but he does it to this day.

I sat there, hungry, tired and broke. I glanced at my Felix the Cat clock with the swinging tail and rolling eyes. It read 8:30 PM. I might have to do the unthinkable, have dinner with Dad.

I swathed myself in black, black biker pants and T-shirt. I stuffed most of my curls under a baseball cap and slipped into some Jimmy Choo stilettos. I looked cool like Catwoman on a bad hair day.

I pulled up to my father's neat brick house and stared at the manicured lawn. A single row of those cabbage-like plants lined the front. I sighed. *I could snatch the cabbages and run. After all, I liked cabbage, didn't I?* Too late.

My father, Daniel Rhodes (Don't say it. Yes, my maiden name was Rocky Rhodes.) swung the front door open and called out, "What are you doing out there? You're working my nerves. Your food will get cold. It's been on the table for five minutes." He stood there, waving me in like he was standing at the shore, and I was being chased by Jaws.

I formed a semblance of a smile on my lips. I checked the rear-view mirror to be sure I didn't grimace.

I visited my father on rare occasions, like his birthday, Father's Day, or Christmas, when guilt would hurt more than the actual encounter.

Dad had fixated on me after my mother died. He watched my every move and dictated my life. Dad's draconian rules added to my high school miseries. He didn't allow after school activities, boyfriends or phone calls after 7:00 PM. No wonder I remained friendless through my school years. I reached a point where I hated school and loathed home. Of course, I had escaped to Holy.

My father ushered me inside, slammed the door and dragged me to the dining table. The rush of the cool air soothed my skin but not my nerves. My hunger fought my knotted stomach as the aroma of a home cooked meal enveloped me. A plate heaped with baked chicken, brown rice with gravy, and a pile of green veggies big enough to feed a cow awaited me.

Dad circled me, scanning me over from head to foot. He said, "Why are you dressed like a ninja?" He looked down. "In heels."

I pulled my lips into a smile and said, "I felt like a warrior tonight."

My father pulled out my chair, and we sat opposite each other.

Despite my tension, I drooled with hunger. I grabbed my fork, only to have Dad snatch it out of my hand and slam it back to the table.

He said, "What about grace? Didn't we teach you to say grace before a meal?"

As the gravy congealed, I said, "Sorry, Dad." When Mom was alive, we said grace at each meal. Once she passed, Dad's prayers lengthened into sermons letting the food cool on the table. On my own, I said grace most of the time, albeit a quick one like "Thanks for the food, God."

Dad lowered his head and embarked on a long prayer. I snuck a few forkfuls of rice before he finished.

We ate in our usual uncomfortable silence, broken only by talk about the weather. Miles Davis played in the background. I gulped the food without savoring the warm spices like I wouldn't get another bite for a month. I needed to fill my belly, but I also wanted to escape before Dad could delve into my life. If he thought I needed him, he'd launch an intervention to change my life in major ways. I had lied my way into dinner by saying I wanted to see how he was doing. I knew I employed an obvious ruse, but Dad would grab any chance to dig into my life.

Dad and I played a game of hide and seek about my life's details. He tried to find out what I'd been up to, and I didn't share a thing. We engaged in this contest each time we met. So far, I have been winning.

To stave off any questions, I posed one of my own. I said, "Dad, why don't you ever talk about your parents?" I usually saved this topic to bounce our conversations from my personal life to his own. I couldn't take the chance of blurting out something about a repo job.

Dad's relationship with his parents remained a mystery to me. He and mom never spoke about my grandparents on Dad's side. I took this annoying diversion to allow me to exit the meal without delay. Dad would release me without question. I often wondered if I had kids, would I talk about Dad?

As expected, Dad rolled his eyes and kept eating without a word. That worked for me.

As I scraped the last veggie from the plate with one hand, I grabbed my handbag with the other.

Dad glanced at his watch. He said, "So, you're running out again. Fine. It's time to call my friend anyway."

I paid him no mind. Good. He had a friend, someone else he could focus on.

I had forgotten my usual Tupperware bowls. Not to worry. Dad had loaded containers with enough leftovers to last me until the next family meal. I threw them into my trunk and took off.

I drove to the address scribbled on the invoice. It, indeed, looked abandoned. I parked a few doors down to throw off suspicion, although I doubt anyone on this street cared.

The silent street made my skin crawl. The click-clack of my heels produced the only sound. Every third or fourth house had boarded windows. I gave the high bushes a wide berth to avoid any lurking ax murderers. The occupied homes had their blinds shut tight. Not one soul walked the street. I reached the house. I crept up the weedy, cracked sidewalk and climbed the rickety steps. At this point I realized my Catwoman costume sorely lacked gadgets of any sort. How would I get through the door?

I searched for an unboarded window. Of course, there were none. Moonlight and a stench led me to a junk pile at the side of the house. I pulled my tee shirt over my nose. The moonlight highlighted peaks and valleys of the heap, but nothing more. Stupid, stupid, stupid. Why didn't I bring gloves? For the first time in years, I wished I had those filthy work gloves I used to use at the junkyard. Twenty minutes later I had picked my way through the pile. I found a biohazard bag, nipple tassels, a raccoon carcass and an urn marked 'Aunt Kitty.' Nothing useful. I almost gave up hope when my synapses kicked in. I traipsed back to my car and rooted around in the trunk. Voila. I yanked out my tire iron.

Back on the porch, the flat end of the tire iron slipped between the door and frame. I counted to three, shoved and fell on my face as the unlocked door swung open. Catwoman would have died of shame.

I got up, choking on the dust. I tested my fingers one by one to be sure they weren't broken. *Good to go.* I squinted my eyes against the darkness and took a tentative step. Something brushed over my Jimmy Choos. I let out a scream that should send people rushing into the streets. Rats. I hate rats. I put my hand to my chest to calm my thumping heart. I refused to be this pathetic. I peeled my shirt neckline from my damp body and fluttered it for air. Sweat rolled down my back, making me shiver. I scrounged around in my Catwoman pockets. On my key ring I found my treasure, a penlight. I pushed the button and, low and behold, light.

The floorboard creaks echoed in the cavernous rooms. The thin light beam guided me through each first-floor room. My toes tentatively tested the floor for debris. No more face-plants for me. I reached a scarred wooden door. The hinges squealed as I dragged it open. I shined my light into the opening. A rickety stairway led down into the depths of the house. No way would I go into a basement. Basements are spooky.

So far, I haven't found anything, no papers, no mail, and no statuettes. I decided to tackle the second floor. A towering flight of steps covered by a worn flowered runner led me to the second floor. I almost lost my penlight in a coughing fit as I kicked up dust on the steps. I turned left on the second landing and entered a room. I swung my penlight around, illuminating about one square inch at a time. My tiny beam landed on a huge steamer trunk sitting in the middle of the floor. A sheet of yellowed paper was adhered to the top of the trunk. I leaned close and read it. It was a copy of the handwritten invoice Mrs. Depew had given me. Eureka. I had found it.

I did a little jig in the middle of the floor. This was the first good thing to happen to me in weeks. Too exhausted to dance for long, I got back to work. A thick padlock secured the latch. I hustled downstairs and found my tire iron by tripping on it. I wiped my hands on my shirt which did little to dry them. I tucked the tire iron into the padlock and yanked. My hands slipped and I plunked to the floor. Ten minutes of pulling and tugging. Nothing. Dust choked me as I panted in exhaustion. I raised the tire iron and whacked the padlock. This sucker was on for good. I had one option; take the trunk to the client.

I jostled the trunk and heard a dull clink-clunk. *Why are the statuettes clinking? Wouldn't expensive ivory pieces be bubble wrapped or something?* I pushed the trunk with all my strength. It moved an inch. I had long been out of the habit of lifting heavy boxes. My current fitness initiative entailed watching exercise videos while eating ice cream. It took fifteen minutes of back breaking labor to push the trunk to the head of the stairs.

I got in front of the trunk, braced my entire 5'3", 105 pounds, grabbed the worn handle and pulled. My clammy hands slipped off of the handle. My chokehold on the banister prevented another fall. I wiped my hands on my pants and grasped the handle again. Tug. The trunk clumped down one step, another twenty to go.

I rolled my eyes to the ceiling and said, "Please, God, a little help." A drop of sweat rolled down my eyelid, stinging my eye. My shirt stuck to me like a second skin.

Tug, clunk. Creak. I froze. *What the hell creaked?* I listened in the dark for a few seconds. Nothing. *Note to self: don't have a heart attack before getting out of here.*

I sucked in gritty air and gagged. *How is it possible to be so dry on the inside and drenched on the outside?* I leaned against the grimy banister. It wobbled. I almost plummeted down the stairs.

I took another step and a creak sounded from the floor above. What the hell was that? Not one breeze flowed in the house to swing a door. A running

23

rat wouldn't be heavy enough to creak the floor. My adrenaline peaked with the knowledge I had company.

I released the trunk. It stayed in place, wedged against the step. I tiptoed to the upper floor. I didn't know why I bothered. I had been making enough noise to wake the dead. Whoever shared this space with me, knew I was here. I clicked my pen light on. I said, "Who's there?" I swept the landing, my light illuminating an inch at a time. I said, "I won't hurt you." Who was I kidding? No one would believe my weak attempt at bravado. Creak. I turned toward the sound and screamed.

A sallow-skinned, skinny man with a dirty beard and pock-marked face stood inches from me. He swayed and leaned against the wall. His ragged tee shirt and jeans reeked of urine and sweat. I held my light out like a gun and said, "What do you want?"

The man pushed off the wall and staggered past me, down the steps. He steadied himself against the trunk with one hand. The trunk clattered down the steps with enough fanfare to wake the entire neighborhood. The man somersaulted down the stairs, crawled onto the porch, got up and wobbled down the street.

I limped down the steps, opened the door and gulped the fresh air. I prayed the statuettes hadn't broken in the fall. I stood for a moment surveying the neighborhood. The blinds were still shut, doors were still closed. How unique, neighbors who minded their own business. I could get used to this.

I eyed the gargantuan trunk. *I hope this job doesn't kill me.*

A half hour later, I bungeed the trunk into my car trunk and drove away.

FOUR

Mrs. Depew and Ernest were at her front door when I arrived. I had called ahead with the news that I had found their merchandise. She looked happy and so was I. My fee would be enough to cover my back mortgage and support me for another two months.

With relief, I watched Ernest hoist the trunk out of my Corolla and carry it into the house with little effort. *Mental note: bring muscle on next job.* I closed my trunk, noting the smashed remnants of leftovers and styrofoam from my dinner with Dad.

Ernest deposited the trunk in the middle of the sitting room, and we all gathered around it. Mrs. Depew smiled and wrung her hands, though I didn't understand her worry. Her troubles were over and so were mine.

I said, "Well, Mrs. Depew, I delivered your merchandise." I puffed out my chest and grinned. Rocky Recoveries had triumphed in its first job. Also, I had done what the best people do, undersell, and over deliver. I had beat my estimated time frame to return the statuettes. Lucrative jobs would line up at my door. I had secured a bright future. I stood there smiling, hoping she would get the hint and pay me so I could go home and collapse.

Mrs. Depew said, "I think we should open the trunk first to see what's inside."

My voice rose an octave as I said, "A copy of your invoice is stuck to the top of the trunk. What else could it be?" I attempted to cross my arms but a twinge in my bicep defeated me. I tapped my foot on her Tabriz carpet.

Mrs. Depew said, "We want to be sure."

A hot shower followed by aspirin, chocolate, and bed, awaited me. Meanwhile, these two were holding up my money. I lowered my tense shoulders and smiled. "That's fair. Do you have any tools?" I would have addressed that question to Ernest, but I didn't even know if he could talk.

Mrs. Depew covered a yawn with her delicate hand. "I'm very tired, Dear. Could we do this tomorrow?"

I said, "Is it possible to tie this up tonight?" I pointed to the trunk. "We're here. The trunk is here. Let's finish our business." I smiled my encouragement.

Mrs. Depew smiled up at Ernest and said, "Please show Rocky out and take me up to my room."

Ernest loomed over me. He gestured toward the front door and stepped closer, blocking my view of Mrs. Depew.

My last vestige of energy collapsed. Without another word, I left.

Back home, I made tea while Murphy listened to my myriad of rationalizations. "I arrived late at night. No wonder Mrs. Depew was tired. If I had the forethought to bring tools, I could have opened the trunk myself. Better to acquiesce than to argue with a wealthy client. I could wait one more day for my money. It's not like I could pay my mortgage tonight. Right?"

Murphy rolled over and went to sleep, giving me the attention I deserved.

I drank a large mug of chamomile tea to quiet my thoughts and induce slumber. I dreamed of hundred-dollar bills floating from the sky.

First thing in the morning, I called Mr. Hartness at the mortgage company.

He answered the phone in his usual curt tone. "Hartness here."

I smiled through the phone. "Good morning Mr. Heartless...I mean Hartness. This is Raquel Rollins. I want you to know I'll make a payment this week. Will you please note that on my account?"

Hartness said, "Are you paying all of the back mortgage?"

I giggled. "In fact, I am." I waited for applause. After hearing nothing but Hartness tapping on his laptop, I said, "I'll be in touch."

Hartness said, "Fine. Keep in mind, I cannot stop the eviction if you don't pay. Got that?" He sure knew how to kill a good mood.

I said, "As usual." I disconnected before he could steal my joy.

Beaming with anticipation, I returned to Mrs. Depew's. As I parked, I realized the early hour and hoped she was up. As much as I wanted my money, I didn't want to disturb her. I waited on pins and needles for signs of life, then decided to text Ernest. I pulled out my phone and looked up in time to see Ernest at the front door.

Ernest bent to get the newspaper. He spotted me as he rose and waited. He escorted me to the sitting room where I found Mrs. Depew without her usual smile. She sat in her wheelchair, wringing her hands more than usual.

The opened trunk sat in the same spot where I had left it. Inside, lay a rotted torn canvas sack filled with rocks. A faint minty smell exuded from the trunk, contrasting the dusty contents. My mouth dropped open and my heart sank. "What is this," I asked. My stomach tightened to the point of nausea.

Mrs. Depew said, "This is what we found when Ernest opened the trunk. As you can see, these are not my ivory statuettes. I need you to keep searching."

I stood there for a moment gawking at Mrs. Depew, then Ernest and back at the trunk. I had two days to pay my mortgage and had no clue what to do next. I gave myself a mental kick for not insisting that we open the trunk together last night. For all I know, they could have pulled a switcheroo on me. Words failed me. If I offended her, I'd never get paid. I felt duped. "Mrs. Depew, I know this is your trunk. Maybe that Charles guy switched the goods. What do you expect me to do about that?" The words rushed out like I had sucked on a helium balloon. My hands flapped about like I was waving down planes.

Mrs. Depew's eyes widened. "You don't expect me to pay you for rocks. Do you?"

Ernest stepped closer and hovered over me. His hot breath toasted the top of my head. The blood drained from my body.

Mrs. Depew had a point. If I were her, I wouldn't pay for something I didn't order. Like when I ordered a pair of Louis Vuitton pumps and received a pair of size thirteen men's sneakers.

I tried another tact. "Mrs. Depew, would you consider paying me half my fee to cover my expenses to date?" I had no idea where this strategy came from, but I hoped it would work.

Mrs. Depew said, "What expenses have you incurred?"

I had no answer. What could I say? Gas, mileage, labor? Also, Mrs. Depew had much more business experience than I did. She would want a written invoice before she paid me. My eyes rolled over the rich interior of the Depew home. The place exuded money but didn't fill my empty pockets.

Mrs. Depew shrugged. "You should get started, Dear." She waved a hand toward the front door.

Ernest placed his huge hand on the small of my back and propelled me down the hallway, matching me step for step. He shoved me out the door and slammed it closed behind me.

While driving home, I reviewed the developments. I beat my hands on the steering wheel in frustration and confusion. Was there something I could have done to protect myself? We didn't have a written contract. I hadn't had the forethought to create one. Then again, Mrs. Depew had a written contract with Mr. Charles, and she never got paid. I could have asked for half the fee up front. At least, I'd have some money in the bank. I wanted to trust Mrs. Depew but my Shitty Kitty voice, the one I often ignored, told me something was off.

When I arrived home, I stopped by Lusty's house.

Lusty ushered me in and hustled back upstairs to finish a client call.

I followed her up to use the bathroom. I emerged from the bathroom just as Lusty said, "Okay, Spicy. I'll talk with you soon, bad boy."

My cheeks flushed and I dashed downstairs and into the kitchen. I didn't want any details on Spicy. I distracted myself by scanning the room.

Lusty loved pink. She had painted her rooms in various shades of hot pink, coral, fuchsia, peach and salmon. Shiny objects accented every table and shelf. Her kitchen appliances could blind a person. *Where the hell do you buy a hot pink microwave?*

When Lusty returned, we sat at her kitchen table, Lusty's favorite spot, while I gave her the update.

Lusty listened with patience while popping cream puffs into her mouth. She nodded in all the right places, so I knew she was listening. When I finished, she licked chocolate off her fingers and asked, "So what's your next move?"

I shrugged my shoulders. "I guess I have to start asking questions, sort of like an investigator." I figured I had watched enough Columbo to know what to do. I could be clever and sly, and I loved puzzles.

Lusty said, "Whom are you going to question?"

My blank expression said it all.

Lusty said, "See if you can track down that Charles guy on the invoice."

I grimaced. "I have no idea how. Besides, people aren't going to answer my questions. They're going to tell me to get lost."

Lusty huffed. "Use your femininity. Be nice to people. Smile. You're a naturally sweet girl. People will respond to you."

Lusty's impression of me contrasted my self-view. I thought I was obstinate and a bit cynical.

I said, "What if that doesn't work? People are skeptical these days. They don't talk to random people."

Lusty splayed her hands. "Add a little pressure. Get tough like you have the authority to question them."

"I don't have that kind of power. People will laugh at me."

Lusty said, "You need a badge or something that gives you permission to interrogate people."

I waved off the suggestion. The image of me flashing a badge made me giggle.

Lusty said, "Now let's look at motives. If someone took the statuettes, they'd want to get paid for them. Maybe Mrs. Depew wanted to get paid twice for the same merchandise. Where would she sell them? Let's make a list. If you find the goods, you may be able to trace them back to her."

We ended up with a list of high-end pawn shops, auction houses, and collectors. Lusty added one independent contractor who, by her description, sounded like a low-life fence. I crossed him off the list. Satisfied with a sketchy plan, I rose to leave.

I wanted to start my investigation first thing in the morning, but I had another worry. I had lost a day and only had two more days before Murphy and I would be eating our Friskies on the pavement.

Satisfied with a sketchy plan, I rose to leave.

Lusty said, "Before you go nosing around in people's business, take some precautions. Get some mace or something for protection. Also, keep your phone charged and keep me in the loop. I know you're independent and all, but I need to know you're okay. Got that?"

Lusty's orders bristled, but also comforted me. Everyone needs someone to care about them. I said, "No worries. Holy gave me a stun gun."

Lusty closed her eyes and clasped her hands in prayer. She said, "I'm gonna pray for you. Holy should know better than to give you a weapon."

I laughed to hide the memory of stunning myself.

Lusty said, "Speaking of prayer, how did Holy get his name? There's nothing spiritual about him."

I said, "When I met Holy, he told me he got his nickname by being the best altar boy in church. A whole year had passed before I realized people had been calling him 'Homely'. By then I had acquired the habit of calling him Holy and it stuck."

Lusty laughed until tears rolled down her cheeks, making rivulets in her blush. "Now that makes sense."

I turned to leave but Lusty took one look at my face and pulled me back into my seat. She said, "What's wrong?"

I scanned my list of leads. "This assignment may take me longer than I thought. I need to make some fast, sure money."

Lusty tapped one pastry-filled cheek. She said, "Well, I do know someone who needs something retrieved."

I said, "I don't have time to start a new adventure. I need something I can do and get paid for sure now."

Lusty said, "No investigation necessary. All you would need to do is pick up the item and bring it to them. No drama."

My eyebrows inched toward one another. I said, "If it's that simple, why don't they just pick it up or have it delivered?"

Lusty wiped her mouth and said, "It's a large shipment."

I was missing an element. "Why don't they get a U-Haul? Exactly what is the item?"

Lusty said, "He said he needed to move some horns. He wants someone he can trust to move them to ensure they are not damaged. They must be valuable."

That made sense. So Lusty agreed to arrange the pickup for the next day.

I thought Lusty's auction house suggestion was promising. Back home, I went online and searched for auctions in the Newark area. A proliferation of auctions for property, jewelry, sports memorabilia, comic books, and fine art popped up. I narrowed my search to fine art and found a public auction happening that day.

I had never been to an auction, but it sounded fancy, so I dressed up. I put on black dress pants and a silk blouse and strapped on my black Louis

Vuitton heels. The auction was held in a Victorian house. A greeter took my contact details and handed me a catalog and a number card.

I entered a large room packed with people seated in rows of chairs. I took a seat near the back of the room so I could leave after my purchase without disturbing people. No air circulated in the hot, stuffy room. People fanned themselves with their number cards. Sitting on the aisle gave me little relief from the heat. Attendees pointed to items in the catalog. They conversed with their partners in hushed, secretive voices. A couple seated in front of me bickered about the price of a painting.

A bell chimed and the auctioneer went to the podium. The stately, gray-haired man wore a tailored navy suit and a bow tie. He studied the audience with an air of superiority. All conversation ceased. He waved his hand, and a young man brought the first item to the podium. The oil painting in a baroque gold frame reminded me of the art hanging on Mrs. Depew's walls. The auctioneer started the bidding at $1,000. I watched in fascination as the bidding rose in increments of $500.

The auctioneer banged the gavel for a final sale at $5,000. Everyone applauded the buyer except me. Sweat ran down my back as I realized I had no money to buy the statuettes, even if they came for sale. The hot room closed in on me. After some deep breathing, I concluded I only had to find the merchandise. I would relay that information to Mrs. Depew, and she could take it from there. If someone bought the ivory, I'd get their contact info for her. Satisfied with my plan, I settled back in my chair for the next round.

Next, they offered an antique chair for sale, again not my stuff. It began to dawn on me that this might take a while and I didn't even know if I attended the right auction. I fanned myself making my curls flutter around my face.

The auctioneer pointed at me and said, $2,000.

My mouth dropped open.

The man to the right of me nudged my arm. He said, "Nice chair. Are you buying for yourself?"

I said, "No, no, no. I'm not buying a chair."

He said, "You signaled the auctioneer with your card."

I glowered at my makeshift fan and dropped it to the floor.

The auctioneer pointed to someone on the opposite side of the room and said, "$2,500." Then, he looked back at me in anticipation.

I shook my head.

The man next to me said, "That's too bad."

I said, "I want to purchase ivory statuettes."

He nodded and said, "Which ones?"

We both opened our catalogs and flipped pages.

That's when I realized I didn't know what the statuettes looked like. Mrs. Depew never showed me any pictures nor gave me descriptions. Were they carvings of animals, trees, people? How big were they? How many? I took my catalog and left.

I needed more courage for my next move. I returned home and summoned bravery by donning a pair of red Louboutin calfskin stilettos. I didn't need an exact description of Mrs. Depew's merchandise to make this connection. I checked myself in my full-length mirror, pulled my shoulders back and lifted my chin. I wore the demeanor of a confident woman.

I didn't frequent bars as a habit, but if I did, this place wouldn't be one of them. The black awning over the shoddy corner bar read "Happy Legs." I opened the wooden door and got hit in the face with the smell of stale beer. Ripped vinyl seats lined a long, pitted bar. Two barmaids in booty shorts and sheer tops served the few patrons at the bar. I was grateful no one glanced my way. I didn't want anyone to see me in this establishment. I headed to the pool tables in the rear as Lusty had instructed me.

A man sat in the corner hidden behind an open newspaper. As I approached, he folded the paper, revealing his balding head. He gave me a slow, appraising leer that pissed me off. I remembered I needed him to cooperate, so I smiled. I stuck out my hand and said, "Hi. I'm Rocky. I believe Lusty told you I was coming."

He stood and shook my hand. "Yes, she did. People call me Freddy the Fence."

I didn't bother to ask his last name. I didn't intend to interact with him after this conversation.

Freddy pulled a scratched chair next to his own. He gave a jaunty nod, offering me the seat.

I shifted the chair an extra foot away from Freddy and sat.

Freddy said, "How can I help you today?" He glanced at my feet. "I just got some Versace crystal embellished sandals." He raised an eyebrow and smirked.

I drooled a little at the thought, then caught myself. After all, did he snatch the shoes off some woman's feet? I said, "I'm looking for ivory statuettes. Have any come onto the market recently?"

Freddy leaned back and eyed me. He said, "What kind of statuettes? I don't have any now, but I could arrange to get you what you want. Give me details. I know people who could bring you your heart's desire." He reached over and touched my hand, making me flinch.

I said, "I don't want you to steal things for me. Either you have them or you don't."

Freddy laid a hand over his heart. "You offend me. I'm not a thief. I'm a merchant servicing the community. You have a need and I can fill it."

I said, "Yeah, right. Has anyone mentioned ivory pieces for sale? Maybe your buddies?" I pictured a raggedy den of thieves with a warehouse of stolen goods.

He shook his head. "No. Perhaps I could interest you in some platinum jewelry."

I dug in my bag and pulled out a sticky note with my name and number. I handed it to Freddy and said, "If you hear of ivory statuettes coming on the market, please contact me. I'd appreciate if you reached out to your friends for information."

Freddy grinned and leaned forward at the word 'appreciate'.

I stood and stepped back. I didn't like the way he ogled me. It didn't matter if he wanted money or something more. I wasn't offering either.

I was about to walk out when Freddy said, "Did that guy send you?"

My eyebrows twitched. I said, "Who are you talking about?"

He said, "The guy who came here asking about the same merchandise. I figure he sent you in to soften me up." His eyes lingered on my hips.

I waved my hands about. "What guy? What's his name."

Freddy leaned back and appraised me. "Those statuettes must be hot stuff for two people to come here searching for them. If I find them, I'm selling to the highest bidder." He picked up his paper and opened it, ending the conversation.

I left, defeated and confused.

FIVE

I jumped up the next morning, eager to make the fast cash Lusty had promised. I stopped by her house to get the address.

She opened the door and gave me a shy smile which made my eyebrows screw up. There is nothing shy about Lusty.

I gave her a sideways glance and said, "What's up? You have a funny look on your face."

Lusty said, "You may need a little help with this transaction, so I'm paying my friend's son to help you today."

I said, "Why?"

Lusty said, "The client said this was a big shipment of horns. He wanted to be sure that you had a towing hitch on the back of your car." Lusty stuffed the client's information into my hand and slammed her door before I could say another word.

I stomped down the path to my car and stared at it. I loved my Corolla. It was 12 years old and although reliable, wouldn't tow anything. I walked around to the trunk and stared at the fender. I had no idea what a towing hitch was or where to get one. As I rubbed my temples to get my synapses to fire, a black SUV pulled up behind me.

The vehicle rocked as a pair of Steve Madden work boots emerged. Mmmm, about size 14? My eyes slid up a pair of well-filled khakis. I craned my neck up to see a "6'4", muscular, Black man in his twenties. The sun gleamed off his shaved head and tiny diamond earring as he peered up and down the street. Tattoos rippled on his Herculean arms. He wore a T-shirt that said, "Logical Man Inside."

I held my breath. The man seemed to block out the sun as he moved into my personal space.

He said, "Are you Raquel Rollins?"

I gulped. "Yes. Can I help you?" My breath caught in my chest. I would help this guy in any way he asked, and I hoped he had imaginative needs.

"Aunt Lusty asked me to meet you here this morning. I'm Malik."

I said, "*Aunt* Lusty?" *Back to reality.*

He said, "I've grown up calling her that. She's just a nice lady my dad knows."

I rolled my eyes. *I bet.* I had to admit my arms still ached from the previous night's adventure and this sounded like it would be a big job. I looked at my Corolla and eyed his SUV. I asked, "Do you know anything about towing hitches?"

Malik smiled and opened his passenger door.

I climbed into Malik's Escalade, and he tapped our destination into his GPS. We took off. Malik already had a hitch on his car for who-knows-what. I didn't know and I didn't care. I just checked it off my list of things to do in the next 48 hours.

We tooled along listening to, of all things, a Beethoven symphony, and began to get acquainted.

Malik rattled on about his doctorate studies at Rutgers. The dichotomy between his appearance and his intellect fascinated me. Books on computer science littered his back seat.

I tried in vain to listen to Malik's melodic voice, but the growls from my empty stomach kept drowning out his words. I said, "Would you mind if we picked up some breakfast? I'm starving."

We pulled up to the neighborhood bodega and I hopped out, cracking my knees in the process. Escalades are high.

Malik caught my arm and said, "I was coming to help you down."

It had been so long since I had been treated like a lady. I had forgotten that some men opened car doors and helped women in stilettos down from trucks. Malik had been trained by the best.

Inside the store, the aroma of greasy bacon and egg sandwiches on thick buttered rolls drew me to the grill. I ordered the same and an extra-large coffee with lots of cream. I skipped the sugar packets to offset the calories in the sandwich. I turned to Malik who lingered by the door. I said, "Do you want anything?"

Malik shuffled his feet and stroked his close-cropped beard. He said, "Well, no. I didn't think I'd need to buy anything this morning."

Light bulb. Malik had no money. I scraped the bottom of my coin purse and said, "My treat. After all, you're helping me out. Right?" I gleamed my friendliest smile, no easy feat this early in the morning.

Malik grabbed an orange juice and a boiled egg, and we headed to the register.

A dirty corkboard hung behind the counter displaying local flyers. While waiting for my turn to pay, I perused the mishmash of posters and advertisements. Missing person flyers and wanted posters cluttered one side of the board. I could have lived a long, happy life without knowing this much crime existed in my neighborhood.

I ignored the wanted posters. I knew I did not have the courage to get involved with criminals in any way, shape, or form. However, missing people fascinated me. Where did they go? Were they abducted in the middle of the night, or did they escape to a tropical island? That's what I'd do. Lay on some beach in Fiji with a cool, creamy drink that you had to sip from a pineapple with a little paper umbrella.

Back on the road, Malik pulled onto the smooth blacktop of I-95. I munched my sandwich, being careful not to drip grease onto Malik's immaculate leather seats. I took a bite and said, "Meow."

Malik gave me the side-eye. "Did you say something?"

"Oops. that's how I express myself when something's delicious."

Malik shrugged his shoulders. "Okay."

I said, "Don't worry. You'll get used to me." I hoped.

My thoughts returned to the posters in the bodega. One of them displayed a grainy image of an old man with a long gray beard. Strange. He seemed familiar. Maybe I'd seen him in the neighborhood, although like most people, I didn't pay much attention to seniors.

Younger people drew my attention these days, men to be exact. Holy had battered my image of love. My heart, and sanity, needed a long hiatus from romance before I considered dating again. I thought my marriage had killed my sexual longings for the rest of my life. Even the thought of casual dating used to make me nauseous. But lately, construction guys and landscapers caught my eye. Their healthy, muscular bodies glistened in the sun making my thighs tingle. I have decided that not all men are poison and maybe I'll give love another try. I haven't made any physical effort to meet someone, but I've kept my eyes open.

I finished my sandwich. Yum. Now I could focus on Malik's conversation.

Malik said, "I grew up in Cherry Hill. My family made decent money, so I received a good education."

I said, "So you get to see your family often?"

Malik hesitated and then said, "We don't stay in touch."

Not wanting to intrude, I changed the subject. "Maybe you could help me. Can I bounce something off you?" I summarized my adventures with the Depews.

Malik said, "What a scam. I wouldn't trust anything they said. They could have switched the goods as soon as you left."

I sighed. "Yeah, I know. I feel kind of dumb. This was my first retrieval job, actually the first time I worked for myself. I wasn't prepared for duplicity. Besides, Mrs. Depew might be telling the truth. She's just a little old lady."

Malik said, "You don't know her. Haven't you ever had someone smile in your face and undermine you when you turn your back?"

I had traveled that road many times.

Malik said, "And Mrs. Depew's nephew sounds strong enough to load rocks into the trunk. Right?"

I nodded and I fidgeted with my breakfast bag.

Malik said, "Aunt Lusty said you were a nice girl. You don't know them well enough to know what they're up to. They may have taken advantage."

I needed to change the subject. I took the opportunity to try my investigative skills. "So, Lusty is your aunt?"

Malik smiled. "Aunt Lusty is a mother to me, closer than my real one. She was friends with my dad, and she had a huge influence on my life. I love her like you must love your parents."

It was my turn to reflect. My mother held a special place in my heart. My dad and I had a rough relationship that I couldn't define. Families are messy.

Ninety minutes later, the Escalade pulled off the highway and rolled into Pemberton.

Pemberton, New Jersey is a sprawling municipality of luscious lakes and stunning scenery. Riding over the sunlit roads and smelling some of the freshest air in Jersey put me to sleep like a baby in a stroller. I awoke to Malik nudging my arm. I put my hand to my mouth and sighed with relief. *No drool.*

We climbed out of the truck. Well, I climbed, Malik hopped out. *Darn, I forgot to wait for him to open the door. I've got to get used to this gentleman thing.* We stood in front of a modest white house with a cobblestone path, wrapped in a railroad tie fence. A couple acres of lush greenery surrounded the home. A red barn sat behind the house.

Malik waved a hand toward the house and said, "Shall we?"

Before we reached the steps, the front door swung open and an old woman said, "Good morning. Elustria told us to expect you. I'm Alice." She considered us with sunken, gray eyes. She wiped her hands on her apron and said, "Pull your truck around back. My husband Henry has your cargo." She handed me an envelope of hundred-dollar bills and the delivery address. She said, "Elustria said you'd accept cash."

I grinned so hard my cheeks hurt. Were they growing marijuana behind the barn? I said, "Thanks so much."

Alice said, "Thank you for helping us."

I surveyed the property and said, "You could play all the horns you wanted to out here. No one would hear you."

Alice glanced around and shrugged. "I guess you could." She winced and put a hand to her back. "Good luck." She turned and went inside.

Henry came out of the barn and said, "Thanks so much for comin' all this way. I just can't do the things I used to do. After 25 years, we thought it was time to give it up."

I said, "Was music your hobby or your profession?"

Henry said, "Music? No. My hobby is carving animals from tree branches. Would you like to see them?"

Malik and I glanced at each other.

I said, "We should be on our way."

At Henry's direction, Malik backed his truck up to the barn door. The hitch ca-chunked into place with the trailer. Malik pulled forward and hopped out to secure the connection.

I put one foot in the Escalade when Malik said, "Rocky, you should see this."

I rounded the side of the trailer. The white trailer was oddly shaped, round in the front with doors on the side and back. My first thought was that it would take a lot of instruments to fill a trailer of this size. Then the trailer shifted.

Malik stood to one side. He said, "Rocky, you may want to rethink this." He attempted to hide a smile with one beefy hand.

I stood tiptoe and peeked inside the trailer window. Inside stood a horse, an honest-to-goodness horse. My eyebrows twitched. *Oh no.*

I bit my cheeks to stop my facial contortions before facing Henry. I drew a deep breath and said, "What is this?"

Henry said, "It's the horse I sold to Lusty's friend. She knows so many people. If I have a problem, Lusty has a solution. She found a buyer for old Billy Boy here and she found you. Ain't she great?"

Malik leaned close to my ear and said, "Close your mouth and unclench your fists."

I answered with deliberate calmness. "Henry, there's been a misunderstanding. I was told we were transporting a shipment of horns. You know, musical instruments?"

Henry scratched his head. "I don't know what you mean. Lusty and I talked just this morning about the hitch for the horse trailer. If this horse isn't delivered today, I'll lose the sale."

I said, "I'm sorry. I have no idea how to transport a horse." I turned away. "You'll have to find another way."

Henry looked at the ground, holding his hat in his hands before him. He sniffed and said, "Ma'am, we had to sell Billy Boy because we need the money real bad. Alice and I can't work the farm anymore. We're scraping by on social security. Our bills are piling up. And now Alice needs to go into the hospital." Head still bowed, he wiped away a tear.

I sighed.

Back on I-95, Malik said, "Stop grinding your teeth. You agreed to transport Billy Boy, so make the best of it."

I said, "I can't believe we're towing a slump backed horse in a rattling trailer. That noise is driving me crazy."

Malik smiled. "Who are you mad at? Henry? He made a good faith transaction. Lusty? Once she realized her mistake, she sent me to help you."

I said, "Your logic is killing me."

Malik said, "You're angry at yourself for taking the horse."

I said, "I shouldn't have done it. I should have held my ground. What kind of businessperson am I?"

Malik said, "Human."

To ease my frustration, I turned my thoughts to the missing person posters in the bodega. Why did that old man's image nag me so? Then the proverbial light bulb lit. Of course. I turned to Malik to share my revelation when a cacophony of screeching tires filled my ears. The truck jolted.

Malik hit the brakes and we both turned to see our cargo rolling backwards down I-95. We waited until traffic squealed to a halt, then we leapt out of the Escalade. We sprinted after the trailer ignoring shaking fists and cursing motorists. The side of the trailer crumpled into the grill of a Mack truck with a sickening crunch.

Malik ran to the tail of the trailer and peered in. The doors had swung open, and Billy Boy was trotting down the highway. Thank God he was too old to gallop.

We wove our way between the tangle of cars and caught up with Billy Boy. Then we stood for a moment looking back and forth between the horse and each other.

I said, "What the hell happened with your trailer hitch?"

Malik remained as calm as possible under the circumstances. "My hitch is good. The front of that rusty trailer broke off."

"Well, what are we going to do now?"

Malik said, "I'll have to fix the front of the trailer and rehitch it."

We returned our attention to Billy Boy. Neither of us was horse savvy. We had no idea how to get Billy Boy back into the trailer. He wasn't wearing a bridle, and we had no clue how to guide him.

I said, "Do you think we can get out of here before the cops come?"

We surveyed the area. No cops in sight, but sirens wailed in the distance.

I said, "Maybe if we get behind him and push, we can get him back into the trailer."

Malik shrugged. "Sounds good to me."

I got behind Billy Boy and put my hands on his ass. He responded by ejecting the biggest horse apples I'd ever seen, not that I've seen many. I gasped as I watched horse shit rolled down the front of my shirt and jeans, and land on my Gucci stilettos.

Malik said, "Oh shit." He slapped his hand across his mouth but could not stifle the laugh rolling up from his belly.

Fuming, I stomped back to the truck to find a rag to clean up my shoes. The hell with the rest of my clothes. I had tons of sweatshirts, T-shirts, jeans, and shorts. But the shoes mattered. I found some napkins left over from breakfast. As I bent down to wipe my stilettos a megaphoned voice called out. *Here we go.*

A police car had stopped some distance away due to the blockade of jackknifed cars. The uniformed officer stood next to his vehicle hands on hips. He pointed at Malik. "You with the horse, get over here now."

Malik held his hands away from his body and approached the officer leaving Billy Boy on his own.

I could see him speaking to the cop and pointing toward the Escalade. The officer was doing some pointing of his own, first at the horse, then at the trailer, followed by the Escalade. They both turned and stared at me. *This was not good.* From what I could see, Malik took all the precautions Black parents teach their sons. Keep your hands visible at all times. No matter how angry you are, be polite. Answer all questions.

Five hours and thirteen explanations later, Malik and I had secured Billy Boy in the trailer. We hooked it up to the Escalade and moved north. We rode with the windows down so we wouldn't pass out from the stench of my clothes. We still had a long drive to Washington Township to deliver Billy Boy to the end buyer.

We made a quick stop at a big box store so I could buy some clean clothes and take a bird bath in the ladies' room. I stood at the end of a long line of people waiting to pay.

The woman ahead of me held her little boy's hand and pushed a cart laden with food. The boy pointed at me and said, "You smell." His mother inspected me with a wrinkled nose. She asked, "Would you like to go ahead of me?"

I stepped up. I turned to thank her as she dragged her kid to another cashier.

The other people ahead of me sidled away, one by one, until I was first in line. In minutes, I had washed up in the ladies' room and changed clothes. I dumped my old clothes in the trash can and returned to the Escalade. We hit the road again.

Darkness approached as we reached our destination. I rubbed my aching neck. Every time we hit a bump, I had whipped my head around to check Billy Boy. Malik had assured me the trailer hitch would hold this time, but I couldn't help myself.

Washington Township is a beautiful collage of hillsides and farmlands, that is by day. This was night and we couldn't see a damned thing. I'm used to living in the city. City nights are filled with traffic lights, streetlights, and apartment lights. Night in the country is just dark.

Malik and I rolled past houses and farms searching for the Johnson place. Malik's GPS didn't get a signal, so we winged it.

I squinted at the passing homes. "I can't see the addresses anymore. The mailboxes are near the road. You're going to have to drive closer to them so I can see the numbers."

Malik reached over and opened the glove compartment. "We need a flashlight."

I held up a finger in triumph. "No need. I bought a high-powered flashlight. Not only is it super bright but it has a radio, a siren and a cell phone charger. Searching for the trunk with a penlight taught me a lesson." I tapped a finger to my temple.

Malik looked at me like I was nuts. "Why didn't you just use the flashlight on your cell phone?"

Damn his logic. I searched through papers, hand sanitizer, pens, tissues, and chocolate. I found the flashlight at the bottom of my bag. I pushed the button. No light.

Malik took the flashlight and slapped the bottom. Voila. Light.

We crawled along unfamiliar roads until we found a mailbox marked 513-Johnson.

I aimed the flashlight on my papers to confirm the address and said, "This is it."

We inched up the long driveway, rolling on and off of the grass in the darkness. We stopped in front of the large ranch style house. No lights were on. No surprise there since it was almost midnight. I rang the doorbell twice before the porch light flicked on. The door opened to reveal a 6'3" thin, angular man rubbing his eyes. He opened his baby blues, hooked his thumbs into his shorts and said, "Are you lost?"

I said, "We have your delivery." I gestured toward the trailer.

Malik peeked out and waved from behind the trailer.

The sleepy man said, "What? What delivery?"

My eyebrows tried to twitch, but they were too worn out. I sighed and said, "Are you Mr. Johnson?"

He said, "Yeah, but I'm not expecting a delivery. What is it?" He eyed Malik who was unhooking the trailer.

I said, "It's Billy Boy, your horse."

Mr. Johnson's blue eyes darkened. He said, "Listen here. I didn't order any horse."

I held the delivery paperwork in front of his face and said, "But it says 'Willie Johnson, 513 Okburgh Road.

Mr. Johnson snatched the paper out of my hand, leaned into the foyer light and read. When he turned back to me, his face had transformed into a reddened grimace. He thrust the paper into my face and said, "Look, Lady."

The paper was so close to my eyes, I couldn't read it.

As I took it, Mr. Johnson said, "My name is Lester Johnson. You want Willie Johnson across the road at 518." He pointed to a house atop a hill on the other side of the road.

I sputtered an apology as the wrong Mr. Johnson slammed the door in my face. Sure enough, the delivery paper said 518.

Two and a half hours later, I stood in my hot soaking shower. After delivering Billy Boy to his rightful owner, I awoke to Malik opening the Escalade door. I yearned for him to carry me to my bed and tuck me in, but that would have sent the wrong message. Instead, I climbed down, crawled to my door and waved goodnight.

The water splashed over my face and body, removing the last vestiges of farm life and Billy Boy poop. My eyelids drooped and my head fell forward. If I didn't get to bed soon, I'd fall asleep in the shower. I stepped out of the shower and caught my blurred reflection in the steamy mirror. My breath caught in my throat.

SIX

The missing person's flyer broke through my exhaustion. No wonder it had nagged me so. The grainy photo portrayed Mr. Depew.

I had no chance to run my theory by Malik, because I fell asleep as soon as I reached my bed. I didn't have the ability to form a sentence anyway. And why would Malik care, unless I hired him to help me find Mrs. Depew's goods? This was my last thought until the morning sun shone through my bedroom windows.

As soon as I could pry my eyes open, I called Malik. I ran down Mrs. Depew's original request and my subsequent revelations. He agreed to work with me for a percentage of my fee.

Malik rolled up in the Escalade fresh and rested.

I dragged my tired behind out to the curb, looking like a bedraggled rag doll. I had tied my bushy curls back with an orange scarf and slipped on my favorite gold hoops. I wore my most comfortable jeans, a loose tee shirt and Christian Dior black suede stilettos.

Malik reached over and opened the door from the driver's seat. I guess he'd given up on the gentleman routine.

I climbed into the Escalade being careful not to scuff my shoes.

Malik said, "Why do you wear those goofy shoes to these jobs? You'd have a much easier time with sneakers or work boots. They look nice but they sure aren't functional."

"Don't ever criticize my shoes."

Malik's eyes widened and his lips snapped shut.

With a lump in my throat I said, "Sorry. I didn't mean to snap. Stilettos remind me of my mom. She was my rock and I really miss her. Whenever I put on stilettos, I channel her spirit. She was badass and that's what I want to be." I turned and watched the passing scenery. Grief is a funny thing. It appears out of nowhere when you think you have it under control.

Malik broke the uncomfortable silence. "I never got close to my mother. She didn't behave like other mothers. She'd disappear for days at a time with no explanation. She'd come back, hug me, and leave again. My dad was my champion. He loved me. He loved her too, but she broke his heart. Dad left when I was only ten, and I haven't seen him since. Aunt Lusty has been more of a parent to me than my mother ever was."

His words jolted me. It never occurred to me that Malik and Lusty's relationship was that deep.

He said, "I've cut all ties to my mother. I used to feel guilty about that."

"But not anymore?"

"Sometimes feelings creep in but I swallow them down and keep moving. She doesn't deserve a relationship with me." He bit his lip and turned away.

I said, "Don't you want to mend your relationship with your mother? I struggle to spend time with a father I don't like. He represents everything I detest in a man. He tries to control me like he tried with my mom. I get a knot in my stomach with every visit, but I still try. I believe family is worth saving."

Malik turned away. "I don't know." After an uncomfortable pause, he said, "So, what makes you so sure that poster was Mr. Depew? You only saw the flyer for a moment and you, yourself, said it was grainy."

I accepted the subject change. "Haven't you ever had a gut feeling?"

Malik smiled and said, "Yeah, when it's based on fact."

I thought a moment and said, "I think there was something fishy about that trunk of rocks."

Malik said, "Now you're thinking. What exactly gave you doubt."

I allowed my eyebrows to knit together to help my synapses connect. I said, "The rocks were huge. There's no way I could have moved a trunk with that much weight."

Malik smiled. "Now that's analytical thinking. Doesn't that feel better than going with your gut?"

He was right. The trunk had been heavy, but movable.

Malik tapped his temple, then said, "You can try tracking down the guy on the invoice."

I said, "Lusty mentioned that too."

Malik said, "Now about the poster. Even if it is Mr. Depew, he could have been missing before he died. How did he die?"

I bit my lip. That was a good question. I didn't know anything about Mr. Depew. How can I assume he died in a bad way. Still, something was going on. The whole situation felt wrong. I said, "Let's get breakfast and think on it."

Malik said, "Sure and while we're at the bodega, we can take a look at that flyer. Right?" He winked and pulled away from the curb.

My cell phone purred as we headed for the bodega. I'd installed the purr ringtone on every phone I'd owned. If nothing else made me smile that day, my ringtone would. My grin disappeared when Lusty's name glared on the screen. I gripped the phone so hard my knuckles cracked. The horse incident still burned in my head. My fingers relaxed as I remembered my fee. I had earned enough money to pay a month's mortgage. That payment would hold off the eviction for a moment, but I was still two months behind. I sighed and answered the call.

Lusty said, "Good morning, Rocky. How are you this fine morning?"

I said, "Fine morning?" *Uh oh.* "What's up?"

Lusty's smile beamed through the phone. "You did such a good job with the last client; I wondered if you'd be interested in making some easy money?"

I said, "What do you get out of these referrals?"

Lusty said, "I get to help out a good friend."

I said, "And?"

Lusty said, "Rocky Recoveries is like one stop shopping. You provide a valuable service for my clients."

I said, "I'm not buying it."

Lusty cleared her throat. She said, "And Malik told me he loves working with you and that you're going to split your fee with him. That money will help pay for his school needs. He was getting ready to drop out because he couldn't even afford the books. He matters to me, and he needs you."

I glanced at Malik from the corner of my eye. I said, "You have another referral?"

Malik and I made one stop on the way to the bodega. The print shop did a good job with my business cards. I grinned and giggled as I handed a few to Malik. The simple black and white card brought joy to my heart. Rocky Recoveries, We Pickup & Deliver, followed by my email and cell phone.

He shook my hand and said, "Congrats on the official beginning of Rocky Recoveries. Do you have a website?"

I shook my head. A website sounded complicated.

Malik said, "I can help you with that."

Some guys offer to fill your needs to get close to you, but Malik didn't seem to have ulterior motives.

Malik flipped the card over and said, "Why did you put your home address on the back?"

I shrugged. "I figured people might want to mail me checks."

Malik covered his mouth and shook his head. He said, "First, people don't write checks anymore. They pay by credit card or an app. Do you have a card reader on your phone?"

"I used to have a device I stuck in my phone to swipe cards. I'd need to change the banking link before I use it. It's in a drawer somewhere."

Malik said, "Let's get you a couple of phone apps for contactless payments. Also, your home address leaves you vulnerable to anyone who has this card. Any knucklehead could find you. For your own safety, I recommend you print new cards."

He was smart. I figured this was a good time to offer Malik a permanent position. My words caught in my throat. Did I have the chops to be a boss? I was still seeking my own way. I plunged on. "Would you be open to working for me?"

Malik said, "You mean working *with* you?"

My mind hiccupped, then recovered. "Okay, with me under my direction."

Malik shook his head and laughed. "Sure. I have flexibility with my classes. I take some courses online but have to go to the campus for exams. We can work it out...on your terms of course."

We agreed on Malik's cut.

The agreement seemed like a win-win for both of us. In minutes, Malik set up several apps on my phone so I could take instant payments. We ordered a mobile reader for credit card transactions. What a rosy day. Rocky Recoveries started forming before my eyes with me as the CEO.

As we reached the bodega, I detailed Lusty's latest referral. The client, Mr. Belch, needed a crate transported to him. He would pay us upon delivery.

The bodega bustled as usual. I found myself grinning as the aroma of ham and eggs burst into my senses. The owner rang up his customers, greeting some and snatching money from others.

Malik pushed past me toward the grill in the back as I stopped to peer at the missing person flyer.

When there was a lull at the register, I spoke to the owner. "Are these flyers current?"

He turned to inspect the posters as if for the first time. He said, "I don't know. Who cares? People bring these flyers in or the cops drop them off and we slap them on the wall. I never look at 'em twice." He peered over my shoulder as people approached the register.

I didn't move, blocking his cash flow. I said, "Can I see that flyer?"

He said, "Lady, you have to move over so these people can pay."

I stayed put. "That missing person flyer there."

The line grew.

The owner shot me a dirty scowl and said, "Take it, dammit. Take whatever you want."

I went behind the counter, snatched the flyer, and jammed it into my bag.

Malik joined the end of the line and said, "I got you an egg sandwich and coffee."

Back in the Escalade, we studied the flyer.

I said, "This is definitely Mr. Depew." I read the flyer aloud. "Missing Person. Perry Wadsworth Depew. Age at disappearance: 83. DOB: March 15, 1939. Sex, race, hair, eyes, height, weight were all consistent with the portrait in Mrs. Depew's living room. The physical description was followed by "Perry Depew was last seen in his residence on..."

Malik pulled his laptop from the back seat. He said, "Let's check news stories." He tapped a few buttons and said, "Boo-yah, here we go."

I leaned in. The scent of Malik's musk after shave distracted me. I shook my head to clear my senses. I turned to the local news stories on Mr. Depew.

We read the first story.

Perry Wadsworth Depew, age 83, left his Forest Hills residence at 2 p.m. Tuesday. When he failed to return by midnight, his family reported him missing. Due to his advanced age, the Newark Police instituted an immediate search. Those with information on the case can call the Newark Police at 555...

The next day's follow up story quoted Lilac Depew. "Someone has to know something." The article displayed a photo of Lilac wringing her hands in her typical fashion. Ernest stood behind her, holding her shoulders in a supportive gesture.

No news appeared for three weeks. Then the Star Ledger ran a story.

Perry Wadsworth Depew, a local collector of rare goods, disappeared three weeks ago. Detectives are compiling a timeline of Depew's movements after he left his Forest Hills home.

Detective "Pepper" Brimley examined Mr. Depew's work and family life. "We found no signs of conflict. However, new evidence raises suspicions that Mr. Depew may have been harmed."

Mr. Depew's wife, Lilac, declined to comment on the possibility of a suspicious act.

I looked at Malik with raised eyebrows. "Suspicious act?"

Malik scrolled down to the most recent story, posted only one week ago.

The Newark Police detained Ernest Depew, nephew of Perry Depew, as a person of interest. They released him after three hours of questioning. Ernest Depew declined to comment.

I said, "Wow. I didn't know Ernest could talk."

Malik gave me a quizzical look.

I said, "Never mind. Let's take care of the new job. I'll explain later."

Malik said, "Wait. There's more."

The NPD are also searching for a possible accomplice in this incident.

I said, "What? Do they mean an accomplice outside of the family?" My stomach churned and my eyebrows twitched. *Oh boy.*

Malik said, "I thought you said he was dead? I don't see anything in here that says he's dead. This says he's missing."

"Maybe they just found his body and it's not in the papers yet."

Malik gaped at me like I was stupid. "This article is a week old. You started working for Mrs. Depew a week ago. Is that right?"

I didn't need to answer.

"And she told you a week ago that her husband was dead. Right? So, why is Mrs. Depew saying her husband is dead when the papers say he's missing?"

The blank expression on my face said I had no idea.

Malik said, "And what about this guy Ernest? He looks dangerous and the police detained him."

I shook my head. "I don't know what to think about either of them."

Malik pointed to the screen. "Look at the picture. He's standing there holding her shoulders like he's controlling her. Plus, he's huge. I bet he has enough strength to kill a bunch of people."

Malik had a point. Ernest hadn't spoken a word to me, but I didn't know what happened behind their closed doors.

Malik closed the laptop, and we moved on to our next job.

Lusty's latest referral was from Mr. Joseph Belch. She said he wouldn't discuss what he needed transported. Lusty wouldn't have gotten it right anyway. It was something he couldn't trust a regular shipper to protect.

The pickup was in Hillside. We pulled off Route 22 onto a street of small, older homes. The residents seemed to do the best they could with the distressed neighborhood. We pulled up to a gray, two story house with peeling paint and broken brick steps. Low handrails, suitable only for a child, bracketed the steps.

On the porch we found a large wooden crate. Someone had scrawled the word "fragile" on all four sides and the top. A large manila envelope marked Rocky Recoveries was taped to the crate. Inside, a folded sheet of paper revealed the delivery address.

I smiled at Malik and said, "This seems harmless."

Malik said, "Great, a simple job. No live animals."

We both examined the box one more time to be sure.

We loaded the box into the Escalade. Well, I held the door open and Malik carried the box.

We had to deliver the box to Budd Lake, so up Route 280 West we went. In a little less than an hour we rolled up a green-lawned street lined with garden apartments. Budd Lake was a rural community surrounding a beautiful lake. It was large enough to have its own beach, but small enough to have a volunteer fire department.

We pulled up to a small white house with blue shutters. Wildflowers lined the stone path. I rang the doorbell as Malik started to unload the crate. The door swung open and out popped a muscular, mustached, four-foot-high man. He wore a black leather vest over tattooed skin and the smallest jeans I'd ever seen. His blond ponytail reached his little round butt.

I pulled out my manifest and held it in front of my face to hide my smile. I said, "Mr. Belch?"

He said, "Call me Belch. Everyone does."

Before I could say another word, Belch waved his arms at Malik and said, "Don't take that out here. Back the truck up to the rear of the house."

Malik sighed and complied.

The little man and I met Malik in the back yard. Belch's eyes darted back and forth like a hunted animal. We completed our transaction on Cash App as Malik opened the Escalade. Belch peeped in, pumped one tiny fist and said, "Alright." He slapped the side of the crate twice. The crate rattled and shook. Malik jumped back, knocking me on my ass in the grass. We both stared at the box as the back panel popped open and a tiny woman in full bridal regalia jumped out.

Belch opened his pudgy arms wide and said, "Baby, you made it."

Malik and I gaped at each other and then at the tiny couple.

When I found my voice, I said, "What the hell? You had us transport a human being in a crate? Are you out of your mind?"

Ignoring me, Belch turned to Malik and said, "Could you please help my bride down?"

I said, "Do you know how much trouble we could've gotten into if the cops had stopped us?"

Belch put his hands on his little hips and glared up at me with a scowl. "That's right. If you tell anyone what was in this crate you can get into a lot of trouble." He arched one eyebrow which made him resemble an evil cartoon mastermind. "Human trafficking is a huge offense."

I said, "Is that a threat?"

Belch stepped to me. He pointed a tiny finger and said, "If one word of this leaks out, we're all going to jail. Besides, you had no idea what you delivered. Did you? I bet you never know what's inside the packages you carry."

I said, "Now wait a minute..."

I felt a tug on the back of my shirt and jumped.

Belch's bride had tears in her eyes. She said, "We had to do it this way."

Malik asked, "Why didn't you just take a train?"

The bride said, "I'm hiding from my family. My parents don't approve of Belch. They think he's dangerous, but he's really a sweetheart."

The idea that this little biker man was dangerous gave me a case of the giggles. I raised my manifest in front of my face again, hoping I could compose myself. From the corner of my eye I could see Malik turning his back to us, his shoulders shaking. This didn't help matters. Tears started to roll down my cheeks. I guess the laughter had come out some way.

Thankfully, the bride mistook my tears for sympathy. She said, "If I had taken a train or bus, my family would have tracked me down and prevented our marriage. It's hard to defy my parents."

I could relate to that. As much as I had wanted to oppose my father, it was a hard thing to do. My dad still held it against me.

Belch wrapped his arms around his bride and gave her a bear, or should I say cub, hug. He wiped her tears and gave her a passionate kiss, so hot that my cheeks flushed.

I cleared my throat and said, "Belch if you could please sign the manifest, we'll be on our way. Don't worry. I understand your situation and will not breathe a word to anyone."

We climbed into the Escalade, and I watched as Belch escorted his bride up the kiddie stairs to his back door. As we drove away, Belch scowled over his shoulder and gave me the evil mastermind look one more time. I couldn't get out of there fast enough.

On the road back, Malik said, "Belch gave you an out."

I said, "What do you mean?"

Malik said, "You can't be prosecuted when you didn't know what you transported. Think about it."

I thought about the trunk of rocks.

I arrived home to a business card stuck in my door. It read Detective Brimley, Newark Police Department. His contact details followed. Inside, I tossed the card aside. I needed chocolate and sleep before facing the police. I glanced at my cell phone. A little phone icon appeared at the top of the screen, indicating a message waiting. After a moment of waffling, I listened to the call. The gruff voice of Detective Brimley delivered a terse phone message. He required my presence to answer questions about Perry Depew.

My last ounce of strength drained from me. I stood there staring at the screen. My mind raced over possible outcomes of an interrogation. Images of hot lights, steel chairs and hulking cops swam through my mind. I could taste bad coffee and see the lie detector needle bounce up and down. This is the curse of watching too much Law and Order.

I pressed the return number and hesitated over the call button. I exited from the screen and threw the phone on the couch. In the kitchen, I opened the fridge, stared blankly at the offerings, and slammed the door shut. I returned to the living room and picked up the phone. I punched Detective Brimley's number again. This time, I hit the call button. It rang. And rang. I was about to disconnect when a jarring voice stated the detective had gone for the day. I blew out a breath I hadn't realized I was holding. In my relief, I fell back onto the couch and nodded off.

The next day, I awakened to an incessant knocking at my door that caused me to roll onto the floor with a thump. I tried to orient myself as the morning sun streamed through the living room windows. I mumbled, "I'm coming." and opened the door to find a fat, rumpled, mustached man flashing a badge.

He said, "Miss Rollins?"

I wiped away a piece of eye crust and said, "Yes?" I wanted to say as little as possible since I have horrific morning breath.

He said, "I'm Detective Brimley of the Newark Police. I'd like to ask you some questions in connection with an ongoing investigation."

I ushered him in, appalled at the state of my living room. Usually neat, this morning it must have resembled a bordello. My stilettos lay toppled over in the middle of the floor. The sofa cushions were askew as if I'd had wild sex there five minutes prior.

Brimley's eyes dropped to my waist.

I jerked my shirt down over my unzipped jeans.

Brimley stepped around my shoes, whipped out a pad and pen, and stood in the middle of the room. He inspected the space, his eyes wandering to the top of my head.

I reached up and felt a tangle of wild hair covered with a dangling scarf. I snatched off the scarf and stuffed it into my back pocket. There wasn't much

I could do about the hair until I could use a mirror. I caught a whiff of my underarm. Not good.

With an almost imperceptible shake of his head, he said, "I understand you've been doing some work for Lilac Depew."

I said nothing since this was not a question. Again, based on what I've seen on Law & Order, it's best to only speak to cops when asked questions.

He raised his eyebrows and said, "Is that correct?"

"Yes."

"What was the nature of this work?"

Uh oh. Images of breaking into an abandoned house in a Catwoman suit swam through my brain. *What had I done?* Until now, I'd only thought about getting a cool utility belt that I could fill with handy gadgets. I looked up to see Brimley squinting at me as if reading my mind.

I cleared my throat. "Mrs. Depew asked me to locate some of her husband's artifacts."

Brimley scribbled something on his pad and said, "What kind of artifacts?"

"Some ivory statuettes." A trickle of sweat rolled down my back. I needed a shower and definitely, a toothbrush.

Brimley stepped closer. "And did you find them?"

What do I say? Yes. No. I thought so, but it turned out to be a crate of rocks from the abandoned house I'd broken into? "No."

He scribbled again, something much longer than "No." Brimley stopped writing and said, "Is there any reason you aren't giving me full answers?'

I gulped. "I'm telling you all I know."

"Trust this. We will speak again. Going forward, I advise you to be forthright with me. We'll get along much better."

I said, "I'm answering your questions."

Brimley said, "You're giving me one-word answers. When someone does that, it usually means they want me to leave them alone. That makes me curious. You don't want me delving into your personal life."

I turned away from his stare.

"I have a job to do, and I intend to complete it to the satisfaction of my superiors. Don't make me push you."

I said, "I read in the paper that you questioned Mrs. Depew's nephew. Is he involved?" *Damn! I broke my own rule.*

"Why do you ask? What do you know about Ernest Depew?" Brimley said, "How did Mrs. Depew come to contact you? Or did Ernest reach out to you?"

Now what? Do I explain that the phone sex operator next door referred her to me? That I agreed to work for Mrs. Depew before I even had business cards? That now I run rampant, picking up horses and trafficking miniature brides? I was beginning to wonder if keeping the house was worth the trouble. *I won't need a house when I'm hauled off to the slammer.*

Brimley cleared his throat, bringing me back to reality.

I said, "My neighbor referred me to her."

"And your neighbor is?"

"Elustria Magoo. She lives right next door." I jerked my thumb toward her house.

Brimley raised an eyebrow. He slapped his notepad shut and said in a rapid staccato, "We may have more questions. You have my card if you think of something you may want to tell me. Goodbye."

As he returned to his car, I could see him eying Lusty's house. *Good grief. She does know every man in town.*

SEVEN

Alone at last, I picked up Murphy, which was no easy task at his weight. I gave him a squeeze. He tried to wriggle out of it, but I held firm. I needed to feel more powerful than someone today and if it had to be Murphy, so be it. I looked into his eyes and asked, "What the hell am I going to do? The police suspect me now."

Murphy pushed back with his paws, and I lost him. So much for feeling powerful.

I started to strip for a steamy shower when a piece of crumpled paper fell out of my jean pocket. I unfolded the pawn shop list Lusty and I had made. I rolled my eyes and thanked God for the direction.

After a change of clothes and a hearty breakfast, I headed out to hit the pawn shops. Most of them were concentrated in the business districts of Newark with a few in quieter spots. If I were a thief, I would pawn my stuff at the shop with the most foot traffic. Boy, was I wrong. The shops in the center of town had jewelry, designer handbags, smart phones, and laptops. No statuettes.

I stopped at a hot dog vendor near Broad and Market for a guilty pleasure. I struck up a conversation while the guy slapped a dog into a bun and slathered it with mustard, relish, and onions.

He said, "I pawned some of my ex-wife's jewelry and stuff to get this cart. If she wanted her things, she shouldn't have left me for a pond scum tester."

I commiserated with him to get some info. "What pawn shop did you use?"

"There's a place called Neighborhood Exchange on the south side of town. Kinda out of the way for a pawn shop, but I didn't want to run into anyone I knew while pawning a box of my wife's stuff." He wiped sweat off his forehead with a greasy rag and rubbed his hands on his dirty jeans.

I stopped mid-bite, thanked him for the info and looked for a place to toss my dog.

The Neighborhood Exchange stood in a strip of stores on a quiet tree-lined street. This shop stood apart from the gaudy, garish pawn shops in downtown Newark. It resembled an old-fashioned drug store where you could buy an ice cream soda. The brick building's green awning shaded an antique bench. The clean windows displayed jewelry and designer handbags. No guns, knives or fat gold chains that spelled "Gangsta." Only the three-sphere pawn symbol on the sign belied the true nature of the business.

Inside, I spotted a gray-haired man who looked like a golfer in his blue polo shirt, khaki pants, and loafers. He said, "I'll be with you as soon as I finish with this gentleman."

I eased my way around the quiet atmosphere of the store. High quality merchandise filled the glass cases and covered the walls. I passed golf clubs, laptops, smartphones, and flat screen TV's. One corner held an entire section of electric guitars, keyboards, and other instruments. Lots of starving musicians must live in this town. I examined a section of mystery power tools and tried to decipher their purposes. He displayed a lot of jewelry in locked cases.

The corner case held an array of official-looking badges on a black velvet tray. Lusty's suggestion replayed in my mind. Karma. Lusty spoke and badges appeared. I was meant to have one.

A blond girl in her early twenties emerged from a back room and approached me. "Can I help you?"

I pointed and she laid the tray of badges on the counter for me to see. I said, "Are these real?" The shiny badges read Police, Border Patrol, Secret Service, FBI.

The girl shrugged. "I don't know but they appear real, and isn't that the point?"

I had to agree. I purchased a counterfeit gold Private Investigator badge. It featured an American flag emblem and the words 'Liberty and Justice for All' in the center. I tucked it into the money section of my crossbody bag for quick access.

As the girl relocked the counter, I asked about the statuettes.

She pointed at the store owner. "You should ask my dad about that. He inventories everything."

He was still helping a customer, so I wandered a bit more. I halted at a pair of Miu Miu turquoise, crystal-embellished, five-inch stilettos. They looked way too big for me, but I'd try walking in them anyway. Usually going for a grand, these were priced at $500. Who was this demented woman who gave up her shoes? She must be desperate. My mind raced through my possessions to see what I could hock in exchange for the shoes. To my heartbreak, I didn't own anything of value except Murphy and of course, my stilettos. I didn't even think I could get $500 for my car. I was deep in thought when I felt a tap on my shoulder. I whirled around to see the salesman standing behind me.

He said, "How can I help you?"

I whipped out a Rocky Recoveries card and used my most professional voice. "Have you received any ivory statuettes recently?" I itched to use my new badge but there was no point trying to fool the man from whom I'd purchased it.

The man read the card and then squinted at me. "What's going on? You're the second person to ask me this today."

My voice went up an octave. "Who else was asking you?" *Oh no, I hope Brimley wasn't here.*

He pointed toward the door, "He did."

I raced out the door just in time to see the man drive off in a steel blue BMW. I got a glimpse of the back of his head. I kicked myself for not paying attention to him in the shop. I returned to the pawn shop.

The owner gawked at me like I had two heads.

I said, "Do you know that man?"

The owner shrugged. "No and I don't know you." He crossed his arms over his round belly.

I needed to play nice. I flashed a smile and batted my lashes. "I thought he and I could work together since we want the same merchandise. Do you know his name?"

The pawnbroker relaxed and leaned close to me. "I believe his name is Charles but since he's gone, maybe I can help you." He laid a hand on my shoulder.

I jumped back knocking over a set of premium golf clubs. As he leaned down to get them, I dashed out the door.

I needed more details from Mrs. Depew. I had been flailing around trying to piece clues together. It was like putting a jigsaw puzzle together in the dark. I waited until Malik got out of school and had him drive me over. His logic might come in handy.

On the way to the Depew house, I told Malik about Charles.

Malik said, "Are you crazy? You were going to confront this guy? You could have gotten hurt. I want you to exercise some caution. You don't know what he's capable of."

I shrugged and said, "Okay."

Malik said, "I don't think you're hearing me. You need to be careful when dealing with strangers."

I suppressed a giggle and sat erect. "Yes, I understand."

Malik and Ernest eyed each other as we entered the Depew home, neither speaking. Malik matched Ernest's long strides down the hall as I played catch up.

In the sitting room, Mrs. Depew waited. She welcomed us but did not offer us seats.

I made the introductions.

Ernest gave Malik a curt nod of acknowledgment.

I gave Mrs. Depew a business card.

She handed it to Ernest without reading it. Mrs. Depew considered us with bright eyes and said, "Do you have news, Honey?"

I moved forward with mixed emotions. How could I suspect an old lady in a wheelchair of malicious intent? She looked so hopeful when we came in and I had no new information for her. "No, Mrs. Depew, no new news. A photo of the statuettes would be helpful in my search. Do you have one you can share?"

Mrs. Depew said, "No, Dear."

I sighed. "How about a description? I need details for my investigation. How many statuettes? What are their sizes? What kind of carvings are they? Are they antiques?"

I felt Malik's gaze on me.

Mrs. Depew said, "Mr. Depew handled that transaction. I only know the trunk contained a sizable shipment of African ivory carvings. You will have to discover the rest. After all, Elustria said you're an expert."

Malik and I glanced at each other and at the rug.

I said, "I have a question unrelated to the statuettes."

Mrs. Depew smiled. "Yes, Dear?"

"When did Mr. Depew pass away? I've been reading news reports and they say he is missing."

Ernest shifted.

Malik stepped closer to me.

Mrs. Depew's smile disappeared. Her eyes watered. "The police still believe he is missing, but I know in my heart he has gone to his heavenly rest. He would never stay away from me this long unless he had no way of returning." A tear rolled down her cheek. She reached into the cuff of her blouse and pulled out a lace hanky. She sniffed and dabbed at her eyes and nose. Then she gazed at me. "Why are you asking? This is the most distressing situation I've ever had to face. The police call night and day, and I don't have any answers for them. And now you..." She began to snivel.

Oh boy. My chin hit my chest and my lip quivered. What the hell was wrong with me? "I'm sorry Mrs. Depew. I didn't mean to add to your stress."

Ernest's eyes bore into me.

I thanked God for Malik's presence.

Ernest sneered like he wanted to rip my throat out.

I said, "We'll be leaving now. I hope to have good news for you when I return." I hustled Malik out of there before I started bawling myself.

Back outside Malik said, "I can't believe you don't know what you're searching for."

I said, "I was hired to find a trunk and I delivered it. I didn't need a description of the contents. Then, when I saw the rocks, I got so mad, I didn't think clearly enough to ask questions."

Malik said, "And did you call that an interrogation? I thought you were going to grill her."

"I couldn't. Did you see her? She's so sad."

"All I saw was her eyes water on cue as soon as you mentioned Mr. Depew. That could be an act." Malik stood with his hands on his hips. "If you're going to be an investigator, you'll have to toughen up. I'm not buying this performance. And what about Ernest? He never says a word, just hovers over her. How do you know what he's up to? Silent people are thinkers. Also, with his size he could kill someone with ease. He could be the one in control."

I had considered that possibility. Granted, Ernest was scary, but he seemed like a dim bulb to me. I could be wrong. Back in the car I said, "I still feel bad for making her cry. She's a little old lady who lost her husband."

Malik said, "Money makes people do funny things. You don't know what Mrs. Depew and her nephew are up to. It must cost a lot to keep up a house like that and did you see all the expensive stuff she has?"

Malik made a lot of sense. Mrs. Depew could have faked her sadness. I've mustered up a few tears when needed to get myself out of trouble. Maybe I was being too soft. I had to get more evidence. I said, "I'm sure she has money from her husband. I can't see this little old lady being a criminal."

Malik said, "You don't know anything about her finances. Haven't you ever known anyone who seemed like they had it all but was broke as hell? Maybe, she can't access Mr. Depew's money until she has proof of his death."

Malik's logic beat my emotions again. Just once, I'd like to be right.

Malik said, "Also, sometimes people fall into crime. by chance." He went silent for a moment. "You asked me about my family. I separated from my family because I couldn't tolerate their criminal activity. I come from a family of intellectuals, but they fell in with a criminal element.

My mother and her brothers own several antique stores and conduct estate sales. We had some lean times but did pretty well. My mother had a gambling problem and ran into financial troubles. My mother's bookie let her get deep in debt. Then he forced her to launder money through our stores."

Malik's voice chilled as he spoke of his mother. I made a mental note not to mention her in the future.

Malik said, "She was too scared to ask the family for help. She didn't want to let us down. We took pride in our stores. We had been able to maintain an affluent lifestyle that many envied. My uncles discovered my mother's transgressions. At first, they were pissed. My mother had singlehandedly, dragged the family into crime. They couldn't extricate themselves. I pleaded with them to go to the police, but they were afraid of tarnishing the family name. Also, they were her brothers and felt as you do, that family is worth saving. Even in their anger, they protected her. They swallowed their pride and accepted their fate. I thought that was the coward's way out. I couldn't stomach the criminal activity and I severed ties with my family. I'm telling you this so you understand that good people can become criminals. All people don't start out that way. The crime is in staying that way."

On the drive home, Malik lectured me about my naivety. As we neared my house, I said, "Don't overreact. I feel safe as a kitten."

He pulled to the curb and shut off the engine. He said, "If you felt safe, you wouldn't have asked me to go with you to the Depews."

I said, "True."

Malik's voice crescendoed. "You're a nice person so you think everyone's like you. You don't know a person's character until you get to know them. Stop being so trusting."

I said, "But Mrs. Depew's a little old woman in a wheelchair."

Malik said, "I'm done talking. If you don't toughen up, you'll get hurt." He reached over my lap and opened the door. Then he turned away from me. As soon as I stepped on the curb, he pulled off.

I tossed and turned all night. Malik had shown concern for me, and I had refused to listen. The next morning, I pulled out my cell phone to call Malik, but thought better of it. Instead, I scrolled down to find his address. Half a mile separated our homes, a long walk or a short drive. I drove so if our conversation ended in anger, I could get home in a flash. I would need chocolate.

Malik lived in a pre-war apartment building with great architecture in University Heights. I had never been there, although I'd thought about dropping by some lonely nights. The neighborhood bustled with college students heading to early classes. I drove to the parking lot behind his building. I parked in a visitor's spot and walked around to the front. At the doorbell panel, I pulled my shoulders back and took a strong, wide stance. I stuck out my finger and pushed Malik's bell. I didn't realize I was holding my breath until Malik said, "Who is it?"

"It's me. Can I please come in?"

He said, "Second floor," and buzzed me in.

As I climbed the carpeted steps, I scanned my mind for my humblest apologies. When I reached the landing, I saw Malik leaning out of a doorway, waiting for me.

He stood back and let me in.

I came face to face with a voluptuous, cocoa-skinned woman with straight black hair and big brown eyes. I hoped he didn't hear my sharp intake of breath at the shock. Not only was I surprised at her presence, but at my reaction. My cheeks flushed with jealousy as Malik introduced us.

"This is Valerie," he said and smiled at her. "She was on her way out."

I held out my hand. "I'm...I'm..."

Malik helped me out. "Rocky."

"Miss Beautiful" and I shook hands and murmured greetings. I sucked in my stomach, mimicking her tiny waist.

I busied myself by surveying the living room as they talked by the doorway. Malik's apartment was full of books. Bookshelves lined the walls, and every shelf was filled. Neat piles of books filled corners of the room and more lay on his desk and coffee table. Despite all that, the room was clean and comfortable. As my breathing slowed, I realized classical music played in the background. Thank God. I don't think I could have taken it if he had been playing Barry White.

As Valerie left, she brushed Malik's cheek with a kiss. I could have strangled her. I turned away and pretended to be engrossed in a book about IT Infrastructure. When she left, so did Malik's smile.

He said, "What's up?"

I took a deep breath and let her rip. "I'm sorry. I know you have my best interest at heart. I promise to be more discerning, especially with new people. Your message sunk in last night. I hope you can forgive me."

Malik smiled down at me. "No problem. I'm glad you got the message."

I relaxed a little. "Was that your girlfriend?"

Malik tilted his head and smiled. "Why?"

"No reason." I'm sure my attempt to be casual failed since my voice had risen an entire octave. When he didn't answer my question, I moved on.

We chatted a while. A half hour later, my mind at ease, I readied myself to leave.

Malik opened the door for me and said, "By the way, Valerie is just a friend."

As I headed down the stairs, I hoped he couldn't see my cheeks burn with embarrassment.

EIGHT

After my apology, I left Malik's needing to burn some energy. I had embarrassed myself in front of Malik twice. First, by searching for statuettes with no details whatsoever. Second, by acting like a jealous schoolgirl. I had to restore my pride.

I drove to Ferdinand's Pharmacy. I'd never shopped there before. The unappealing piles of junk I'd seen through the store windows kept me away. Today, it was the perfect place for my plan.

I parked in Ferdinand's back lot and went through the back entrance. I walked the width of the small store, glancing in each aisle for my desired items. The signs above each aisle read Oral Hygiene, Cold Remedies and so on. They held no relation to the items below. Instead, heaps of dollar store trinkets hung over shelves and lay on the dirty floor in no seeming order. I ended up walking each aisle. I scanned the undesirable and unusable junk until I found my treasure.

A jumble of dusty plastic figurines mixed with dog chew toys stopped me in my tracks. A crudely handwritten sign said, "Ivory Statues." Perfect. I picked up one figurine. It was a bust of an African woman molded in white plastic. I surveyed the area for onlookers, but I appeared to be the lone customer. I used a sock from the next bin to wipe the bust clean to see the actual color. To my relief, it looked like ivory, white with a tinge of yellow. I hefted the weight. Heavy. Most likely filled with sand.

At the front of the store, I found a cart and wheeled it back to my bounty. Of course, only three wheels rolled while the fourth skidded across the floor. I extracted the other busts, twenty in all, and pushed them to the register near the front door. A disinterested boy in his late teens sporting rock band tattoos turned on the register. He offered no greeting, just clicked the register keys.

While he rang up the busts one by one, I noticed a 'Help Wanted' sign in the front window. I hoped they would replace this kid with a courteous salesperson.

The boy handed me a receipt and tossed the loose busts back into the cart.

I said, "No bag?"

He shook his head. "You're supposed to bring your own. Didn't you drive?"

I said, "How'd you know that?"

He shrugged. "Most people who come in the back entrance parked in the lot."

I didn't expect great customer service here and I was right. I pushed the cart into the pitted gravel lot and threw the figurines onto the back seat of the Corolla. I spied a pile of discarded cardboard boxes, grabbed one and threw it into my trunk.

Back in my kitchen, I sprayed and wiped the statues until they gleamed. Then, I packed them into the cardboard box. A huge beetle crawled out of the box. I stomped on it and made a note to check my trunk for bugs.

I texted Ernest that I needed to stop by with important news.

In twenty minutes, I stood in Mrs. Depew's sitting room.

Ernest had carried the box in and set it on a table near Mrs. Depew.

I pulled out the first bust and held it up for Mrs. Depew to see. I said, "I found your figurines."

Mrs. Depew peeped into the box. "These aren't the right statuettes."

I said, "How do you know? You've never seen them, and you don't have a picture or description. These are African figures. You said Mr. Depew purchased them from Senegal. Remember?"

Mrs. Depew took the bust from my hands and examined it closely. She said, "This is plastic."

I stood my ground. "Nope. It's ivory." I wanted to see her next move.

She motioned Ernest to her side and whispered in his ear.

He nodded and left the room.

I gulped, unsure of my next move. For all I knew, she could have told Ernest to get a gun. I was ready to bolt for the door when Ernest returned.

Ernest handed a long hat pin to Mrs. Depew and flicked open a lighter. He held the blue flame to the tip of the pin until it turned black with soot.

Mrs. Depew stuck the pin into the plastic bust with ease. She pulled out the pin and handed it back to Ernest. Then, she showed me the sooty hole left between the eyes of the African bust. She threw the bust into the box with the others with such force that it cracked. Mrs. Depew leaned back in

66

her wheelchair and glared at me. "I'm very disappointed. You tried to take advantage of me."

Ernest stood behind her, watching me behind hooded eyes.

I said, "I feel used, too. I brought you your trunk. Yet, you refuse to pay me until I find merchandise you can't even describe to me." Malik would be proud that I stood up to her.

Mrs. Depew said, "You are overmatched, Dear. You just haven't realized it yet. Leave now and I won't call the police about your attempt to defraud me."

I couldn't wrap my mind around Mrs. Depew's tenacity. Her strength and obstinance outweighed mine tenfold.

I left with the knowledge I needed. I confirmed Mrs. Depew's intentions to withhold my fee no matter what I did. I erased the illusion of a frail, old lady. Her mean personality pierced that notion. I no longer believed any statuettes existed. I had one question in my mind. Why did she hire me at all?

Outside, I sat in my car and stewed. The white lace curtain pulled back from the Depew's bay window as Ernest peeped out. I drove off under his steady gaze.

I turned on my radio, flipped rapid fire through several stations and cut it off. I slowed my breathing and loosened my fingers on the wheel. I've made some disastrous decisions when pissed. I wanted to take smart actions going forward.

I pulled to the curb and turned off the engine. I opened Google on my phone and searched. I'm not an IT expert like Malik, but Google made research easy. In a few minutes, I'd found my next destination.

The attorney rocked back and forth in his faux leather chair. He said, "Ms. Rollins, I'm Harry Sunshine. How can I help you?" The tips of his shiny black pencil mustache accented the thinnest lips I'd ever seen.

I stuck out my hand.

He gave me one limp shake and drew back. He ran his hand over oily, curly black hair, making me glad I'd only touched him briefly.

I laid my business card on his desk. I figured he'd toss it when I left, but I needed to get rid of them. I sat on the faded green, threadbare chair and almost sank through the cushion. I said, "First, I want to confirm this is a free consultation like it says on your website."

Sunshine leaned over the scratched oak desk and flashed a brief smile. "Of course. Please share your plight." He turned and glanced out the window while I started.

I plunged ahead. "I did a job for someone, and she refuses to pay me. What are my recourses?"

He shrugged. "This is a common lawsuit." His bored expression revealed his disinterest.

I brightened. "Great. How much do you charge?"

He flipped his hand. "You won't have to pay up front. I take a percentage of the win."

My lungs loosened and I was able to breathe again. A free attorney would be a blessing.

The attorney glanced at his watch and said, "Let's speed this along. I have a few questions. First, did you bring your contract with you?"

I gripped the chair arms. "It was more of a verbal agreement."

The attorney rolled his eyes. His shoulders sagged. He said, "That makes the suit much more difficult to win. Will the other party dispute the terms of the contract?"

I gulped and stared at my feet.

For the first time during the consultation, Sunshine gave me his full attention. "Let me be honest here. Your case would be an uphill, time-consuming battle. You should have consulted me before you took this job. You would have had to pay me up front, but you would have gotten your fee from your client."

I said, "If I had money to pay a lawyer, I wouldn't be in this predicament."

The attorney shook his head and made a note on his laptop. He looked up and said, "You should have chosen a stable career." He glanced at his watch again. "My pockets will always be lined with cash. I don't think I can help you, but would you mind telling me the name of the defendant?"

I said, "Mrs. Lilac Depew."

The attorney's face blanched. He closed his laptop and eyed me for a moment.

I said, "What's the matter? You know Mrs. Depew?"

He said, "Yes and the interaction was a nightmare. I'm going to share something with you in confidence and then, you're going to leave. If you repeat this, I'll deny it."

I leaned in.

Sunshine rose and closed his office door. He said, "Mr. Depew wanted to put his nephew Ernest in his will, but Mrs. Depew forbade it. They had a huge fight right here in my office. The next day, Mr. Depew called and told me he would not be amending his will."

I said, "I'm not surprised."

He said, "That's not all. A day later, Ernest stopped in asking about the will. I don't know how he knew about it. I had to tell him he would not inherit from his uncle. You can believe he wasn't happy. He left with clenched fists and tears in his eyes. I didn't know if he wanted to kill me or his relatives."

I said, "I bet his uncle told him he would be added but didn't have the heart to tell him what happened."

Sunshine splayed his hands. "Who knows what went on in that household. They're nasty people. I cut ties with that crazy family. I also don't do business with their associates." He stood abruptly, opened his door and ushered me out with a swoop of his hand. As I left, Sunshine said, "Goodbye Ms. Rollins. We will never speak again."

Back on the road, I knew I had to get more information on the Depews. They had the upper hand. I had to flip the script. I needed to spy on the Depews without getting too close. Malik had cautioned me, and I would try to embrace his warnings. But how would I see what was going on from a distance? What would Catwoman do? She would have spy glasses. I hustled to my car and headed to the big box electronics store.

On Route 22, my mind wandered through the details of my case. I sped right past the store, cut over two lanes and swerved onto the U-turn. In my rear-view mirror, I saw another car do the same. At least I'm not the only idiot on the road. My mind returned to Mrs. Depew. I swept past the store again and hit another U-turn. This time I noticed the same car followed my lead. Don't be silly. No, I'm sure. The hair stood up on the back of my neck. Hundreds of cars filled the road. This had to be a coincidence. But still...

Finally, I pulled into the parking lot of the electronics store. The car that I thought was following me kept going and I breathed easier.

As I walked up and down the bright aisles, I mapped out my plan. The house across from the Depews would make a great spy location. Big bushes lined their front yard and would make a secure hiding spot. I was counting on the residents being at work during the day giving me full access to the yard. I wandered up and down the wide aisles until I found a mesmerizing display of binoculars. Big ones, small ones, single-eye telescopes, and neon-colored binoculars held my gaze for twenty minutes. Tucked into a far corner, I spotted the perfect pair. Happy with my purchase, I hit the road.

As I darted back onto the highway, I remembered the creeps I'd felt earlier. I checked my rear-view mirror as I swerved from lane to lane. No cars followed my lead. It wasn't until I jumped onto the off ramp that I spotted it. The same car I had seen earlier still tailed me. Malik's cautionary words echoed in my mind. Reminding myself to breathe, I devised a plan. I drove up and down random streets leading the car to a well-populated location. If I was going to confront someone, I wanted a lot of people around. I pulled into a crowded grocery store parking lot and waited. Sure enough, a steel blue BMW pulled up alongside me. I knew this car.

A man hopped out. He dropped his keys and bent to retrieve them.

I marched up to him. I braced myself to face this Frankenstein, a horrible person who would steal an old lady's stuff. I tapped him on the shoulder, prepared to lay into him with all my fierceness. When he stood, I opened my mouth and said, "Meoooow." My eyes slid over the most handsome slice of chocolate man I had seen in years.

He said, "Did you say something?"

Did I say that out loud? I said, "Is your name Charles?"

He said, "Why yes. How did you know?" He reached out his hand to shake mine.

Of course, I took it. Mmmm, warm. Frowning with what I hoped was a stern face, I said, "What is your last name?"

"My last name is Charles."

My brain dizzied as it bounced from his charming smile to my need for cash. I leaned back on my car and said, "What is your first name?"

He smoothed his 6'3" frame into the space beside me and said, "Let me explain. My name is Charles Charles."

"Is that supposed to be like Duran Duran?" Despite my sarcasm, his athletic physique had my attention, more than his words. His light brown eyes and close-cropped curly hair distracted me from my task.

He said, "My birth name was Charles Ortiz. My father died and my mother remarried a man named Burton Charles. He moved us from Puerto Rico to the U.S. When my stepfather adopted me, he changed my last name to Charles. Hence, Charles Charles."

My hard shell had turned rubbery. I smiled, then remembered Rocky Recoveries. I whipped out the invoice for the statuettes and waved it in his face. "Where are the statuettes?"

Charles rolled his eyes. "Not this again."

I handed him one of my dandy new business cards and said, "I'm here to recover those statuettes. They belong to my client."

He stepped back and said, "I have no idea what you're talking about."

I leaned in closer. He smelled of a heavenly Jimmy Choo cologne I had sniffed once at a shoe sale. "I know you were in that pawn shop inquiring about the statuettes. Don't deny it." I thought my interrogation technique sounded good.

Charles smirked. "That's right. I was."

Wow, this interrogation stuff is easy. He confessed already. "So you admit it."

"Sure. I'm looking for statuettes. So, obviously, I don't have any."

I said, "Oh." I went from being Jessica Fletcher to Lucy Riccardo in one second flat. I felt my eyebrows gearing up for a mighty twitch. I handed him the invoice. "Then how do you explain this?"

Charles Charles scanned the paper. His face contorted into a scowl. "This is bullshit. I ordered some merchandise from Mr. Depew online. I wired the money to his account, but never received the goods. Mrs. Depew has the whole situation backwards. She thinks I have the statuettes and never paid." He crumpled the invoice and threw it to the ground.

I picked up the invoice with a shaky hand. He told a plausible story. My voice squeaked. "Why are you visiting pawn shops, if you're not selling the statuettes?"

"Mrs. Depew is trying to sue me for payment. I want to prove that Mr. Depew took my money and then sold the merchandise elsewhere so I can get her off my back. Hence, I'm searching pawn shops."

I opened my mouth to speak but before I could utter a word, Charles Charles stepped forward and leaned over me. I froze.

He said, "Look lady. I'm advising you now to step back. You don't know what you're doing or what you're involved in. Don't try to contact me again. I'm giving you a pass right now because I don't want to see you get hurt, but you better stay away." He pointed a finger in my face and said, "Stay away."

Charles Charles marched back to his car, leaving me panting in fear. He sat in his car, gripping the steering wheel and staring down at his lap. His shoulders rose with each breath. A minute later, he got out of his car and walked back toward me.

I jumped into my Corolla, locked the doors, and cracked my window an inch. "Why were you following me?"

Charles flashed his smile and said, "Open the door. I want to apologize."

I held my ground. "You can apologize through the window. I'm not getting out of this car. How did you find me?"

He shrugged. "The pawn shop guy gave me your card with your contact info on it. I followed you from your house. By the way, you drive like a maniac."

I said, "That's impossible. You left the pawn shop before me."

He said, "I circled back because I wanted to ask him something else. He told me about your inquiry and gave me your card."

Logical. I said, "If you had my address, why did you follow me out here? Did you just happen to be on Route 22?"

Charles looked down and shook his head. He took a breath before answering. "As I said, I followed you from your house. I didn't want to scare you by knocking on your door. I thought it better to meet you out in the open. You stopped at an apartment building and then you headed for the highway. I thought you'd be comfortable speaking with me in a public parking lot."

I said, "You told me to stay away from you. Now you're here. Why?"

Charles opened his mouth to speak.

I raised a warning finger, and he stopped short.

I said, "You cursed at me and..."

Charles leaned close to my window.

I stopped mid-sentence.

He said, "I just want to apologize."

My mouth hung open. It took a few seconds to process his words. My eyes darted back and forth as I decided how to respond. Thirty seconds later I said, "I don't believe you." Yes, it was a lame response, but what else could I say?

He stepped back and said, "Please, hear me out. We started out on the wrong foot."

I crossed my arms and said, "You bet."

Charles said, "After all, you came on pretty strong."

"What? I didn't..."

He said, "You waved that paperwork in my face and accused me of stealing."

This isn't going well. I rolled my window down.

Before I could defend myself, Charles said, "You yelled at me."

I sighed. "I didn't mean to yell. You wouldn't cooperate."

Charles cocked his head, "Didn't I answer all your questions?"

"Yes." I couldn't look him in the eye.

He said, "Didn't my answers make sense?"

My shoulders slumped. "Yeah."

He smiled. "The least you could do is accept my apology. Give me a chance to start over."

I got out of my car.

Charles extended his hand. "Can we be friends?"

My stomach clenched as I took his hand.

NINE

The next morning, I parked my Corolla a block over from the Depew house. I could see its rooftop from where I stood. It was after nine so most of the residents had gone to work. I sauntered up the driveway of one house, hoping to look like I belonged there. Once behind the house, I scrambled through two adjoining backyards. I tiptoed around a huge doghouse (empty, thank goodness) and onto the next property. There, I ducked behind the Azalea bushes in the front yard and peered at the Depew house across the street.

Even with my fancy binoculars, I couldn't see much motion through the sun glare on their windows. Each time I sensed movement, I leaned forward and squinted to sharpen my vision. This, ladies and gentlemen, is the surveillance game.

I don't know what I expected to happen. In truth, I should have walked away, far away from this family. But they had drawn me into their deceit, and I couldn't extricate myself. I didn't have the full picture of this mystery and I couldn't rest until I solved it.

After some time, Ernest passed a window. Ernest was the key. He was the one person who could tell me the inside story. If he could speak, that is. If he came out, I'd grab his attention. I hoped he would talk to me away from Mrs. Depew's scrutiny. Then again, if Ernest murdered his uncle, that key could unlock dangerous reactions. Should I take the chance and approach him?

I heard a latch click behind me. I ducked down as small as possible hoping to blend into the shadows.

A deep, stern voice said, "Who the hell are you and what are you doing in my bushes?"

I rose on shaky legs.

A tall, middle-aged man stood at the door of the screened-in porch.

I cleared my throat and pulled my shoulders back. "I'm with Rocky Recoveries."

The man ran a hand through his wavy gray hair. "So?" He started down the steps.

I took a deep breath. "I'm on a case." I reached into my bag. I whipped out my shiny badge and held it out for him to see.

He stopped mid-step. "And you're interrogating my azaleas?" He crossed his arms.

I stepped forward. "I'm conducting an investigation into the occupants of the house across the street. Do you know the Depews?"

The man said, "Oh. We don't get many police around here. This is a good neighborhood." He approached in a friendly manner.

I tucked the badge away before he took a closer look at it.

He said, "I don't know them well. Mostly, I see the big guy come out to cut the lawn or run errands. I've only seen the older lady a few times. I don't think she comes out much."

I said, "Did you get a sense of their personalities? Are they nice people? Have you seen anyone else visit? How often do they come and go?"

He scratched his head. "One time I saw the old lady screaming at the big guy about doing the lawn a certain way. He was cringing, but he didn't yell back. She must be his mother or something."

From inside the house a woman's voice said, "Honey, where are you?"

He said, "I gotta go. Please don't take too long. My wife won't like a stranger in the yard." He disappeared into the house.

I blew out a sigh of relief and made a mental note to thank Lusty for the badge idea. I leaned forward and peeped through the bushes again. I stood too far away to see much, and I didn't dare cross the street.

From behind me a voice said, "Why are you using those ridiculous glasses?" Before I could turn, a hand slapped across my mouth and an arm wrapped around my middle, lifting me up. I could feel hot breath in my ear as a voice said, "Don't say a word."

Say a word? I could hardly breathe. Before I could think of escaping, I was being pulled back into the underbrush at the side of the house. I kicked my legs taking care not to damage my Prada heels.

My attacker stopped and said, "I'm going to release your mouth. If you scream, I'll strangle you."

I held very still, dropping my gold and rhinestone opera glasses.

He released my mouth as promised and then, gripping my arms, turned me to face him.

I shut my eyes tight, because in all the movies, if you see your assailant, they kill you.

He said, "Open your eyes."

I shook my head and shut them tighter.

He said, "Rocky, look at me."

At the sound of my name, my eyes popped open. It was Charles Charles. Anger shot through me before I could stop myself and I stomped a stiletto into his instep.

Charles screamed.

I stood there with my arms crossed, glaring at him as he hopped up and down on his good foot. I said, "What the hell are you doing? You scared me half to death."

Charles said, "You didn't have to cripple me." He slipped off his loafer and rubbed his foot. "I had to talk to you. You're in trouble."

"What was your first clue? Was it finding me in the bushes? And how did you know I was here anyway? Did you follow me again?" At this point my words were rolling in a fever pitch. My mouth couldn't keep up with my thoughts.

Charles laid his fingers on my shoulders and smiled. "Calm down. I'm on your side."

That smile. What is it about his smile? I wanted to lay my head on his shoulder and forget my troubles. I wanted him to tell me everything was going to be alright, that he would take care of everything. No matter how strong I can be, I still need someone to lean on in hard times. And these were the hardest of times. I drew a deep breath and agreed to lunch.

Charles' BMW was parked behind my car, its slick exterior gleaming next to my unwashed Corolla.

I pulled out my car keys and Charles said, "You're going to ride with me."

I put my hands on my hips and said, "I'm not getting in a car with you. How do I know you're not kidnapping me?"

He said, "Because you're coming willingly. Kidnap victims are dragged to the car and thrown in a trunk."

I had to admit that's how they did it in movies. I said, "I don't know. Why can't I follow you?"

Charles chuckled, then walked around his car and opened the passenger door.

I could smell the sun-warmed leather and a faint vanilla scent. My eyes darted back and forth between my car and his. I said, "One moment." I leaned into my car and dropped a post note on my seat. I left the Corolla where I parked it and rode in Charles' steel blue BMW.

We stopped at a small café in Montclair. Again, I waited in the car while Charles ran in and picked up lunch. This time I hunkered down. I didn't care if we were in Montclair, people still might recognize me. I didn't want a repeat of what happened at the bodega.

Charles emerged with a large paper tote bag (no grease, and plastic would be a no-no in Montclair). He handed me the heavenly smelling bag and we took off.

We had lunch in Edgemont Park. We crossed the beautiful expanse of greenery and settled on a shady bench near the lake. A cool breeze offset the warmth of the day and carried a floral scent. The setting was so beautiful I almost forgot why we were there. Charles sat the bag between us.

Charles laid a large napkin on the bench. With a flourish, he presented two small quiches, a bottle of white wine and a green salad for two.

I said, "What, no dessert?" at which he whipped out a small strawberry shortcake.

Charles said, "Now, about you."

I leaned in and smiled. "Yes?"

He said, "The police have found solid evidence of Mr. Depew's murder."

Back to reality. I said, "Well, that should be a good thing. Right? I mean the evidence can't lead to me because I didn't kill him."

"They found a cane."

I said, "With an ivory dolphin handle?"

"Yes, a bloodied ivory dolphin."

My mouth dropped open, but I remembered to close it since it was full of asparagus quiche.

Charles said, "The police have confirmed the blood is Mr. Depew's. The case is no longer missing persons; it's homicide."

I asked, "How do you know? Where are you getting your information? Are you a cop?"

Charles said, "No, but an officer may be involved."

I stopped chewing. "Involved how?"

Charles scanned the park, then leaned in close. "Detective Brimley ran the theft case on Mr. Depew's merchandise. Now, he's investigating Depew's murder? Brimley has his hands on all things Depew."

I had stopped breathing. "So?"

Charles said, "Who's to say he didn't take those statuettes himself? That would make a nice nest egg." Charles leaned back and let me absorb his words.

I took a sip of wine and let the cool liquid relax me. I said, "I wish I'd never heard of the Depews."

Charles asked, "How did you get involved with them anyway? You never told me."

I said, "My next-door neighbor Lusty referred me to them."

Charles said, "Is she trustworthy? Could she have set you up?"

I gasped. "Lusty is my best friend. She loves me and would never do anything to hurt me. Don't you ever say anything like that again."

Charles held up his hands in defense. "I'm sorry. I didn't mean to offend you. I want to help you. I know you didn't kill Mr. Depew, but the police think you did, or at least, were an accomplice."

"But why would I want to kill him? I have no motive. I didn't even know him."

Charles laid a gentle hand on my arm and said, "The police found connections between you and Mr. Depew."

A shiver, which I couldn't identify as fear or desire, ran up my spine. "If you're not a cop, how do you know this information?"

He said, "The police questioned me because of the statuettes. They also found the cane at the address on the manifest. Just like you, they assumed I lived there. Once they confirmed my actual address, they let me go."

I said, "The cane was in that house?" I'd lost my appetite.

"Yes, and so were you."

My chest began to heave.

Charles said, "They have a statement from a witness, some junkie, who claims to have seen you in the house."

I could feel my eyes fill and I looked away.

Charles moved the food aside and wrapped his strong arm around my shoulder. I leaned into him and released my pent-up fears, my brave face washed away by tears. I sniffed and Charles handed me a napkin. I said, "Why do you want to help me?"

Charles brushed a tear from my cheek. "Why wouldn't I help a beautiful woman like you?" He kissed my forehead, my eyelids, my wet cheeks, and my waiting lips.

Right there in the midday sun, I fell in love. Here was a man who would shelter me from the evils of the world. I could release my fears and melt into his safe haven, if only for a few moments. That kiss erased murders and police and threats and trepidation. This was a kiss I could dwell in forever.

I opened my eyes and re-experienced the beauty of his smile and the twinkle in his eyes. The tingle I first felt when I met him at the pawn shop returned. We packed up the remains of our picnic and walked back to the car in silence.

Back at my car, Charles said, "Please be careful. The police have another lead they're following, and I don't know where it will take them. Also, the Depews are dangerous. Don't underestimate them. Be sure to share any information you find with me so I can help you. I'll call you later."

I didn't share Mrs. Depew's threat with Charles. A tiny voice in the back of my mind said, "You still don't know him." But damn, I sure wanted to.

It was too late in the afternoon to return to my hiding spot in the bushes across from the Depew house. Adults would be coming back from work and kids would be home from school. So, I packed it in for the day. I hopped in my car and crumpled the post note that said, "If you find this car I've been kidnapped."

Before I drove off, Holy called.

I didn't want to ruin a beautiful afternoon with Holy's nonsense but decided to get it over with.

He said, "Hi Honey."

I said, "Why are you calling?"

Holy said, "Do I need a reason?"

"Absolutely. We don't chitchat. We don't interact. We have no reason to call each other."

Holy said, "I need your help."

I waited, silent. I knew not to fall for his cons. Over the years, he had played on my sympathies in an effort to renew our relationship. Once he pretended to have a broken foot so I could nurse him to health. He hobbled up my walk on crutches with an Ace bandage wrapped around his foot. Murphy bit the end of the bandage and it unraveled to reveal a perfectly healthy appendage. Then, there was the time he said he needed help at the junkyard because he lost his wallet in a pile of garbage. I don't know why he thought I'd fall for that one.

Holy said, "Can I stay with you for a while?"

I almost choked with laughter. "Are you serious?"

He said, "I need a place to hide out. The police questioned me today."

I stopped mid-chuckle. "What did they want?"

"They didn't say what they wanted. A Detective Brimley asked if I'd seen anything strange at the junkyard. A couple of other cops strolled around searching piles of garbage. It seemed casual, but it made me nervous."

I steadied my breathing before I answered. I said, "No. You can't with me. You're not in any trouble. They're probably checking all the junkyards in the area for something."

Holy said, "But Honey, I need you."

I said, "You'll be fine." I disconnected and waited until I stopped shaking before I drove away.

I wanted to sleep off my lunch and dream about Charles, but I was too unnerved. To get rid of my nervous energy, I decided to update Malik on my way home. I floated through Malik's door on a romantic cloud and stopped short.

Malik greeted me at the door and said, "I cooked dinner. I thought we could strategize our next moves." He waved his hand toward the kitchen. An aroma that should have made me drool, instead caused nausea.

He put his hand on the small of my back and ushered me into the kitchen. Blue China topped a white linen tablecloth. Blue and white napkins in bone napkin rings matched the plates. Two long stemmed wine glasses and candles finished the setting.

My stomach bulged as it was. I had eaten a full meal and finished my dessert in Charles' car on the way back. I was about to bow out of dinner when Malik said, "I've been cooking all afternoon. I hope you're hungry." He pulled out my chair, the determined gentleman that he was, and poured red wine.

I fidgeted with my napkin and sipped the wine as Malik ladled beef stew onto our plates. He whipped a towel off a bowl to reveal hot homemade cheddar biscuits.

Malik raised his glass. "What should we toast to? I know, to your safety."

I raised my glass to meet his. The lump in my throat kept me from saying anything. Why do I feel guilty? It's not like we're in a relationship.

My belly protested as I began to eat. Beneath the tablecloth, I unbuttoned my jeans with one hand. I forced down every bit of the stew and two biscuits.

I needed to get to the bathroom and retrieve some stomach space. As I stood, Malik brought down a giant double chocolate cake from the top of the fridge. He said, "Surprise. I know you love chocolate."

Thank goodness, Malik mistook the horrified look in my eyes for surprise. "I knew you'd like it. I bet you thought I didn't know you at all." He let me beg off with a promise to have some cake later that evening.

I excused myself from the table and went to the bathroom. On my way back I stopped cold at Malik's whisper. I flattened against the wall and cocked my head.

Shitty Kitty said, "It's wrong to eavesdrop but you know you can't resist."

Malik said, "I know it's been a while. It's nice to know you miss me." I missed conversation pieces as he paced the living room. Damn. I bet that's the beautiful Valerie. Malik moved closer. "I need you." I bit my lip to keep from screaming my frustration. I wanted to rush into his arms and tear the phone from his hand. He said, "Thank you for understanding." Was he explaining why I was here? Maybe she should understand that I'm here to stay. More muffled words. Then, "I love you too." My heart dropped.

TEN

I waited for Malik to end his call, then entered the living room. I sat on the couch and said, "I need your feedback on something."

Malik's eyebrows rose. He sat next to me and waited.

I said, "I saw an attorney yesterday about the Depews."

Malik said, "You could afford an attorney?"

"Thank goodness, Harry Sunshine offered a free consultation."

Malik chuckled. "You mean that guy with posters on the bus stop shelters? He looks slimy."

I said, "Whatever. Harry Sunshine knew the Depews. He told me Mrs. Depew stopped Mr. Depew from adding Ernest to his will. If Ernest had that good of a relationship with his uncle, he wasn't likely to have killed him. That means Mrs. Depew did the deed."

Malik took a moment to absorb the info. "That's not necessarily true. Suppose Ernest killed his uncle thinking that he would inherit. Then, he found out he wasn't a beneficiary. He might kill Mrs. Depew to ensure he gets their money. She could be in danger."

I bit my lip. "I see what you mean. There's a lot of ways this could play out. I don't know enough about the inner workings of that household."

Malik took my hand. He said, "Someone in that house is dangerous and you don't know who. I've been doing a lot of thinking. You've been good to me, and I want to take care of you. Your safety has been utmost in my mind." He leaned closer. "I fixed up a place here for you. That way I can protect you. We can work together to extricate you from this mess." He smiled and gazed into my eyes. "How does that sound?"

I turned away. "I don't need protection. I can take care of myself."

Malik sat back. "You think you're safe because you're spunky and maybe a little naïve. You're involved in a possible murder. You don't know what these people are capable of or who else is involved. You need someone to watch your back."

I stood up and tried to look stern. "I appreciate your concern, but I like my own space."

Malik didn't give up. "I'll give you space. You'll have plenty of time to yourself while I'm at school."

"I'm not afraid to live alone."

Malik eyed me for a moment, then said, "Did your divorce make you leery of commitment? Why did your marriage end?"

My head hurt at the memory.

Holy had turned out to be a replica of Dad. When I wanted to see a show or go to a craft fair, Holy had always managed to give a logical reason to stay in. When he wanted to do something, we did it no matter how I protested.

Years passed before I saw the pattern of smothering dominance. Our marriage revolved around Holy's wants and needs.

At Holy's insistence we shopped together, ran errands together, did everything together. At first, I loved it. I felt more comfortable with him than by myself.

A couple of years into married bliss, our oneness began wearing thin. His comforting hugs morphed into strangleholds.

The blinders of denial fell from my eyes the day Holy lost his mind and sold my stilettos.

I opened my closet to see my shoe racks missing and nothing but dust balls in their place. My work boots stood alone. I hated those ugly, thick, dirty boots.

"What happened to my shoes," I asked.

Holy shrugged. "I sold them. What do you need with fancy shoes, working at the yard?"

I stepped to within a half inch of his face. Holy's eyes widened.

I said, "Have you lost your little mind?" I had never raised my voice to Holy before. In fact, I had never even considered it, but shoes were worth fighting for.

My anger opened my eyes to Holy's control of my life. I didn't blame him. In fact, I felt sorry for him. He hadn't changed in ten years, but I had. I had thought we had a warm, comfortable relationship. Instead, I had married familiarity. In truth, Holy had dominated me just like Dad. Instead of gaining freedom, I had moved from one controller to another.

I looked at Malik and said, "He sold my shoes."

Malik sighed. "This isn't funny. I don't think you're taking your situation seriously. You take too many chances."

I took a deep breath and plunged ahead. "I can take care of myself. For example, this afternoon I met Charles."

"Charles? The guy on the invoice? Are you nuts? You could have gotten hurt."

I said, "He seemed nice at first. Then he got a little testy."

Malik's biceps tensed. "What did he do? He didn't touch you, did he?"

"Of course not. He just yelled a little and walked away." I filled in a few details, skipping the romantic lunch. "So, you see, I'm very careful."

"Oh yeah? You stole a trunk from an abandoned house. You confronted that Charles guy. You launched your own investigation into the Depews."

"What's your point?"

Malik stood and held my shoulders in his warm hands. He said, "Let me take care of you."

It took all my strength not to nuzzle into him. One tear, then another, rolled down my cheek. What's wrong with me? Why am I crying so much lately? My shoulders sagged. I pulled back and said, "Maybe you're right. I'll move in with my father." *What are these words coming out of my mouth? I need my head examined, and fast.*

Malik's hurt expression broke my heart. If he had only asked yesterday, I would have jumped at the chance to live with him. But now...

Malik said, "That doesn't make sense. You despise your father and I know you like me." He reached for me again.

I stood. "I don't want to put you in danger. The police's suspicions could spread to you. I couldn't forgive myself if you got wrapped up in my trouble."

Malik opened his mouth to protest, but I said, "I'd better go."

I left that evening with half a chocolate cake and a whole broken heart.

Murphy and I parked in front of Dad's house. *What am I doing? This is the last place I want to be.*

Dad swung the door open and said, "What are you doing out there? Dinner is ready."

Oh no. I could smell chicken and garlic.

Dad helped me in with my bags, and Murphy and I settled in.

I scanned my childhood bedroom. Dad had painted it a girly pink color that I hated. In turn, I had hung posters of Tupac and Snoop Dog on the wall. Not that I liked rap, but because Dad hated it. The room represented the tug of war between us that continued today. One day I came home from high school to find a new white Princess bed with a ruffled canopy. I yanked the canopy down and snatched the matching coverlet off the bed. I replaced it with a black blanket that mom had stashed in the back of the linen closet years ago. I hung a Black power flag from one of the posts. This tug of war continued for months before Dad gave up.

As I examined the bedroom, I wondered if it represented me or just my resentment. My posters remained on the wall. The white desk facing the window had been my favorite place. It's where I sat, gazed outside, and dreamed of freedom. Next to the desk hung a cork board to which I'd attached pictures of the feisty Black women. I'd hung posters of the fiery females of Living Single next to Carol Moseley Braun and Venus Williams. In the center, hung a picture of Mom.

With all the conflict in my memories, I still felt a sense of home and comfort. The fact that Dad had preserved my room meant he felt the same or that he had closed the door on that part of our lives.

Dad yelled from downstairs. "What are you doing up there? Dinner's getting cold."

Sure enough, the table was set.

What should have been an enticing aroma sickened me. My stomach already bulged with food. I said, "Dad, I'm too tired to eat."

He glared at me and said, "I cooked for you even though you never call, that is until you need a place to stay in an emergency. It took a fumigation to get you to visit."

"I'm sorry, Dad. I'm just so tired."

He said, "You're so skinny. You need to eat." He looked at my feet.

I could see his temperature rise ten degrees.

He pointed down. "And those shoes make you even thinner. Take those shoes off. You don't need party heels in my house."

I kicked off my Pradas and said, "Am I plumper now? See, I don't need to eat."

"Don't be ungrateful. I've been cooking since you called, and you will eat." He loaded the table with fried chicken, garlic mashed potatoes and cabbage.

I said, "Fine. I brought dessert."

After dinner, I offered to do the dishes. I instantly regretted it. A proliferation of pots, pans and utensils blanketed the stove and crowded the sink. The sight of the remaining food repulsed me. I hoped I could stand long enough to get through it all. I filled the sink with steamy soapy water and got to work.

Dad went to his room to call his friend. I never thought of Dad having friends. In fact, I rarely thought about his life alone. When Mom died, he focused all his energies on me. He never left me with a sitter to hang out with pals or go to the local bar. As far as I knew, he didn't date. For the first time, I wondered if he was lonely. What had raising me alone taken from him? Had I been selfish for leaving him?

I called Lusty and laid my phone on the windowsill above the sink.

Lusty answered in a husky voice. She said, "Hold on while I finish this call."

I heard her cell plop onto a soft surface. In the distance, I heard Lusty say, "You so spicy." She giggled. "I'll talk to you soon." Lusty's voice came through loud and clear on her cell. "How's everything going?"

I said, "I'm trying to spend time with Dad. It's grueling."

Lusty laughed. "Do you want some tips? You know I deal with a lot of men."

I shook my head, then realized Lusty couldn't see me. "No thanks. I can't talk to my dad the way you talk to men. It's different."

Lusty said, "Not really. Just play to your father's ego. Praise whatever he's good at. All men appreciate that. In fact, so do we."

She had a point. I thanked her for the advice and disconnected.

As I dried the last dish, Dad's voice boomed from the living room. "What are you doing in there? You're taking forever to wash a few dishes. Did you forget how? Hurry up and sit with me. I'll pick a show for us to watch."

Back to reality. He eradicated my sympathy with a few words. I entered the living room and said, "How's your friend?"

Dad said, "Fine. Sit down." He clicked the remote.

I sat on the couch, eyes drooping. All I wanted was to lay on my back as my stomach had bloated to the size of a basketball.

My father seemed refreshed. He prattled on about my lifestyle, our lack of communication and my stilettos.

I think I nodded in all the right places. I got up the courage to say, "Dad, I've got to get some sleep. Thanks for dinner." Remembering Lusty's advice, I said, "Your cooking skills are off the chart. You could give lessons." I waited for a warm response as I stood to leave.

Dad grimaced. "I knew you wouldn't tell me."

"Tell you what?"

"The real reason you came here."

"Dad, I told you..."

He stood up, turned his back to me and stared out the front window. "The police have been here."

My blood turned to ice. "When were the police here?"

"Two days ago. They said they wanted to question you about a murder. I felt so stupid, not knowing my own daughter's whereabouts. I've been waiting to hear from you since they came by, thinking you were in danger. Then when you finally call me, you give me some story about fumigating your house."

I shifted my feet. "Dad, I'm sorry. I didn't want you to worry."

My father wiped the corner of his eye and said, "I know you don't love me, but I am your father. I thought you knew you could come to me if you were in trouble."

"Dad, of course I love you." I choked back a sob. How many hearts am I going to break in one day? I love him but I don't like him. Most of us have family like that.

Dad said, "You started this cockamamie business and now you're in trouble."

"What kind of evidence did they say they had?"

"They didn't say. Why should they communicate with me? You don't."

I didn't have an answer for him. What was the point anyway? The reason I left in the first place was because he won every argument.

Dad said, "You are going to scrap your so-called business and move back in here with me. End of discussion."

"I can't do that, Dad. I need my independence. I hope you understand."

As my dad left the room, he muttered, "Just like your mother." He walked into the dining room and kicked my stilettos halfway across the room.

For the third time in one day, I fought back my tears. "Dad..." My cell purred. 'Unknown Caller' flashed on the screen. I hesitated, glancing at it. By the time I turned back Dad had gone.

A medieval rack of men pulled my mind in opposite directions and caused me misery. I needed time to think on my own. I crept up to my room, packed my duffel bag and Murphy, and returned to Paradise. Dad would understand. My absence would give us both peace.

I entered the dark, quiet interior of my home and for the first time in days, breathed tranquil air. The serenity lasted only one night.

ELEVEN

The next morning, I took a rare trip to the grocery store. Usually, I pick up my basics once a month consisting of canned and frozen items. I hit the local farmer's market weekly for fresh veggies and fruit. As I exited my car, I stopped short. My breath caught in my chest.

Ernest strode toward the grocery store entrance. Of course, someone had to buy the Depew groceries. Ernest did everything for Mrs. Depew. It made sense that he buy the food. Then again, Ernest may have Mrs. Depew captive in her home. All he would have to do is lift her out of her wheelchair, rendering her immobile.

I waited until he entered the store, and I ducked inside. Ernest pushed a cart down the produce aisle. When he reached the far end, I ducked behind the apples and watched as he shopped from a list. I stood and walked toward him. He turned toward the fish counter. I jumped back and flattened myself against the salad bar. Come on Rocky, you can face him. What's he going to do? Murder you in the pasta aisle? Shoulders back, head up, I stepped toward the fish counter. No Ernest. I searched each aisle and finally found him checking out. With shame, I watched Ernest march out the door with three vinyl shopping bags. I made the mental note that he only bought enough groceries for a week. That meant he'd return next week. Maybe I could work up more courage by then, or I could bring backup.

The backup idea seemed best, since I didn't know Ernest's capabilities.

I needed to call Malik. I'd asked him to pick me up from my dad's to continue the Depew investigation. I pulled out my phone and set it on the table. I reached for it and pulled back. I needed to come up with a reason why I was back in my own house. I could park in front of my father's house and let him pick me up there as agreed. That would be silly...but it could work. I checked my watch. I can get there just in time. I grabbed my keys and the phone buzzed. I dropped my keys and shoulders as I answered Malik's call. "Hi Malik."

"Are you ready? I'm on my way."

I said, "Well, about that. I'm back at my house." I squeezed my eyes shut to prepare for the onslaught.

Malik said, "What are you doing there? You did move to your dad's, right?"

"Yeah, but I'm home now."

"Why? Did you forget something?"

I braced myself and launched into a replay of last night's argument with Dad.

Malik said, "Are you getting the message that people are worried about you? You're ignoring everyone who cares about your safety. I'm not going to rehash what I've already told you."

"Malik..."

"Sit tight. I'm on my way...to your house."

In a few minutes, Malik rolled up to my curb. My cell phone purred as I climbed into the Escalade. I glanced at my caller ID and answered. "Hi Lusty."

"Hey there. What are you up to?" she asked.

She sounded way too cheery for me, like someone who needed a favor. But it was okay because I needed cheering up after talking to Mrs. Depew. I said, "Malik and I are about to work on our case, I mean job. What's up?"

"Good news. I have another referral for you."

I wasn't sure if this was good news or not. Lusty's last referrals had been a pain in the ass. I had staved off my creditors for the moment, but unless Mrs. Depew paid me, I would be in trouble before I knew it. "Let's hear it."

Malik looked at me and said, "Is that Aunt Lusty?"

I nodded.

Malik said under his breath, "Uh oh."

Lusty chattered on. "My friend needs his fish transported. I told him I knew someone he could trust. He paid for the fish, but he needs to pick them up. He can't do it himself, so I suggested Rocky Recoveries."

She sounded so proud of herself. I knew she wanted to help Malik and me, but frankly, her referrals were killing us. I said, "You say it's a tank of fish? Are you sure?"

Lusty said, "Yes. I double checked with him. Malik told me about your other jobs, and I didn't want you to have any trouble."

I glanced at Malik and said, "Give me the address." We chatted a few minutes more and disconnected.

Malik and I took off.

I sighed. "I know Lusty means well, but I don't trust the jobs she gives us. I mean, she would never deliberately sabotage us, but these referrals get us in trouble. I don't know what mess I'm in because of the Depews."

Malik stopped my roll. "You're correct. Deep in your heart you know Aunt Lusty wouldn't do anything to hurt you. Right?" Malik waited patiently for my answer.

My face flushed with shame. I had let Charles remarks about Lusty seep into my brain. I knew better. I said, "Lusty loves me. I can't blame her for trying to help me. She's doing her best just like me." I bit my lip to stop my flow of stupidity.

When I felt able to hold a decent conversation, I said, "Mrs. Depew uses a wheelchair but there's no ramp for her to get out. There's no way she could navigate those brick steps."

Malik said, "Maybe she's homebound. That would drive me crazy, but some people are content staying inside."

I said, "Her neighbor said he saw her outside, yelling at Ernest about the lawn."

Malik gave me the side-eye. "You spoke with her neighbors?"

I said, "Only one." I searched for a quick change of subject but none came to mind.

Malik said, "How did you get them to talk to you?"

My mind jumped. Badge, no badge, badge, no badge? I said, "The guy was nice."

Malik said, "You lucked out. Going to strangers' homes isn't safe. Anything could have happened to you."

I said, "My whole business takes me to strangers' houses."

Malik jerked a thumb to his chest. "But I'm with you when you go. That's all I'm saying."

I nodded. "Understood." I wanted to get off the subject before words slipped out about Charles' picnic lunch. "Mrs. Depew has been in that wheelchair for years. She needs a way out of the house. Suppose there's a fire?"

Malik said, "Maybe Ernest wants to control her."

"But the neighbor said she was yelling at him. Those actions would say the reverse. She's in charge."

Malik said, "There's a third option. They both murdered Mr. Depew. In an equal partnership people argue."

We both mulled on that thought.

Malik said, "Regarding the ramp, have you ever seen the back steps? They could have a ramp installed there."

I said, "I've never seen the rear entrance, but I could check it out."

Malik said, "Didn't we agree to do things together?"

"No. You declared we had to do things that way. We didn't agree on anything."

We both knew we had the makings of a big argument, so we shut up.

Malik and I were picking up the fish in West Orange. I thought that was good because it wasn't too far. I wouldn't want to drive 100 miles with fish sloshing around in the back of the truck.

Malik asked, "How big is the tank?"

I said, "It couldn't be too big. Lusty said he only had five fish."

"You're assuming they're small like goldfish. Tank size is determined by the size of the fish and how much water each fish requires."

I said, "How do you know that?"

Malik gave me a side-eye. "Because I'm a thinking man."

I started to get that queasy feeling I get when I don't know the logical answers to questions.

We pulled off Route 280 and drove a half mile to a sprawling white ranch style house.

While we backed up the long driveway, a lanky teenage boy ran out to meet us. His red hair and blue eyes accented his pasty skin. The boy said, "Are you here for the fish?"

I climbed out of the car and said, "We sure are. Where are they?"

The boy jerked his thumb toward the back of the house. "The tank's in the backyard but I couldn't carry it without your help."

I smiled at the boy thinking, *he's too skinny to carry anything more than a quart of milk.*

Malik said, "Show me where it is."

The boy peered into the car. "Didn't you bring help?"

My eyebrows began to twitch. I said, "How big is this tank? I thought you only had five fish."

The boy said, "Yeah, but these fish need a lot of room." He jerked a thumb toward the backyard and said, "Come on. I'll show you. Better yet pull the car back there."

Malik and I hesitated. By now we had developed a symbiosis and we both knew we were in trouble.

I walked around the side of the house with the boy while Malik moved the truck. As we rounded the bend to the back of the house, I saw a six-foot-long glass tank filled with water and yes, only five fish. I walked up to the tank and peered at the fish. They had grayish blue bodies and red stomachs and teeth, lots of sharp teeth. I asked, "What kind of fish are these?"

The boy looked at me like I was addle-brained and said, "Piranhas."

My head snapped back at the word.

Malik stood erect with his jaw dropped open.

I said, "Piranhas? Are you serious?"

The boy hooked his thumbs into the loops of his jeans and rocked back on his heels. "Red bellied piranhas to be exact."

I said, "What do you expect me to do with these? And this tank is huge. How are we supposed to get this into the Escalade?"

The boy shuffled his feet. He said, "I thought that was your specialty." His head swiveled from me to Malik. "You have to take them. I already sold them to Mr. Hooper, and he paid a good price. If you don't deliver these, they'll drum me out of the Piranha Enthusiast League. You don't know what it's like to be blackballed." He sniffed and blinked rapidly.

My shoulders sagged. I gave Malik a forlorn look hoping for sympathy.

The boy said, "If I get blackballed on the forum, my life is over." His eyelashes turned dewy.

Malik wasn't falling for it. "Are you kidding me? A Piranha League?" He crossed his arms and said, "There is no way I can get this tank into the trunk by myself." He glared at me, then the boy. "Neither of you would help much." He turned to the boy and said, "How much does this tank weigh anyway?"

The boy said, "About 1400 pounds give or take."

We stood in silence for a moment and then the boy snapped his fingers. "I know. My dad has a ramp in the garage that we can use to roll the tank up into the truck."

I pulled the corners of my mouth up trying to smile and said, "That doesn't sound too bad."

Malik said, "Are you crazy? I can't push 1400 pounds up a ramp by myself. We need help."

I asked the boy, "Isn't there anyone around who can help us?"

The boy said, "My uncle lives down the street. I'll see if he's home."

As soon as he disappeared from the yard, Malik stepped to within an inch of my face. He said, "I know my Aunt Lusty gave you this referral, but don't you ever take a job like this again." He glared at me for what seemed centuries, but I'm sure was only seconds. At that moment the boy reappeared with three men behind him.

Malik muttered, "Thank God" under his breath.

I said, "See? This turned out okay."

Malik said, "Oh yeah? Are they coming with us to help unload?"

I thought it best to keep my mouth shut for the rest of this job.

The boy introduced us to his uncle and his uncle's two friends.

Malik took one look at them and raised an eyebrow at me.

The uncle sported a large cast on one arm and a brace on the opposite ankle.

The boy said, "Uncle Max tripped over his Chihuahua and broke his arm."

Uncle Max grinned at us and said, "That's alright, the other arm works."

Malik pointed at his ankle and said, "What about your leg?"

The uncle shrugged. After all, what could he say?

We scrutinized the other two men. One looked to be about eighty years old, and the other was so skinny that his tee shirt sleeves flapped around him.

Malik's shoulders slumped. He stared at the ground a few minutes before saying, "Okay let's do this."

Uncle Max, who had the same red hair as his nephew, opened the garage and pulled out a roller conveyor. It was about five feet long with a series of rollers and hooks on each end. He went to the Escalade and leaned one end in the open back. He stomped the other end into the ground to secure it. He ruffled his nephew's hair and said, "See, I told you I would handle this."

Malik rolled his eyes. He cleared his throat and said, "Let's get started."

The four men managed to lift the tank off of the ground just enough to put it on the conveyor. Then they began to push. The tank inched up the rollers about a foot and then stopped.

I asked, "What's wrong?"

Malik said, "One of the rollers is out of place." By this time the men were straining under the weight of the fish tank. The piranha swam around in a furious flurry of activity.

The boy said, "We need to get the piranhas into the truck. I don't want them to get stressed."

I swear if that boy's uncle wasn't there, I would've slapped the crap out of him.

Malik said, "I have a wrench behind the front seat. You should be able to use it to push that roller back into its place. Hurry up." Sweat rolled into his eyes causing him to squint.

I crawled into the back of the Escalade, conscious that my fanny was in everyone's faces and found the wrench. It was huge and heavy. I crawled back out the way I came, dragging the wrench. I knocked the wheel into place with a satisfying click. I stood grinning, waiting for my applause and compliments. Instead, Malik said, "Please move so we can shove this thing in the truck." A few sweat laden minutes later they tucked the tank into the trunk. We left our helpers hugging each other in congratulations.

As we headed back to Newark with our cargo, Malik asked, "You didn't leave my wrench in the yard, did you?"

I said, "No. I leaned it against the inside of the trunk."

At that moment a car swerved in front of us, and Malik jerked the wheel to the left, missing the car by inches. A crisp crack assaulted our ears as Malik righted the Escalade. In one voice, we said, "Oh no." Malik pulled to the side of the road.

I covered my eyes with my hands. I couldn't look. I should have covered my ears. A soft gurgling sound that would normally soothe me, instead horrified me. "Noooo." I peeked between my fingers. Water dribbled out of the tank where the wrench had slammed into it. The fish swam in frantic circles. The water level was going down fast. I climbed over my chair into the back of the Escalade. My hands and knees got wet and smelly fish water ran through the vehicle. "What do I do?"

Malik said, "How bad is it?"

"It's leaking dammit. What do you think?"

Malik said, "Plug it up."

"With what? I can't use my hands. These are piranhas. I need my hands."

Malik said, "Let me think."

"We don't have time for thinking. Suppose they escape?"

Malik reached under his seat, pulled out a clipboard and handed it to me.

I said, "I don't have time to write anything."

Malik said, "Hold the clipboard against the hole in the tank."

I slapped the clipboard against the tank and held it tight with both hands. Water dribbled from beneath it. The fish slammed against the side of the tank like they saw an opportunity to flee.

Malik pulled back onto 280 and floored it.

I dared to release one hand to reach into my crossbody bag.

Malik glanced into the rear-view mirror. "What are you doing?"

I said, "I'm going to stun these fish. They're trying to get out of the tank. If I knock them out, they'll sleep until we deliver them." I pulled out my cell phone stun gun.

Malik said, "You're going to stun the fish with a phone?"

"It looks like a phone but it's a stun gun."

Malik said, "Where the hell did you get a stun gun? Forget that, just don't use it."

The fish thrashed against the cracked tank.

I said, "Why not? I have to stop them. I'm not going to make it to Newark."

Malik said, "Think about how electricity and water mix. You'll either kill the piranhas or yourself. My money's on the piranhas to survive."

Damn his logic. He probably saved my life. I'd already stunned myself once. I shoved the stun gun into my bag and resumed my stance. I pushed against the tank with all my might for the twenty-minute ride back to Newark. We pulled up to a shabby house with a weedy yard. Despite the peeling paint, the porch was neat and clean, and the windows sparkled. A graying man in his forties came out as soon as we pulled into his driveway. Malik opened the back of the Escalade.

Mr. Hooper glared at me and said, "What are you doing to my fish?"

Amazed at his stupidity, I said, "I'm keeping them in the tank. Isn't it obvious? We need help here. The tank cracked and the piranhas are trying to escape." My arms had moved past pain into agony. Spasms stabbed my shoulders as I held fast to the clipboard.

He climbed into the Escalade and squeezed behind the other side of the tank. He said, "I don't give a shit about the tank." His eyes darted back and forth as he peered into the water. "You're short a fish."

I almost dropped the clipboard. "What the hell do you mean 'short a fish'?"

Mr. Hooper said, "I only see four piranhas in this tank. I'm supposed to get five. Did you let one escape?"

I dropped the clipboard and scrambled out of the truck. Malik and I peered inside the back and only saw water.

Malik said, "All I see is my truck getting ruined." He shot me a dirty look.

Water ran freely out of the back of the truck. I was soaked to the skin and so glad I didn't get eaten, that for once, I hadn't thought of my shoes.

Malik and Mr. Hooper decided the best thing to do was to get the tank out of the truck pronto.

Luckily, Hooper had enough sense to bring some manpower. He waved to someone in a window and four men hustled out his back door. These gents were ready. They wheeled a heavy-duty trolley cart to the back of the truck.

One guy approached Malik and said, "What happened, Man?"

Malik pointed to me and said, "She's the boss."

All six men looked at me.

I stammered. "Well, you see, we were on 280..."

The men ignored me and went to work. In short shrift they pulled the tank onto the cart and taped the clipboard to the side with duct tape.

I rubbed my sore arms. *Why didn't I think of that?* I would have apologized for the hole in the tank, but thought if I did, they'd want me to pay for it.

As if reading my thoughts, Hooper said, "I don't need this tank anyway. I've been preparing my tank for six weeks for this shipment."

Six weeks? That tank must be room sized.

Hooper peeked into the truck again and confirmed no fish remained. He examined the tank and said, "I see the problem. See those bones at the bottom of the tank?"

I squinted and nodded.

Hooper said, "They ate the fifth fish."

I gulped. "They eat each other? Are you kidding me?" *Damn, I guess they'd have had no problem eating me if they had the chance. I wasn't even part of their tribe.* I gave him my brightest smile. "Mystery solved. Well, we have to be going." I started to get in the truck.

Hooper stepped in front of me. "Problem not solved. They ate him because you stirred them into a frenzy along the way."

Malik and I talked to Hooper and his band of fish men for half an hour before he agreed to let the matter go.

Malik gave me silent treatment on the ride home.

I said, "Watching you guys move that tank made me think. I couldn't have moved Mrs. Depew's trunk of huge rocks. I had a super hard time moving the trunk as it was. If it had been filled with big rocks, I wouldn't have been able to budge it."

Staring straight ahead, Malik said, "I'm glad to see some logic sinking in."

We rode with the windows down in an attempt to air out the fish smell. I knew it would take more than a little air to remedy this. I was afraid to say a word. I kept giving Malik little side glances to see if his mood changed. It didn't.

TWELVE

I climbed out of the Escalade and squished my way into the house. Malik hadn't spoken to me the entire drive home. He just pulled up to my house and stared straight ahead.

Murphy greeted me with inflamed interest, probably because I smelled like fish. I peeled off my heels and clothing in my foyer, unwilling to leak a trail of dead piranha juice through the house. I padded into the kitchen and grabbed a garbage bag for the clothes. I stopped cold. Something creaked on my back porch. I spun around to see Detective Brimley peeping in through the door window. I screamed so loud that Brimley jumped back and covered his ears. I pulled the garbage bag to my body and backed out of the kitchen. I dashed upstairs and grabbed my robe. Somewhat covered, I ran downstairs where Brimley now pumped my front doorbell.

I swung the door open wide. "What the hell do you want? You scared the crap out of me."

He wrinkled his nose. "I did, didn't I?"

"Is that supposed to be funny? What do you want? I'm in no mood for your shit today."

Brimley held his hands up in a defensive posture and walked past me into the living room. He pulled a newspaper from under his arm and opened it to a full-page ad in the center of the first section.

"$10K reward for tips leading to an arrest in the suspicious disappearance of Perry Depew."

Mr. Depew's photo and Detective Brimley's contact information centered the page.

I stood there with my mouth hanging open. I would have snatched the newspaper from him if my arms weren't so damn sore. My tired brain couldn't make much sense of anything at this point.

"Why are you showing me this?"

Brimley shoved the ad close to my face. "Because this made my job 10,000 times tougher. Because now every nut in the county will call me with clues. Because you're my most likely suspect. So, the sooner I bring you in, the better for me."

"Did you ever consider I'm innocent? No. Maybe you should spend your time investigating real suspects. Or even better, try to find Mr. Depew." I jabbed the newspaper. "After all, this says he disappeared. How do you know he's not holed up with some woman or soaking up sun in Fiji?"

Brimley chuckled. "You and I both know that's not likely."

I crossed my arms and stood flat-footed. "Weren't you the detective on the theft of Depew's statuettes?"

Brimley said, "Yes."

I stepped closer. "And now you're investigating Mr. Depew's murder?"

"So?"

I said, "I think someone should check you out. Where were you when Mr. Depew went missing?"

Brimley snorted.

I said, "Why did you go to Junior's Junkyard?"

Brimley said, "So your ex told you? We always check people close to our suspects. You two could have acted together. If so, you'd be the mastermind. He's not the brightest bulb on the tree." He eyed me up and down. "Pack your toothbrush. I'll be bringing you in before you know it. He crumpled the newspaper with one hand and threw it onto my couch. Brimley stomped to the door and turned back. His red face conveyed anger. "You don't understand what's at stake here." He turned and left.

I stood in my living room smelling like fish with Murphy hungrily licking my leg. I wrapped my arms around myself. My eyes searched for nonexistent safety. I couldn't help it. My bottom lip began to quiver, and my eyes filled.

I took the hottest shower I could stand. Then I crawled under my covers and pulled them over my head, blocking out all signs of outside life.

Charles' call woke me. I pleaded for help to trap Ernest. "I feel safe when you're around. Promise you'll back me up."

Charles chuckled. "Back you up? You sound like you want me to hold him down while you interrogate him."

I pouted. "I hate to admit it, but he scares me. He's so big and creepy. I've never heard him speak. He's like a silent Frankenstein."

Charles said, "Okay, Baby. I'll protect you. You know you can count on me. I'll keep you safe."

A brilliant idea lit my brain. I sat straight up in bed. I said, "Would you teach me how to fight?"

Charles chuckled. "Who do you plan to engage in combat?"

I said, "I'm serious. I should learn how to handle myself. I want to feel secure when I investigate criminals."

This time Charles howled.

I gripped my phone so hard, I thought the screen might crack. "This isn't funny. I never learned how to fight."

Charles muffled his laughter. "How did you fight in high school?"

I leaned against my headboard. "I never fought in school." I almost disconnected in my shame.

In high school, my dad hadn't allowed me to perm my hair. So rather than ruin it with a hot iron, I had fluffed it into a natural style I thought was funky. My classmates taunted me, pointing me out in the hallways. I ducked into the girl's room only to run into the mean girls. You know, the beautiful ones, cheerleaders with perfect legs and shoulder length hair. They surrounded me and pushed my face to the smudged mirror taunting "Kinky head, kinky head." I ran and hid behind the school dumpster where Holy had found me while picking through the trash. That summed up my lack of courage and my path to the present day.

Here as an adult, I craved defense skills. Charles' laughter made me determined to stand up for myself, not run like in high school.

Charles must have felt my conviction. He said, "I'll be glad to teach my girl some moves."

We set a time to meet the next day.

I hung up and snuggled into bed with a satisfied feeling. I'd never had a man I could lean on. I slept in that security for the first time.

The next afternoon we met in our prearranged spot, a spacious area in Weequahic Park.

I wore an old pair of biker pants and a loose tee for the occasion.

Charles scrutinized my outfit and pointed at my feet. "Are you kidding? Do you plan to fight in heels? Why didn't you wear sneakers?"

I guessed he had a point, but stilettos were my natural footwear. I said, "I should be able to fight however I'm dressed. Besides my power comes from my shoes."

In the end, I kicked off the shoes and stood in my best power stance.

Charles' mouth ticked up at one corner, but he kept his composure. "Who is your enemy?"

I said, "I want to help you take down Ernest."

Charles stood, hands on hips. "We're taking him down? This is not a SWAT operation. I thought you just wanted to talk to him."

In the end, Charles showed me how to use my elbows and knees instead of my fists which he said were too delicate. He demonstrated easy kicks to sensitive areas.

We drank lots of water and ate some questionable protein bars during my training session. We rested in the grass a few minutes to catch our breaths.

Charles rose and said, "I have to get going."

I slipped on my heels and Charles pulled me to standing.

I said, "You didn't show me any choke holds."

This time Charles didn't hide his grin. He said, "You're not ready for that."

I said, "With a choke hold, I can knock out the bad guy and tie him up."

Charles took my hand and led me back to my car. He said, "Let's we'll try that move another day. For now, practice what I've taught you." He kissed me on the cheek and walked away chuckling.

Back home, I fired up my laptop and watched YouTube videos on how to execute a choke hold. I practiced on pillows until I perfected my move. After all, you can't train Catwoman halfway.

I met grocery day with a hot mug of coffee and a smile. Charles and I had spoken several times, mostly because I wanted to reinforce the plan. I would stop Ernest in the grocery parking lot. While I had his attention, Charles would flank him from the back. Ernest would be forced to reveal what was going on in the Depew home. Together, we'd make him spill his guts.

I arrived at the grocery store earlier than the previous week to stop Ernest before he entered. I stood inside the doorway and watched the parking lot until I spotted Ernest. The moment had come.

Ernest paced around errant shopping carts left in the lot by thoughtless shoppers. He walked like a man on a mission.

I kept my head down as I stepped out of the store. I walked up to Ernest and stopped him mid-step. I stuck my finger in his face and said, "I want to talk to you."

Without bending, he looked down at me and glared.

Ice ran through my veins, and I couldn't breathe. That's when I realized Charles had not arrived. My eyes darted around the parking lot. Where the hell was my muscle?

Ernest stepped left and so did I. Charles must be late. I'll have to keep Ernest in the lot until he gets here. We two-stepped back and forth several times. I danced around Ernest until I reached his back. I leapt on his back and wrapped my arm around his throat. Ernest leaned back and shook. I hit the pavement hard. Ernest grabbed me by my shoulders and lifted me off my feet. My breath caught in my throat disabling my screams. Ernest took two long steps and sat me in a shopping cart. He shoved the cart, and I careened across the lot, smacking several cars in my path. My carnival ride ended when I banged into the back of an SUV. The cart stuck, tilted with one wheel still spinning. No one came to my aid or even took notice of my adventure. I climbed out of the cart and stood, shaking with adrenaline. Ernest was nowhere in sight. He had probably finished half his shopping by the time I could walk. I inched to my car on wobbly legs.

As I opened my car door, I felt a tap on my shoulder. I spun around and screamed.

Harry Sunshine took my panic in stride. He smirked and said, "I told you they're nasty people." He hoisted his grocery bag over his shoulder.

I said, "You saw Ernest assaulting me and you did nothing?"

Sunshine shrugged and strolled to his Mercedes.

I thought of the injustice of a creep like Sunshine driving a shiny Mercedes. Why do bad people get good things? I leaned against my car and took deep breaths. I needed to shake off the adrenaline before hitting the road.

Sunshine rolled up next to me. "I see you're admiring my car. She's a beaut. For a small fee I can put you in touch with a guy. Freddy could put you behind the wheel of the car of your choice. Of course, I got this baby for getting him out of a jam. You would need to pay cash, but you'd get a great deal." He cruised away, leaving me standing, mouth open.

Back home, I paced back and forth from the living room to the kitchen. I stomped upstairs and laid on the bed for two seconds before jumping up again. At that moment, I hated all men. Ernest had scared me. Sunshine had angered me and Charles had deserted me. I was sure Malik would scold me if he'd known what I did. The whole lot of them could piss off.

I had been home for hours when Charles called. I debated on declining the call for a millisecond then smashed the accept button. "Where the hell were you?"

"Now Baby..."

"Don't 'Baby' me. You left me out there with that monster."

"But you're alright."

"How do you know? Can you see me through this phone? You really let me down today. You said I could count on you, but you lied."

"Let me explain."

"Keep your explanations. I can't believe anything you say. Ever. A real friend like Lusty would never have abandoned me like this."

Charles said, "Please calm down and listen."

My chest tightened with ragged breaths. "That's the problem, isn't it? You sweet-talk me in your charming way, and I believe you. But what you say isn't true. They're just words. And you never listen to me, to my wishes. I should have seen this coming. I've dealt with men like you all my life."

"What does that mean?"

Tears washed my face and cleansed my mind. "Men who control the conversation, interactions and inevitably, my life. Men who expect me to be a good little girl and do as I'm told because they know best. Well, I've had enough."

Charles said, "Please give me a chance to explain."

"No. You have the perfect words to soothe me and draw me back into your web of lies. That's a scenario where I lose. I'm not listening anymore. We're done." I disconnected. I sobbed, head in hands, for a long time. I rolled to my side and slept.

THIRTEEN

I awoke the next morning with a new determination. I didn't have the courage to call Malik. Even though I had promised to pay for professional cleaning of his vehicle, he was still pissed off. I'd have to do this on my own.

Three cups of coffee later, I tooled over to the Depew house. I was fuming. I had had to throw out a pair of fishy Stuart Weitzman stilettos. My right-hand man wasn't speaking to me, and the dumpy detective was on my ass.

Ernest ushered me in with no acknowledgment of yesterday's events. Mrs. Depew sat in her wheelchair as usual. I didn't waste any time. "Why did you put that ad in the paper? Do you know the police are questioning me because of my association with you?"

Mrs. Depew's usual smile disappeared. She pushed a button on her motorized wheelchair and sped over to face me. "Look, Honey, the police aren't investigating you because of that ad. They're checking you out because that's where I'm pointing."

"What?" Coffee and adrenaline surged through my veins. "Why would you do that? I never did anything to you."

Mrs. Depew's giggle sent shivers up my spine. "Because you've been asking questions about my husband. The other day you asked me outright whether he had died or not. You're suspicious, but at this point, you can't prove a thing. I thought about having Ernest visit you at home to shut you up." She waved my business card in front of my face. "After all, you conveniently handed me your address. But Ernest might bungle the job. So, the best thing for me to do is lead the police to you."

"The police have no reason to suspect me of anything." I said, "Mr. Depew went missing long before I ever met you."

Mrs. Depew smiled. "I don't know who killed my husband, but I'd rather point police to you than have them accuse me. Soon the police will find evidence of his death and they will find it on you. He may have disappeared before we met, but that doesn't mean he died before we met."

I turned and started walking toward the door. "I had no reason to kill Mr. Depew, no motive. Only you or Ernest could have had a motive to kill him."

Mrs. Depew said, "Or Mr. Charles. After all, he was on the manifest. He wanted those ivory statuettes at all costs."

My breath froze in my chest. *Possible, but I don't believe it. Had I been drooling over the killer?* I turned back and stared at her.

Mrs. Depew pointed a bony finger toward me. "You didn't think of that did you? You see, the police have a number of suspects."

I sucked in a big gulp of air. "I'm innocent. That's all I know."

Mrs. Depew said, "And you don't have to actually kill him to be an accessory."

"Accessory? The police need a suspect to have an accessory. Are you willing to be a suspect?"

Mrs. Depew smiled. "Not me, Dear. Ernest." She looked up at her nephew. "I'm going to do what I can to protect him. I'm not letting my Ernest go to jail."

Ernest had been standing in the corner with a sullen expression on his face. He said nothing.

I said, "Ernest, I don't think you'd kill your uncle. Would you?" I didn't know what Ernest might do as he never spoke or showed a smidgen of emotion. But if he murdered his uncle, I didn't want to know, at least not while I was in the house with the two of them. I thought I'd better sound like I was on his side. "Are you going to let your aunt frame you?"

Ernest turned and gazed out the window.

At least he heard me, I think.

Shaking my head, I turned back to Mrs. Depew. "You can't make me an accessory. I didn't do anything."

Mrs. Depew rolled her wheelchair to the door and opened it. The bright sun highlighted the grit on the soles of her sneakers. She said, "Suppose I tell them Ernest killed my Perry by accident. Then he paid you to dispose of his bones. What do you think was in that trunk? Ernest is addle-brained. He could go to a sanitarium instead of jail. But you?"

I left Mrs. Depew's feeling scared and isolated. I missed Malik's protection. When I examined my life, I realized I had few friends, few people I could trust.

Again, I owed Malik an apology. I drove to his place before I could chicken out.

Malik buzzed me in.

I fumed at myself for being so flustered. "I didn't see your car. I'm glad you're home."

Malik nodded toward the sofa, and we sat. He said, "It's being cleaned. They'll probably have to replace the carpet."

This isn't going well. "I stopped by to apologize for all the trouble and for messing up the Escalade."

He said, "Don't worry. It'll get fixed. Besides, you're paying for the cleanup. Also, the job came from Aunt Lusty. It wasn't your fault."

I briefed him on Mrs. Depew's threat. "Will you help me? I don't know what to do." I hated sounding like a damsel in distress.

He said, "You're seeing her true colors now. I'm not sure what I can do but let me think about it. Can you take me to pick up my car?"

"I'll do you one better. Let me buy you lunch on the way. I'll pick up some cash at my house and we'll be on our way."

As we turned the corner of my block, I spotted Detective Brimley standing on my front porch. I raced past him, keeping my face averted.

Malik said, "What's up? Why'd you pass your house?"

I told him about Brimley's earlier threat.

Malik said, "Damn, you're a real fugitive. I tell you what. Drive to the bodega." When we arrived, he said, "Why don't you stay in the car and let me buy lunch? Then we'll pick up the Escalade and go back to my place to brainstorm."

That sounded wonderful to me. So, we went with his plan.

I tuned into some smooth jazz while I waited. My morning caffeine had worn off and my eyes started to droop. I jerked awake to the sound of the bodega owner tapping on my window. I lowered it.

He said, "You stay right here. I called the cops. They've been asking about that Depew guy, and I remembered you taking that flyer."

I said, "What are you talking about?"

He said, "Do you know what I could do with that reward money? I could take a long vacation." He clasped his hands and rolled his beady eyes up to the sky.

I dug my investigator badge from my bag and slammed it against the window. "Back up. I'm doing an investigation of my own and I'm authorized to do it."

Bodega Man glanced at the badge and said, "Phooey. That's a fake."

I revved my engine and scanned the bodega door for Malik.

The man grabbed the top of my open window and said, "You're not going anywhere."

At that moment, Malik emerged with two greasy bags and walked over to the car. He gawked at the bodega man, dumbfounded.

I said, "Get in."

Bodega Man held on with one hand and started waving with the other.

I spotted a cop car turning the corner.

I said to Malik, "Get your ass in this car right now."

Malik jumped in and I sped away, almost taking Bodega Man's hand with me. We drove past the cop car going in the opposite direction. He didn't even look my way. That's the beauty of living in Newark. The police have much more serious business than speeding cars.

Malik gripped the bags as I spun around the corner, out of the cops' sightline.

I said, "I can't afford another encounter with the police. Brimley is trying to frame me for the Depew murder."

Malik said, "Why would he do that, besides the fact that you're making yourself an easy target?"

I said, "Did it ever occur to you that he's covering his own actions? Maybe he's the murderer."

Malik gave his head a little shake as if clearing his mind. "What makes you think that?"

I ran down Brimley's connections to the Depew theft and murder.

Malik chuckled. "That's quite the theory. How did you find out Brimley investigated the theft? Did Mrs. Depew tell you? If Brimley was involved, no way would he share that info."

We reached the auto shop, and I pulled over.

Malik sat patiently, awaiting my answer.

Once again, I had talked myself into a corner. The selfish part of me wasn't ready to tell Malik about Charles. Supposed Charles didn't work out. Besides, I wanted both men in my life. I shrugged. "I just know."

Malik smiled. "Why don't I get the police report to check out your theory."

My mouth dropped open. "You can do that? I thought police information was private."

Malik shook his head. "Many police reports are public records. Anybody can get them."

I thought Charles had used his superpowers to get me information when I could have gotten it myself. I said, "You better get your car."

I waited in my car while Malik ducked into the auto shop.

While I waited, Shitty Kitty had a field day with my emotions. "You can't tell Malik about Charles. You could lose Malik. You know you want them both. It's not a crime to love two guys. They don't have to know about each other. Don't tell me you're a one-man woman. Your heart flutters for both of them. Just keep them. You're still a good girl." Kitty shut her trap when Malik emerged from the shop.

The Escalade was good as new, much better than my bank account. Only a few bucks remained and since I knew I wasn't getting any money from Mrs. Depew, I needed cash.

We sat in Malik's kitchen munching on cheeseburgers and fries, downing them with big gulps of soda. Malik said, "I don't think it's safe for you to go home."

I stiffened. Was he going to ask me to move in again? My confused heart didn't know what to do. I could easily slip into Malik's comfort, but would that be fair to him? At least Malik's reliable and I do care for him.

My bubble burst when he said, "You should go into hiding. Is there someplace you can stay where the police won't think to look?"

I hid my disappointment. "If I had money, I'd stay at a hotel. But that's not an option. In fact, if I don't make some money soon, Murphy and I are out."

Malik took my hand. Then he pulled a brown envelope out of his pocket and presented it with formality.

I took the envelope. "What's this?"

Malik said, "It's a month's mortgage. I want to take some pressure off you."

I said, "I can't take this. You're as poor as I am. In fact, I'm paying you."

Malik said, "I have some savings. Do you think I live off what you pay me?"

I had to admit no one could survive off my jobs.

I opened my lips to protest, and Malik said, "Take it."

I did.

Malik said, "Now, don't get mad. Aunt Lusty told me about your financial troubles. She's concerned for you and so am I."

"I'm two months behind. By the time I can make another payment, I'll still be two months behind. It's only a matter of time before they evict me."

Malik said, "You may want to think about retaining an attorney. I mean a real lawyer, not Harry Sunshine. You need to be on the offensive now. If Mrs. Depew continues to push the police in your direction, you want to be prepared."

Attorney? That's all I need, another bottom feeder in my life. But Malik was right. My brain had numbed to the point that all I could do was nod.

Malik said, "Well you know what this means."

I sighed. "It means I need another job."

Malik said, "You mean *we* need another job."

"I wasn't so sure you'd work with me again after the last incident."

Malik smiled. "I like working with you." He picked up his cell and called Lusty.

I clutched the envelope to my chest. A mix of shame and relief swept through me. I turned away from Malik as he chatted with Lusty. I went into the living room and stuck the life-saving envelope into my bag. I grabbed my phone and speed-dialed my mortgage company.

Mr. Hartness picked up on the first ring. "Hartness. How can I help you?"

I kept my voice steady. "This is Raquel Rollins. Please note on my account I will send you a payment in two days."

Mr. Hartness paused, then said, "Is that it? No pleading? No begging? I'm disappointed."

I said, "There's no need for sarcasm. Please just note my account."

Hartness said, "How much? The full two months back mortgage? You know you have another month coming up soon."

I swallowed hard, tamping down my anxiety. "One month. I will send the rest shortly after."

Hartness laughed. "I'm not going to stop the eviction with one month's payment."

My voice squeaked. "Why not? You've stopped it before."

Hartness said, "That's the voice I wanted to hear. I tell you what. I have a way to stop your eviction."

I could barely speak. "How?"

Hartness said, "I can be reasonable. You need to pony up an extra $1,000 in cash for me. I'll wipe the eviction off your record...for a month. The same process each month you're late will keep you off the foreclosure roles."

I stepped into the guest room and closed the door. I didn't want Malik to see the tears flowing down my cheeks. I said, "But that's a half month's mortgage. If I pay you that on top of my mortgage, I'll never catch up."

Hartness chuckled. "That's the plan. You will pay me $1,000 a month until you can bring your account up to date. You see, unlike you, my pockets will always be lined with cash."

I said, "Supposed I pay your blackmail instead of paying my mortgage."

He said, "That won't fly. If your mortgage passes three months overdue, alarms will ring in the upper office. You'll get kicked out anyway. There's only so much I can do to help you."

I sniffed. "You call this helping me?"

Hartness said, "Take it or leave it. With your record, I can start proceedings today. You'll be out on your ass before you can say 'money'. So, we have a deal?"

I said, "Yes."

He hung up without another word.

From the kitchen, Malik said, "Aunt Lusty got us a job."

I wiped my eyes and emerged from the guest room. "That's great." My shaky voice didn't seem to alarm Malik.

He said, "I've been thinking, you need a place to live. That Detective is probably waiting at your house. You might get taken in for questioning or even arrested on suspicion. Can you stay with your ex-husband?"

Is this a test question? I slumped back in my chair and fiddled with my sandwich. The little fantasy of Malik and me that had danced in my head shriveled up and died. "That would be the last place I'd go. I'd have to be pretty desperate to do that."

Malik asked, "Well, aren't you?"

"Aren't I what?"

"Desperate."

Actually, I was. I said, "Maybe we could think of someplace else." I wiped a little bit of ketchup from Malik's mouth with my napkin. *Hint, hint.*

Malik said, "I know. You can stay with your dad."

I almost choked on my burger. "Now that you mention it, a stay with Holy might not be too bad."

FOURTEEN

I concocted a story about fumigating my house and Holy was all too happy to have me stay with him. I arranged to come by the next day.

Malik and I headed to Port Newark to pick up a shipment of party favors. We would deliver it to a party store on Ferry Street in the Ironbound section of Newark. Simple. To our great relief, Lusty assured us there were no live animals in this shipment.

The hot afternoon sun flared over the Escalade. The warmth released a new car smell from the fresh carpet that had emptied my bank account. As we neared our destination, I felt a slight quiver in my stomach. I scrutinized myself in the visor mirror. "Someone might recognize me. I should camouflage myself."

Malik said, "Nobody's gonna notice you. You're not an international fugitive. Your picture's not hanging in the post office."

I crossed my arms over my chest. "I need a disguise."

Malik rolled his eyes. "You should have thought of that before we left. Do you think I carry disguises in my car?"

My eyes swept over Malik's neat car. I said, "Most guys have a lot of junk in their car. You don't have anything." By this time Malik had stopped speaking to me. I dug through his glove compartment. Voila! I pulled out a baseball cap and some oversized sunglasses. I put them on and rechecked the mirror. "Perfect."

At Malik's request, I opened the back of the Escalade. Malik backed up the truck to the port door. A burly guy who smelled of sweat and cigars stood in the bay door. He hurled one large carton into the back of the truck. It landed with a whoomp. The carton seemed undamaged, so I closed the back door, signed the manifest and hopped back in the car.

Malik said, "This is going to be easy money and we both need it. What kind of merchandise is it?"

I read the manifest. "It says eyeball party favors. That's creepy."

Malik said, "I went to a campus party once where they had fake eyeballs floating in the punch bowl. It was a hoot."

I rolled my eyes. Maybe he was too young for me.

The afternoon was going smoothly which, given my track record, should have given me pause.

Ferry street is in the Ironbound section of Newark. It's also known as Down Neck because of its location on the bend of the Passaic River. The Portuguese population had built a proliferation of stores and great restaurants. These attractions drew a mix of cultures to the area. The heat had drawn everyone out, shoppers, diners, strollers, and kids. Between the gridlocked traffic and the pedestrians, the Escalade moved at a crawl. We turned onto Ferry Street, the most heavily trafficked street in the area.

Malik said, "The store is a straight shot from here. All that's left to do is to get paid."

I glanced at the huge box in the back. Nothing moved. No noises emanated from the box. We were home free. We stopped to let a woman with a stroller jaywalk in front of us. When she passed, we had a few yards of space between us and the next car. Miraculously, no one was crossing at that moment. Malik took that opportunity to speed up. Bam! The Escalade pitched sideways and bounced back up as we hit a huge pothole. The back of the Escalade flew open, and our cargo slammed onto the pavement. Screams emanated from behind us. Malik and I jumped out and ran to the back as eyeballs rolled down the street.

As people ran screaming from the scene, cars screeched to a halt to avoid hitting them. One woman fainted dead away as an eyeball rolled onto her open toe sandals.

I waved my hands in the air. "Calm down people. These are just party favors." But no one paid attention to me. They were all pointing, running, and screaming, lots of screaming.

Malik said, "Forget them. Let's pick up this merchandise and get out here. We don't want to draw attention to you."

I said, "Are you kidding? We couldn't have drawn more attention if we were a marching band."

Malik started scooping up the eyeballs and throwing them back into the box. He stopped, stared at his hands and said, "Uh oh."

I dreaded those words. I said, "What you mean 'uh oh'?" But in the next second, I understood. These weren't just any eyeballs. They were made of candy and were melting on the hot pavement. Flies and children had landed on our cargo. Somehow the kids instinctively knew this was candy. Frantic mothers dragged crying children away. Some, too late, watched their kids pop sticky eyeballs into their mouths. Flies and a proliferation of other bugs torpedoed down from the sky. Ferry Street soon became a mob of screaming, crying, and swatting. Sirens wailed in the distance. We had one blessing. Patrol cars could not get through this mess to reach us.

I said, "Let's get out of here."

"You don't have to tell me twice," Malik said. He hauled the box up, threw it into the trunk and slammed the back shut.

We jumped into the Escalade and made our way down Ferry Street to deliver the remnants of the cargo.

We parked down the block from the Penny Party Shop and surveyed our cargo to see what we could salvage. We had lost about half of our eyeballs. Malik pulled a roll of duct tape out of his glove compartment and resealed the box.

I didn't want to ask, but I had to. "Didn't you see the pothole?"

Malik said, "Did you lock the back of the truck?"

At that standoff, we decided to take the box to the Penny Party Shop and see if we could get paid. This small shipment would normally earn little money. Because it was a rush job, I'd get at least half a month's mortgage.

We walked the half block to the back door of the Penny Party Shop. A runny nosed clerk let us in and examined the manifest. He said, "We've been waiting for these eyeballs. They were special order for a guy who's having a party. He's been calling every day."

I gave him my cheeriest smile and held out my tablet. I hoped he would sign the manifest and we'd be long gone before he opened the box. He had poised his finger to sign when he cocked his ear and said, "What's that buzzing sound?"

Malik said, "Oh, that's me. I have a sinus condition and sometimes my nose makes this humming sound."

I said, "If you'll just sign, we'll be on our way."

The clerk said, "I could've sworn the buzzing was coming from this box."

Malik hummed out loud. Both the clerk and I stared at him. Malik said, "This is the only way to make my nose stop." He gave the clerk a big grin.

The clerk said, "Good luck with that, Man." He signed the manifest and paid for shipping.

We got the hell out of there.

I spent the night in Malik's guest room.

The next morning, I threw on yesterday's clothes and tiptoed out while Malik slept. As I entered my car, my cell purred. I feared Malik had caught me. Instead, Harry Sunshine's name appeared on the screen. Could he have had a change of heart? Did he take pity on me and decide to take my case? I answered.

He said, "Good morning Ms. Rollins. Harry Sunshine here."

I hoped he heard my smile when I said, "Good morning, Mr. Sunshine. Did you change your mind?"

He paused, then said, "What do you mean?"

I said, "About handling my case. Remember?"

Sunshine said, "Ms. Rollins, I'm calling because your home is up for foreclosure. Stopping evictions is one of my specialties. I'd like to help you."

I said, "How do you know about my eviction? I didn't mention that to you."

Again, he paused. "Ms. Rollins, have we met?"

I gripped the phone so hard my knuckles cracked. "I was just in your office. Remember, we talked about the Depews."

Sunshine said, "Oh, I see. Well, this is another matter. I help people stop evictions."

I said, "On contingency?"

Sunshine snickered. "No. Contingencies are only when you're suing for money. My foreclosure service is for a fee."

I shook my head to clear it. "You must not remember my predicament. My client wouldn't pay me. Also, doesn't the fact that I'm losing my house tell you I have no money?"

Sunshine said, "Most people can get the money to save a precious item like their home. For a mere $1,000 you can stay in your house. I'll email you a contract for my service. You just email the signed form back to me with payment and I'll get started. Better yet, bring the contract to my office with cash and I'll give you a $100 discount. How does that sound?"

I disconnected. I thumped my head on my steering wheel hoping the pain would replace my anger.

When I could breathe normally, I drove to a hardware store and picked up a prepaid cell phone. Then I went back to my post in the Azalea bushes across from the Depew house and sent a text.

Two minutes later, Ernest emerged from the Depew house and lumbered down the street.

My text worked. I ran back through the yard to the parallel street, made a quick right and ran to the corner. I saw Ernest's tall body striding in my direction. I stood with my back to the brick building like I had seen in many detective movies. I waited for Ernest to reach me. When he did, I reached out, grabbed his elbow and pulled with all my might. Of course, I only succeeded in jerking myself off my feet. Nonetheless, he stopped and gasped when he saw me.

I said, "Here I am. Let's talk."

We walked the half block to a small park. The area was deserted enough for privacy but public enough for protection. We must have made an odd couple, a herculean man and a diminutive woman toddling along on stilettos. Even with four extra inches, I didn't reach his shoulder. We sat on the green and white bench.

Ernest clenched his hands so tight that his knuckles turned white. He said, "I only came because you said you had evidence against my aunt."

I almost fell off the bench because I had never heard Ernest speak. His voice came out in a high squeak like a nervous little girl. I almost laughed in his face, but I remembered the gravity of my plight. I said, "That's right, but my main concern is clearing my name. I know you have inside info. I don't expect you to go against your aunt, but if you don't help absolve me of blame, she's going down." I sounded like something out of a gangster movie, but it was all the toughness I could muster. I didn't have any other references.

Ernest said, "I'll help you. I'll do anything to get away from my aunt."

I said, "What? You seem so loyal to her. I'm grateful for your help but I don't understand why you stay with her if you want to leave."

Ernest sighed and stared at the ground. "I'd leave Aunt Lilac in a heartbeat, but she has my mother in her grip."

"Your mother?" It never occurred to me that Ernest had other family, and I'd never thought about his feelings. To me, he was just Mrs. Depew's dim-witted muscle.

Ernest said, "You see, my mom is Uncle Perry's sister. She's been sick for a long time. When my mom got sick, we lost everything. We sold our house to pay the hospital bills. The doctors said my mom would need round-the-clock care for the rest of her days. I couldn't afford that. Uncle Perry stepped in. He's been paying for an expensive nursing home so Mom could be comfortable. Now Aunt Lilac threatens to stop paying for the home unless I help her. I don't have any money. My mom would be shipped to a state home and left to die. So, you see, I can't go against Aunt Lilac, but you can."

Now I understood Ernest's compliance. It felt good to get some kind of control, because lately I sure hadn't had any. I said, "So your uncle took care of both you and your mom?"

Ernest nodded. "Uncle Perry said he'd add me to his will so I would be taken care of in case he died. I don't know what happened, but I'm sure Aunt Lilac prevented that transaction. Soon after, Uncle Perry went missing." Ernest's eyes moistened. "I've been so scared. The police questioned me. Aunt Lilac is watching everything I do. You're the first person to really listen to me, to care."

I blinked my looming tears away. I gathered my strength for Ernest. I said, "Did the police tell you what kind of evidence they have?"

"No. They won't tell me anything. They don't talk to my aunt either which tells me that they don't trust her." Ernest jumped at the jangle of his cell phone. His face blanched. "It's Aunt Lilac." He started to rise, but I jerked him down hard.

I said, "You have to face your aunt sometime. Are you going to live your whole life in fear?"

Ernest's eyes bounced from the phone to me and back to the phone. The screen glowed 'Aunt Lilac'. The ringing stopped and Ernest gasped. He sat frozen, holding the cell midair. The jangle resumed causing Ernest to drop the phone into the dirt. He reached for it.

I grasped Ernest's arm and said, "What you do now may change your path forever." I don't know when I became Yoda, but my words seemed appropriate.

Ernest pulled his shoulders back and punched the green button to accept the call. "I'm sorry. I dropped the phone."

I punched Ernest in his side. I flexed my muscles and said, "Strong."

Ernest put the phone on speaker.

Mrs. Depew said, "Where the hell are you? I didn't send you on any errands. Get your ass back here."

Ernest inhaled deeply, then said, "I needed some air, and you were napping."

Mrs. Depew said, "You don't go anywhere unless I send you."

Ernest said, "Aunt Lilac, the time has come for some changes. I'm not going to be your slave anymore. I need some freedom."

Mrs. Depew snickered. "You want to be free? How are you going to care for your mother without my money?"

Ernest said, "I'll get a job and take care of her myself."

Mrs. Depew laughed. "Nobody's going to hire you. You're stupid and most of all, you have no backbone. You get back here right now, or I'll call the home and cancel your mother's room. They'll put her on the curb with her bags. Do you want that?" She hung up.

Ernest's shoulders sagged. Tears glistened in the corners of his eyes. He broke my heart.

I had no answers for him. I had been all rah-rah at the start, but now realized that was all I had. Words. I could barely finance my own life and definitely couldn't bankroll his. I had pushed him to the end of the plank and couldn't pull him back. I turned away to let Ernest wipe his tears in private.

Ernest returned his phone to his pocket. He said, "She hung up. She's furious."

I said, "I'm sorry I pushed you so hard. Maybe you shouldn't go back."

Ernest said, "I'm going home to face her. I should have done it long ago."

I asked, "Is your uncle dead?"

Ernest stared at the ground. "Yes."

"Did your aunt kill him?"

Ernest's eyes welled up. "You're next."

I stopped breathing. With all that was going on it never occurred to me that Mrs. Depew would kill me too. "I need to know two things. How did she kill your uncle and where is his body?"

Ernest stood.

"Where are you going?" I asked. "We haven't finished."

Ernest said, "I have to get back right away. I was only able to get out because she was asleep. I shouldn't have come."

I said, "Wait, I need one thing from you."

Ernest looked over his shoulder and back at me.

If I didn't get his concession, this risky meeting would be worthless. I took Ernest's rough hand in mine and got his full attention. I said, "Would you meet with me and Detective Brimley? I want you to share your story."

Ernest snatched his hand from mine and stepped back. "No way. Suppose Detective Brimley charges me with murder? Lots of innocent people end up in jail."

I said, "If we stick together, we can clear both our names."

Ernest shook his head. "Brimley might believe Aunt Lilac's story. She would serve us both up to stay out of jail. Her age is her superpower. People think she can do no wrong because she's a little old lady in a wheelchair."

I had fallen for her act early on and suffered her abuse later. I said, "You're stronger than you think. I need you. If you don't help me, we could both suffer the consequences." I held my breath. Then said, "Please."

Ernest's shoulders sagged. "Okay."

I texted him the time and place of the meeting, and prayed Brimley would agree. It would be too dangerous to call Ernest back with any changes.

Ernest jumped up. "I have to go and face my punishment. I don't know what she's going to do to me."

My mouth dropped open. "Think. What would she do without you? She depends on you."

Ernest started to walk away. He turned back and said, "I'm afraid. I'm not helping you because you're threatening my aunt. I'm helping you because this may be the only way to get her out of my life. My uncle was a good man. I miss him. She's evil." Without looking back, he broke into a trot and disappeared around the corner.

FIFTEEN

I picked up a dozen frosted donuts and returned to Malik's.

Malik agreed to take me home to pack a bag for my stay with Holy. I laid down in the back of the Escalade while Malik rolled up my street to see if someone was watching the house. Sure enough, Detective Brimley was sitting in his car across the street from my house. We drove to the next street over and parked.

Malik said, "I don't see why you have to do this. You made enough cash to buy a few things for your stay with Holy."

I said, "I didn't make enough money to buy shoes."

Malik raised his eyebrows. "Is that what this is about? Shoes? You're going to risk your freedom for shoes?" He shook his head.

I knew it sounded silly to him, but if I had to spend time with Holy, I would need some kind of comfort. Also, I needed my cash to pay my mortgage. I got out of the car and cut through the yard of the house behind mine. I climbed over the wire fence that separated our backyards, ripping my jeans in the process. I used my Catwoman stealth to creep inside through the back door, staying low so Brimley wouldn't spot me.

Murphy greeted me with a growl. I hadn't fed him on a regular schedule, but I surmised he would raid the fridge anyway. In fifteen minutes, I had grabbed enough clothes, shoes, and cat food for my stay with Holy.

Now for the real problem, Murphy. I've used a cat carrier on rare occasions to take Murphy to the vet. The problem was that Murphy would only submit to the carrier if he was too sick to fight back. That was not the case today.

I piled my conglomeration of bags and cases next to the back door. Then I focused on Murphy. He had been eyeing my process as I gathered my things but kept a safe distance away from me the entire time. He knew something was up.

I smiled. "Come here Murphy." I took a step toward him. He took a step back. I held my breath and lunged for him. He took off down the hall and up the steps at jet speed. There was no way I could catch him. I was Catwoman, but he was a genuine cat.

121

We zigzagged through the second floor knocking over anything in our paths. We made enough noise to attract the entire neighborhood. My bedroom floor lamp crashed against the front window. Without breathing, I stood behind the curtain and peeped out. Sure enough, Brimley had emerged from his car. He peered at the house as if deciding whether to break in or not. I ducked down as he approached.

At this point I had no choice. I had to get Murphy out of there or leave him. Murphy had hunkered down in a corner of my shoe closet. On an average day, this would've brought me near hysteria, but I had already removed my favorite shoes. I took the opportunity to slam the closet door shut, then searched for a Murphy container.

I glanced out the window again. Brimley was climbing my steps. I tiptoed to my bed and snatched the pillowcase off my pillow. I opened the pillowcase and then the closet door. As I knew he would, Murphy dashed for the exit and right into my pillowcase. I slung the sack over my shoulder. *Now, how do I get downstairs with Brimley at my door?*

My front door had one of those little windows that I thought silly. The purpose of a front door was for privacy and to keep people out. Those windows let people see in. Even though I had a curtain over the window, it was sheer, and Brimley would have no problem seeing me come down my steps. I went to the bathroom window and peeked out. *Hallelujah.* Malik stood in my backyard with a worried look on his face.

I opened the bathroom window and waved. Malik spied me, and I pressed one finger to my lips to signal him to be quiet. Then I stage-whispered, "Catch this." I dangled the pillowcase out the window. By this time, Murphy had worked himself into a frenzy. Malik held his hands up defensively and shook his head. I ignored him and dropped the bag. *Oops. Maybe I should've tied the bag shut.*

The pillowcase flapped open in the air and Murphy burst out like a dive bomber, all claws out. Malik's eyes widened like saucers. Murphy landed on Malik's chest and held on with every claw. Malik screamed like a girl.

I heard Brimley clump down my front steps. I was sure he would head to the backyard. I waved Malik away. He held Murphy to his chest and rounded the side of the house just as Brimley reached the yard. I ducked inside, clunking my head on the windowsill. *That's gonna hurt tomorrow.*

I raced to the first floor. Staying low, I crept to my kitchen window and peeped out from the lower corner. Brimley stood in my yard, hands on hips, craning his neck from side to side. I glanced at the conglomeration of bags and suitcases I had piled by the back door. I had no idea how I would get them all to the Escalade. When I peeped back at the yard, Brimley had vanished.

It was now or never. I cracked my back door open and stuck my head out. I glimpsed side to side. I saw nothing. I heard nothing. I grabbed the most important bags first, the ones containing my shoes and Murphy's food.

I ran across my yard to the back fence and threw the bags over the side. I repeated that action until I had all my bags on the other side of the fence. Then I leapt over. Well, I didn't really leap, but it sounded better than crawled.

The Escalade was a straight shot from where I stood. I took the bags, two by two, until they were all in the Escalade. Just as I loaded the last bag, Malik rounded the corner with a pile of wriggling fur attached to his chest. I extracted Murphy from Malik's grasp. Malik shot me an angry look and got into the driver's seat. Little specks of blood and multiple holes spotted his white T-shirt. There was nothing I could say. We took off to Holy's house.

I had never seen Holy's new house. In fact, I wished I hadn't seen Holy since the divorce. Using Malik's GPS, we drove through the back streets Down Neck searching for his abode. Holy had told me he wasn't far from the junkyard. Great. At least no one would look for me there. We turned down Holy's street to find a row of dilapidated houses, most of them boarded up. It was hard to tell where the junkyard ended, and the houses began. We stopped in front of a gray house with peeling paint, rickety steps and a bent chicken wire fence. I gaped at the house and shifted my eyes to Malik.

Malik shrugged. He said, "It's up to you."

As I got out of the Escalade the front door of the house popped open and Holy appeared with a big bouquet of flowers. I sighed. This was not gonna be easy.

Holy bounced down the steps, pushed open his gate and shoved the flowers in my face with a big grin. He said, "Welcome back home."

I said, "I'm not coming back home. I never lived here. You do understand this is temporary. Don't you?"

I couldn't tell if he heard me. He busied himself hustling my bags into his house.

A sea of junk drowned his front yard. Moldy chairs, rusted tools and deflated tires scattered across the dirt. I would say lawn, but that would be way too generous. A few brave weeds sprouted between the debris. Holy had cleared a small path through the rubble to his porch.

Murphy had been hunkered down behind the driver's seat. I reached for him and was met with a low growl. Malik's eyes widened when he heard that. He got out of the car with his hands raised in a defensive motion. This was going to be up to me.

Holy had returned to the car. He peeped inside and said, "Oh, you brought Murphy. How wonderful."

I said, "You hate Murphy. You always have."

Holy said, "That's not true. I can't wait to have you both here."

I rolled my eyes. "Then why don't you get him out of the car?"

Holy said, "I'll hold the door for you." He hustled his stocky body up to his front door and stood there holding it open.

I said, "Here I go." I gave Malik a wistful look. *Please take me home with you.*

Malik said, "Call me if you need me."

I hugged Murphy to my chest and crept through the maze of junk into the house. Inside the foyer, my jaw dropped. Boxes of bolts, screws, and metal objects I couldn't identify, heaped higher than my head. Murphy's claws tightened into a death grip. He tried to claw his way over my shoulder to the door. I bit my lower lip to fight the pain and walked on.

I entered the living room and stopped short, letting Murphy clump to the floor. A dilapidated refrigerator stood wrapped in chains. An old TV with a wire hanger antenna leaned next to it. A musty, stained couch supported three feet of old newspapers on two of the three cushions. Two contrasting rugs covered the floor. Several rolled up carpets leaned against the wall in one corner.

Murphy scrambled away kicking up a cloud of dust and making me sneeze. I touched the shade of a tilted floor lamp and jerked back from the grit. My nose scrunched up from the musty air and I blinked back itchy tears.

From where I stood, I could see the kitchen. A small, bent leg, vinyl topped table centered the room. Four mismatched chairs surrounded the table.

I jumped, when from behind me Holy said, "I see the tears in your eyes. I knew you'd love it." He puffed out his chest and said, "Pretty great, huh? This house has everything we could possibly need. Welcome home Honey."

I whirled around and said, "Are you crazy? This house is a health hazard. If you think I'm staying here, you're out of your gourd."

Holy surveyed the room and shrugged. "This is good, salable stuff. It's like having a second bank account. Besides, I cleaned up for you." He pointed to the empty spot on the sofa.

I said, "Is the rest of the house like this?"

At that moment I heard a low growl. I said, "Murphy? Where are you, Baby?" I tracked the sound to a pile of torn chair cushions at the bottom of the stairs. As I pushed them aside, Murphy shot past me up the stairs. I ran after him, tripping on a can of motor oil and spilling forward onto an old pair of army boots. I pulled myself up and resumed the chase.

From the bottom of the steps, Holy said, "Be careful, Honey."

Three rooms plus the bathroom composed the upper floor. I listened for signs of Murphy but heard none. I started with the first room. This room had undefined usage. It could've been an office or a den, but it resembled a salvage yard. A table holding an old computer and a chair sat near the window. An overflowing wastebasket sat on the floor next to it. It could have been a workspace, but a quarter inch of dust lay over the computer screen. A conglomeration of envelopes, letters and bills lay on the table in no seeming order. A mix of boxes and crates of miscellaneous debris filled the rest of the room. Holy would call it salable trash. Murphy didn't seem to be here.

The next room mimicked the first, minus the office components. Then I entered the bathroom and stopped in stunned amazement. The sink, although a 1970's sage green, gleamed and smelled of pine. Holy must have remembered this was one of my pet peeves. I couldn't stand when he left hair or little globs of toothpaste in the sink. The rest of the bathroom reflected a mix of salvaged and newly purchased items. The medicine cabinet door hung at an angle and featured a spotted mirror. A frayed bathmat and moldy shower curtain curling at the hem hid the tub. The towels, however, were brand-new. I refused to look in the toilet. In his own fashion Holy had prepared for me. I moved on in my search for Murphy.

I entered the last room, the bedroom. The bed was neat with turned-down covers. A single red rose and one Hershey Kiss lay on one pillow. Holy must've seen that on TV. He wouldn't have thought of it himself. In this room Holy had pushed the junk against the walls, leaving space around the bed. Makeshift nightstands made of wooden snack trays stood on either side of the bed. One held our framed wedding picture. Mismatched lamps topped the nightstands. Shades covered the unadorned windows, one white, one beige, both dusty.

I heard a rustling sound - Murphy. The closet door sat askew. Murphy loved to hide in closets. I closed the bedroom door. Then I crept to the closet, opened it, and forgot all about Murphy. The half empty closet held a row of wire hangers which I assume were meant for me. Holy's clothes filled the other half. My wedding veil hung on a nail inside the closet door. My eyebrows started to twitch. Something wasn't right, something more than the horror of this house.

From behind me, Holy said, "How do you like our room? I changed the sheets for us. Did you notice?"

I said, "What do you mean *our* room?"

Holy ignored me. "I'm so glad to have you back. I'm gonna make you happy, Honey."

"I am not back. I told you this is temporary while I have the house fumigated. We are not sleeping together. In fact, I'm not going to stay here at all."

Holy got down on one knee and clasped his hands in front of his face. He gazed up at me and said, "Honey, give me a chance. If you're not ready to sleep together, I understand. I'll sleep on the couch for a few days until you change your mind."

"I'm not going to change my mind." From the corner of my eye, I could see Murphy creeping out of the closet. I said, "Quick, close the bedroom door."

Holy's eyes lit up. "See, I knew you'd change your mind. Come here, Honey."

I straight-armed Holy in his chest, and he fell back. It took some convincing for Holy to understand I was serious.

He was about to leave when I noticed a matchbox topped with a tiny stick-on bow atop the dresser. I tried to ignore it, but Holy pointed it out with a flourish of his arm.

I said, "I'll look at it later." I didn't want to know what the box held. The only gifts Holy had ever given me were polished bits of garbage abandoned at the junkyard. I stepped toward the door and Holy blocked my way. I said, "Holy, I need to get my duffel bag."

Holy bowed at the waist. "I'll fetch it for you, my lady." He disappeared out the door and thumped down the obstacle course of steps.

I sighed. This was going to be a long stay. I picked up the box. The bow fell off. No glue. I slid the compartment open and gawked at an exquisite ivory ring. The vintage sepia-toned ring was carved with tiny roses around the perimeter. I wanted to slip it onto my finger, but feared Holy would take that as a sign to renew our vows.

From behind me I heard, "Isn't it beautiful? Just like you. Let me slip it onto your finger."

I said, "No way. Besides, someone probably discarded this by mistake."

Holy raised his eyebrows. "How do you know I didn't buy it for you?"

I threw him a look that said, "Really?"

Holy lowered his head. "Okay. But I gave it to you rather than sell it."

I put the ring back in the matchbox and handed it to him. "Thanks anyway. You should try to find the rightful owner." I felt sorry for Holy. He tried hard to please me, but my heart had closed to him a long time ago.

Dejected, Holy left me to settle in.

I resigned myself to sleeping at Holy's until I could find another safe haven. Exhausted from the day, I slipped into a deep sleep with Murphy at my side. About 4 AM I awoke with a feeling of imminent danger. My eyes flew open to find Holy standing over the bed staring at me. I sat up so fast I pulled a muscle. "What the hell are you doing in here?"

"Baby, I miss you. I know you want me too, don't you? Come on, admit it." He leaned forward and tried to kiss me.

I flipped on the tattered lamp. "You're naked."

Holy splayed his arms in a helpless gesture and said, "I didn't want to waste time."

"Well, you're wasting your time right now." I pulled the covers up to my neck.

Holy took a step closer.

I stuck out my hand and pushed him back.

He said, "Ah, I missed your touch. I know you miss me, too."

"You're not getting the message, Pal and if you don't get out of here, I'm going to sic Murphy on you. You know how he likes to play with things that dangle."

Holy inched back and cupped his hands between his legs, but he still hovered.

I knew what to do. I opened my mouth and blew a huge gust of morning breath into his face.

Holy jumped back. "Damn, Honey."

I said, "If you don't stay away from me, you're going to get worse than that."

Holy raised his hands in a defensive manner and backed out of the room.

He was gone for the moment, but I knew he'd be back. My morning breath was putrid, but it wouldn't keep him away forever. Murphy and I had to get out.

It had taken a half an hour of shouting to get Holy out of the room. I spent the next hour sitting up with Murphy snoozing in my lap. Then I pushed some of the junk boxes against the door (although this might be a problem if I had to pee). Even then, I couldn't sleep. At 5:00 a.m. I got dressed and took Murphy downstairs for breakfast.

One glimpse at the kitchen and I called Malik.

Malik's voice sounded muffled. "Who is this?"

"It's me. Please come and get me."

"Rocky?" A pause. "It's five in the morning. Did something happen?"

"I'm sorry. I can't stay here another minute." By 6:00 a.m. Murphy and I had our baggage at the curb. I could see Holy peeking out between dirty blinds.

Malik rolled the Escalade to a stop and shot me a sleepy look.

We decided to drop Murphy and my stuff at Malik's apartment while I found a place to stay.

I piled myself, Murphy, and my bag into the car. Murphy retook his sanctuary behind the driver's seat, and we took off. *Hallelujah*.

SIXTEEN

Malik said, "Where to?"

I had only one option – Dad. Last time I stayed there, I fled in the middle of the night. I hadn't spoken to Dad since. I hated being the ungrateful child who only called when I needed something, but today I had no choice.

Dad spoke in even tones. "Good morning, Raquel."

I hoped my smile would add warmth to my voice. "Hi Dad. You're up early."

Silence.

I said, "Dad?"

He said, "I'm waiting. You wouldn't call unless you needed something."

My soul deflated. I couldn't fool him if I tried. We knew each other too well. I took a deep breath and said, "Dad, can I come back and stay with you a while?"

Malik turned his back to me and looked out the window.

I ground my teeth as I awaited Dad's reply.

He said, "I wouldn't turn you away." Not exactly a welcome, but at least I'd have a bed for the night.

Malik dropped me and Murphy at the curb and drove off.

Dad cracked the door open and went back to his lounge chair to watch TV. He didn't utter a word.

I dragged my duffel into Dad's house and up to my room. Then I laid down to take a well-earned nap. My worn-out emotions had wiped me out more than the day's activities. The second I drifted off, Malik called.

Now what? I couldn't take another emotional conversation. I said, "Hi Malik."

Malik said, "I called Aunt Lusty, and she has another job. I wouldn't have bothered you, but I think we should take this one." He spoke in even tones, not exactly cold but not his normal sweetness.

I said, "Thanks for calling. What's the job?" I wanted to say so much more but couldn't form the proper words. It was better to say nothing.

Malik said, "We need to pick up a shipment of mousetraps and deliver them to a trade show. We have to do it early in the morning because the trade

130

show starts at 10 a.m. tomorrow." He ran down the rest of the details and hung up without saying goodbye.

I woke up every hour that night, tossing and turning so much that Murphy chose to sleep on the floor. When I rose that morning, Dad's door was still closed. Murphy and I stood on the curb as the sun rose and waited for Malik. I couldn't leave Murphy behind, because he could get out of control sometimes. Dad wouldn't understand if Murphy raided his fridge.

Malik picked us up and we decided to stop at an out-of-town diner to pick up breakfast. This job was important, not only because of the income, but because the client was a lawyer. I might need one soon.

We drove in awkward silence. My cell purred. I glanced at the display. Charles was calling.

Malik said, "Who's calling you this time of morning? I thought I was the only one that called you this early."

I answered the call. "Good morning." I tried to keep the lilt out of my voice. "Can I call you back?"

Malik said, "Go ahead and talk. I don't mind. Besides, we're at the diner. I'll go in and get breakfast so you can have your privacy." He slammed the Escalade door and left me to myself.

I sighed and said to Charles, "How are you this morning?"

Charles said, "Hey, Beautiful. I'm doing better than you sound."

"I didn't sleep well last night."

Charles' smile shined through the phone. "Thinking about me, I hope."

I said, "Of course." It was one of those things you say to a loved one that sounds good but isn't believable.

Charles said, "Hmmm. That doesn't sound too convincing."

I was too tired to come up with a clever retort, so I said nothing.

Charles said, "I called to give you new information. The evidence the police have on the cane, besides the blood of course, is dirt."

"Dirt?"

"Yeah, whatever kind of soil is on the cane is unique to an area they can tie back to you."

How much more can I take? "That's stupid. I don't have unique dirt; I have neighborhood dirt."

Malik emerged from the diner balancing a huge brown bag and two gigantic coffees.

I said, "I've got to go. Can I call you later?"

Charles said, "Sure. By the way, who's the guy you were talking to?"

Everybody wants to know who I'm talking to. "My coworker. I'm on a job."

Charles said, "Oh." He didn't sound convinced.

Malik was standing at the door, waiting for me to open it.

I said, "Talk to you later," and disconnected before opening the door.

We organized our food so we could eat and travel at the same time. We said little during the ride to our client, mostly awkward small talk. We ignored the elephant in the room of my morning call until we pulled up at the client's door.

I was about to climb out of the Escalade. Malik put his hand on my arm and said, "Was the person on that call the reason you didn't stay with me?"

I blurted it out. "He's a nice guy. We're just starting out."

Malik said, "I thought you and I were just starting out."

I had no reply.

Malik took my shoulders in his muscular hands. "I want you to think. You're mixed up in a murder. Now this new guy shows up in your life. How do you know he's not part of it? He may even be the killer."

My eyes watered. I said, "He's not the killer. In fact, he says Brimley..."

Malik reared back from me as if in shock. "Is that where you got that theory? Did it occur to you he's throwing suspicion on Brimley, so you'll trust him? Did you even bother to ask him any questions about himself? What do you know about him?"

I said, "He and I are getting to know each other. I don't know if anything will come of this, but I want to give it a chance."

Malik said, "You gave him a chance, but not me. I guess that says it all." He put his hands on the wheel and stared straight ahead. "I think we should make this our last job."

My world turned inside out. I must be doing all the wrong things, because when I'm doing the right things, everything falls into place. What could I say? "If you think that's best."

Malik stared straight ahead. He said, "While we're making confessions, I should tell you I got your money from my mother."

My mouth dropped open. "You spoke to your mother? How did that go?"

"It was a hard conversation. I didn't want to talk to her, but your welfare was worth the risk. I don't know if we can mend our relationship but it's a start."

I couldn't look at him. "I'll pay you back as soon as I can."

Malik said, "Don't worry about it. I was just helping a friend." He started up the car and we pulled off. He didn't glance my way the entire drive.

The attorney lived in a huge house with a detached garage in the back. We pulled around to load the truck.

As Malik loaded the truck, he said, "Why are these boxes so cold? It's a warm day."

The attorney said, "I requested a refrigerated unit. The mousetraps are pre-baited. When a customer buys this mousetrap, he doesn't have to worry about setting it or loading it with bait. They just set it out and wait. After this trade show, this product will fly off the shelves. It's my own invention." He puffed out his chest as if he had just birthed a child.

I said, "You should be fine. It's a short trip to the trade show. We'll take good care of your product." I collected the payment, and we took off.

I had been holding Murphy on my lap, but he kept squirming, so I let him go. He scrambled into the back and nestled between the boxes.

Malik looked back at him and then at me.

I said, "Don't worry. He's resting. He likes to fit into small places."

The trade show was downtown at NJPAC, a short half-hour from the attorney's house. We were in the downtown area when a scratching noise emanated from the back of the Escalade. I turned to see Murphy clawing his way through the boxes. I screamed. Malik slammed on the brakes, causing the boxes to tumble on top of Murphy. I expected to hear screeching tires of other vehicles, but it was too early for much traffic. Instead, a series of snaps, followed by a succession of pops and cracks filled the car. We pulled to the side of Broad Street. Malik jumped out and ran to the back.

I said, "Don't let Murphy out."

Malik returned to the driver's seat, and I scrambled over my seat into the back. The boxes bounced around like jumping beans. In the heat of the morning sun, I could smell the aroma of pungent cheese, the kind Murphy loves.

I said, "These boxes smell like cheese. That's why Murphy's trying to get into them." Hundreds of little boxes popped and snapped around me as I searched through them for Murphy. Murphy dug into the boxes, pulling out bits of cheese and smacking as he ate. He was determined to make a meal from those boxes. Each time I grabbed him, he scrambled out of my grasp. I said, "Give me your shirt."

Malik said, "My shirt?"

"Just do it."

Malik tugged off his tee shirt, revealing smooth, sculpted pecs and handed it to me. The vision dredged up a yearning I thought I had reserved for Charles. I lingered for a second then dragged my eyes to the back of the truck to find Murphy. I hated to do it, but I caught Murphy by his tail and yanked. I wrapped him in the shirt and handed the writhing bundle to Malik while I climbed back into my seat. I said, "Give him back to me. You have to straighten up the merchandise."

Malik said, "You made the mess; you clean it up."

I sighed and climbed in the back. I stacked the boxes, hiding the damaged ones in the center of the pallet. By the time I had fixed the shipment, the entire Escalade reeked of Limburger. So did I. Traffic had slowed to a crawl to circumvent us. A scowling cop threatened us with a ticket if we didn't clear the lane. Off we went.

I said to Malik, "Do you have any air fresheners? You know, the little trees that you hang from the mirror?"

Malik's scowl said what I knew to be true. Air fresheners wouldn't do it.

The trade show had been in full force for an hour by the time we got to NJPAC. An angry little man accepted the shipment with a sniff. We got out of there before he could ask any questions.

I unwrapped Murphy and returned the shirt to Malik. The hair covered shirt had a few small holes but was wearable. Malik scowled and tugged it on anyway.

On the way home Malik said, "I need to pick up some cash." We stopped at an ATM. While I sat alone in the car, I checked my phone. No messages from Charles. He had disappeared again. How could I love the Invisible Man?

Malik climbed back in and sat behind the wheel staring at nothing. He gripped the wheel and breathed deeply.

I said, "What's wrong?" I held my breath for his answer.

He said, "My money's gone. All of it."

I didn't know what to say. "What happened to it? There has to be a record of what you spent the money on."

Malik's face turned grim. "I knew I shouldn't have trusted her."

My chest tightened and I dared not speak.

"That bitch. She stole everything from me...my whole life. I had a queasy feeling in my stomach when my mother asked for my bank details so she could wire your money to my account. But I didn't listen to my gut. She wiped me out. I have nothing on now, no school money, no living expenses. Nothing. She had no right. My father left me that money in a trust and thank God he did. It was the only way I could get away from her. I received my trust on my 18th birthday, and I left my mom the next day. I go to school on scholarship. The money my dad left me is just enough to pay living expenses if I'm frugal."

A tear rolled down my cheek. I said, "I'm sorry I hassled you about not speaking with your mom. You were right to cut her off."

Malik said, "I'm past it. In a way, I'm glad this happened. She released me from any guilt. I'm free of her now."

I said, "Going forward, I'll keep my advice to myself."

He grimaced and said, "It's not your fault. I knew she was snake when I reached out to her."

When I returned to Dad's, I found my bag on the porch with a note attached. It read, "You may return home when you're ready to act like a lady should. Let me know when you've closed your business."

SEVENTEEN

I can't take anymore today. I looked at the bags, then back at Malik who waited by the curb, then at the front door. *I can't make one more decision today. Besides my choices are all wrong. Forget this drama, I'm going with Malik.* I picked up my duffel, scooped up Murphy and turned to see an empty space where the Escalade had been. Malik had made the decision for me.

I unlocked the door and dragged my bag into the foyer.

Dad stood at the top of the stairs, arms crossed, face scowling. He said, "So you've decided to close this crazy business of yours?"

I had nowhere else to go. That's how I justified my lie. Malik was through with me (not that we ever started). My house was under surveillance, and I had no idea where Charles Charles lived. In fact, I knew nothing about him which meant I'd abandoned a perfectly good friendship for a mystery. My entire life was upside down.

I said, "Dad, you're right. I'm going to get my life back on track." This wasn't exactly a lie. In fact, it was my full intention to return my life to normal. Did Dad need to know I was pursuing a murderer? No. Did I have to share my romance options? Nope. I'd never reveal my looming eviction. All that stuff's incidental.

Dad said, "Since you've come to your senses, you can stay." He went up to his room and shut the door without another word. *Thank God.*

I dragged my duffel bag up to my room. I could hear Dad talking. Was he telling his friend about his ungrateful daughter?

He didn't sound agitated. He spoke in soothing tones I wished he used with me.

I took a hot shower to erase the aroma of Limburger and dropped my cheesy clothes into the washing machine.

I sat on my bed and called Lusty. Before she could utter hello, I said, "What the hell is wrong with you?"

She said, "What's the matter?"

I said, "Malik didn't call you? The mousetraps were a disaster. In fact, all your referrals are a mess. Just once, I'd like to get a decent job from you. How about something like shoes or books instead of melting eyeballs and horses?"

Lusty said, "I'm doing my best to support you and Malik."

"Well, Malik and I aren't on good terms right now, and I'm about to lose my mind."

Lusty sniffed. Her voice cracked as she said, "I'm sorry, Rocky. I thought you understood I was trying to help a friend." When I didn't respond, she said, "I have to go. I'm on a business call."

I hung up without another word and immediately regretted it. I turned to Murphy for support. I said, "Yes, she's a good friend. I can't blame her for the disastrous jobs. She can't predict the future. Even though she never gets her facts straight, she tries to help. She deserves my understanding. In fact, I would have lost my house by now if it wasn't for her."

Murphy glared at me, turned his back, and curled up to sleep.

I went to the bathroom medicine cabinet for aspirin. My head throbbed like I had banged it with a hammer. On the way back to my room, I heard Dad say, "Are you all right? You sound upset." How could he comfort his friend, but not me?

That morning's emotions had taken their toll. I flopped back on the bed and fell asleep instantly, warmed by the baking midday sun. Sometimes sleep is a blessed escape. Instead, I dreamt of doors shutting in my face. I tossed and turned until I awakened to the smell of coffee and cinnamon buns. My dad's favorite afternoon snack would put him in a good mood. I wiped the drool from my face and went down to join him in the kitchen.

Dad had the classifieds folded next to his coffee mug. He had circled one ad in red. He said, "I'm glad you're up."

Without responding, I poured a steaming mug for myself.

He said, "I called in a favor and got you a decent job."

I froze, with the mug an inch from my lips. "A what?"

"A J-O-B. You start tomorrow."

I tried my best to be casual. "That's great, Dad." Is he nuts? I have a business to run. Then I remembered my promise. Uh oh.

Dad said, "It's a customer service position."

Now there's something I'm good at. "Dad, I don't know what to say." *I'm not doing it, that's what I can say.* Instead, I said, "Thanks Dad. Where is the job?"

The job turned out to be ten blocks from Dad's house at the Nubbin Nut Factory. He wanted to be sure I could get to work on time. A few months back I would've killed for a steady job, but I've had a taste of an entrepreneurship. There is a freedom in choosing your jobs and making your own hours. So, what if I'm still piling up debt? I'll get better at it. Rocky Recoveries is my creation. I'm the boss. I don't want to work for someone else. I looked my father in the eye and said, "What time do I start?"

Dad relaxed back in his chair. "Early."

I said, "My car is at Malik's. Can you run me over to pick it up?" I concocted the fairly coherent explanation that I left it there so Malik could change my oil. *Lies, lies, lies.*

Dad raised an eyebrow. "He's a good friend."

Dad dropped me at my car. I figured this day couldn't get any worse. That made it the ideal time to talk to Hartness. I entered the bank and flinched at his gruff voice.

"Do you have my money?"

I said, "Not yet."

He tapped his laptop keys before I continued. He said, "You haven't paid your mortgage or me. You're testing my patience."

I said, "I can't pay the mortgage yet, but I'm working on it. Can't you give me a break?"

"I'm not in the break business. You should be out making money, not wasting my time. Soon you'll be three months late. I won't be able to help you then. I gave you a good deal. Don't come back without the money."

I returned to my childhood bedroom at Dad's, feeling weak and vulnerable like in my adolescence. I tossed and turned all night. For once, my dreams focused on problems other than my own. Images of Ernest being tortured by the old woman in the wheelchair haunted me.

The next morning, I dressed in a simple black pantsuit and white blouse. I donned a pair of orange silk Sergio Rossi platform stilettos. Dad would be watching me, so I couldn't wear comfy jeans. I hopped into my Corolla and drove right past the nut factory. I returned to my post in the Azalea bushes across the street from the Depew house.

Crouched behind the white flowers, I strained to hear any noises. With relief, I heard no screams and saw no signs of torture. I feared for Ernest's life and didn't know what to do.

A tap on my shoulder made me jump a foot into the air, which was no easy task in those shoes. I whirled around to see Charles Charles. "Where the hell did you come from?"

Charles said, "I didn't mean to startle you, Baby."

Before I could run, he grabbed my arm. I wrenched away from him and stood face to face. A fiery anger I had never experienced rose in me. "You don't get to call me Baby." He reached for me and I quick-stepped back. His touch was my Kryptonite. I said, "I've had time to think, and you are not welcome in my life. I need a man who is there when I need him. I can't count on you. If you cared, you would listen when I talk. Also, we don't spend time together."

"Are you lonely?" He reached out to touch me.

I stepped back. He's not going to suck me in this time.

"That's another thing. When I'm pissed, you don't take me seriously. I'm not a child you can dismiss with a smile and a hug."

Charles shrugged. "I can't be here all the time."

"A real relationship needs two committed people. I want a real, loving relationship. I want to have fair fights that upset us both. I need a man I can wake up to. I want to have breakfast and dinner with my man. I want to spend holidays and birthdays with someone. It's become increasingly clear that person isn't you." I hadn't realized I still held so much pent-up anger. "You treat me like a fling, your little thing on the side. I'm much more than that."

Charles raised his hands in submission. "Please let me explain. I had a job emergency just before our meet. I didn't even have time to call."

I crossed my arms. "What exactly is your job?"

He sighed. "I can't give you details but it's a dangerous job. I do important work and travel a lot. I make good money, but it carries a downside. When they call, I have to go. That's all I can tell you."

I said, "Do you think I'm stupid? You sound like some kind of super spy. I can't have a relationship with someone I can't count on. I can't trust you." I turned to walk away.

Charles circled me and blocked my path. "Rocky, I'm sorrier than you know. I can't promise I'll always be available, but I can assure you I'll have your back whenever I'm here."

I said, "I'm not buying it."

He said, "You're not being fair."

My head jerked back. I must have heard wrong.

Charles said, "I went away knowing you could handle your situation."

My voice rose an octave. "I was terrified. Ernest grabbed me."

Charles said, "He didn't hurt you and I knew he wouldn't."

"What do you mean? How could you know anything from wherever you were?"

He said, "From what you'd told me, Ernest is quiet. He doesn't make a move without Mrs. Depew's consent."

I had to admit that was true.

Charles said, "And then, there's you." His eyes glowed with warmth when he spoke. "You're a tough cookie. You don't believe it, but you're brave. It takes courage to take the chances you do. You've accomplished a lot in life, and you fight every day for your independence."

My barriers started crumbling. He really got me. I thought I was just his plaything, but all the while he had paid attention to my thoughts and feelings.

Charles took my hand and led me back to the bench. "I have news for you. But first, what did Ernest have to say?"

Mrs. Depew's accusation of Charles swirled in the back of my mind. I didn't know how much to share with my mystery man. I said, "You first."

Charles said, "The police have found Depew's body, skeleton actually."

I said, "Hallelujah. Now they'll see I had nothing to do with this mess." I was convinced the police would use their forensic superpowers to root out the real killer.

Charles said, "Don't celebrate yet." He took my hand in his. "The police identified the dirt on the cane as coming from a junkyard and that's where they found the body. Somehow, they're tying this evidence to you."

I gulped. "What junkyard?" *Why am I even asking?*

"Junior's Junkyard, Down Neck."

I removed my hand from his and sat back. "How are you getting your information?"

Charles didn't hesitate. He leaned forward and gazed into my eyes. The sunlight glinted in his amber eyes, reflecting waves of warmth I wanted to dive into. He said, "Trust me. I know you're innocent and I'm here to protect you."

My walls crumbled into dust. In the next moment, his kiss removed all doubt. Soft lips and firm arms transported me to a safe haven where criminals and murder didn't exist.

I shared everything Ernest had told me.

Charles said, "According to what you're saying, Ernest only implied his uncle was killed. He didn't say Mrs. Depew did the deed. We need hard evidence against them."

I said, "You only need confirmation that Mrs. Depew killed her husband. I already told you Ernest is innocent."

Charles kissed my forehead. "We need to know the whole truth. Ernest could have willingly helped kill his uncle. Suppose Mrs. Depew turns up dead next? Would you still believe Ernest clean in this mess?" Charles took my hands in his. "Just because he treats you nice, doesn't mean he's a good person. My main concern is that you are in danger. I want you to call me any time day or night."

He took my phone and entered his number. Then he escorted me back to my car. He had parked his BMW behind my car. My worn Corolla looked like Charles Dickens' Oliver next to Ritchie Rich.

I was about to hop into my car when Charles touched my arm and said, "I have a surprise for you."

EIGHTEEN

Without another thought I slid into the luxurious seats of his BMW. We drove in comfortable silence like an old couple who enjoyed unspoken communication. We pulled up to a small white house on a quiet tree lined street in a neighborhood I had never visited.

I said, "Is this where you live?"

Charles smiled and said, "Let's go."

We entered the house and were greeted by a young blond couple dressed in white scrubs. We followed them down to the most beautiful basement I had ever seen. Pecan paneling and hanging plants lined the walls. Peace exuded from the soft sage carpeting and a water feature in the corner.

The woman gestured to two curtained doors. She said, "You may disrobe here, and we'll be back." The couple left the room.

My eyebrows rose to my hairline. "Disrobe?"

Charles chuckled and said, "No need for alarm. We're getting massages."

We emerged from our dressing rooms in fluffy white robes. The couple guided us to bamboo massage tables. We lay on our stomachs as they kneaded our backs with mood enhancing aromatherapy oils. My mind went south as they placed hot stones along my spine. Soothing new age music played softly in the background. The tensions of the day drained from my body. They served tiny cups of chamomile tea to end the ritual. It was the most romantic nonsexual experience I had ever had. It was like sex without sex.

After the massage, the couple escorted us to a screened in porch that followed the soothing theme of the spa. Tiny birds flitted about in the yard, twittering their joy. Soft sunlight warmed our skin. In our robes and spa slippers, we were served an organic lunch. Codfish fritters, Jasmine rice and Cajun collard greens filled our bellies. We topped off our meal with a creamy banana pudding.

After our meal, the couple removed our dining table with swift efficiency. They converted our chairs to the lounge position and allowed us to nap in the afternoon sun. I awoke to find Charles sitting upright, gazing at me. I wiped the sleep from my eyes.

Charles leaned over and pushed my curls out of my eyes. He didn't say a word.

I said, "What?"

He shook his head and kissed me gently on the cheek. He returned me to my car and tucked me inside. He had been uncharacteristically quiet and calm during the ride back.

As I drove off, I peeped in my rear view and saw him watching me with an enigmatic smile on his lips.

I circled the block and re-parked in the setting sun, this time on the street behind the Depew house. To my relief, Charles had gone. After good food and massage, I could do serious spy work.

Before I could start, my cell jangled with Holy's fire alarm ringtone. Holy had the only distinct ringtone on my cell, appropriate to alert me to upcoming stress. As hard as I tried to separate from him, my troubles had seeped into his life. I picked up.

Without a greeting, Holy said, "They interrogated me. The cops raided the junkyard with dogs. They took a trunk and some other stuff."

I tried to rub the tightness from my chest. I said, "Are you okay? Where are you?"

Holy said, "I'm back home now. They kept me at the station for hours grilling me."

I kept my voice as steady as possible under the circumstances. "What did the police ask you?"

Holy said, "The cops asked when I got the trunk. Who brought the trunk? The trunk, the trunk, the trunk."

I said, "And what did you tell them?"

Holy said, "Somebody left the trunk at the gate. I had no idea when because I wasn't there. How would I know who dropped it there? People leave junk at the gate all the time. I just add it to my stuff. They said my prints weren't on the trunk so someone else must have put it on my property. Then, they stared at me like I did something wrong."

I shivered. *Not you, me.*

Holy said, "My prints weren't on the trunk because I wore work gloves when I dragged it in. Why would they care about getting fingerprints on a dusty, old piece of luggage?"

For one blessed moment, I was glad Holy was dumb as a post. However, with all my brain power, I had left prints for sure. I said, "What else did they want?"

He said, "They wanted video from my surveillance cameras."

I said, "They're dummy cameras."

Holy said, "After a while, they let me go with no charges. I'm eating cheeseburgers to calm myself. Do you want some? You could come by. I'll share."

After declining Holy's offer, I disconnected. My mind shut down. Nothing made sense and I had important things to do.

Shitty Kitty had worked its magic during my massage. With each rub, she purred, "Do it. Do it. You'll be fine. You're a badass super spy."

My post in the neighbor's azaleas wouldn't work this time. I couldn't amble across the wide street and risk Ernest seeing me. Instead, I'd do my backyard thing. I'd sneak through someone else's property into the Depew backyard.

Wealthy neighborhoods are different than poor ones. In my neighborhood, the houses sat close together. You could look out your window and see your neighbor's. In rich areas, more property surrounds the house, thus giving more privacy. Less people could see me tiptoe through the yards, but I had to cover more ground. I had to take the chance.

The house behind the Depew home was even grander. Updates to the exterior gave it a modern appearance with large windows and an asymmetrical design. Only the porch light shone with no lights on in the interior, implying that no one was home. Good for me. I pinned my investigator badge to my waistband like I'd seen on TV. I wanted to look official if I got stopped. I took the cobblestone path around the house and into the backyard like I was their long-lost cousin.

The yard covered more property than my entire house. I could see the Depew house in the distance. Tall and short shrubbery, fragrant flowering bushes and greenery embellished the yard. I crept over the thick cushion of grass, sticking close to the tallest and thickest plant life. To my surprise, no fence divided the two properties. I supposed they had a gentleman's agreement on the property line.

I reached Mrs. Depew's backyard and pulled out my binoculars. No need to alarm them by climbing the steps. I wanted to know if Mrs. Depew had a ramp but I found something more interesting.

The sun had set, and I could only see outlines in the dark. Then, a soft porch light flashed on. I ducked down at the base of a large bush and held my breath. When no one emerged, I assumed the light was automatic. I remained crouched and could now get a good view of the porch. A white object caught my eye. A tiny pair of sneakers sat on the porch steps. I couldn't resist the pull of shoes. I crawled a hundred yards, pausing at the slightest sounds. When I got close enough, I crept up the steps and touched the shoes.

The tiniest Air Jordans I'd ever seen, sat drying on the steps. Mrs. Depew must have washed them and left them on the porch to dry. A question nagged at the base of my brain but wouldn't emerge. At that moment, a light lit inside the house and streamed across the porch into the yard. I tumbled backwards and landed on the stone pathway. I scrambled on my knees away from the blanket of light. I hoped no one could hear my frantic panting. Once under the protection of darkness, I got to my feet and ran back to my car.

Driving to Dad's I gathered my tumbling thoughts. There was no ramp at the back steps of Mrs. Depew's house. Unless Ernest carried her outside, Mrs. Depew remained housebound. I didn't know the significance of that fact and couldn't concentrate on it. My mind kept jumping to the sneakers. I didn't know why but they seemed important.

I returned to Dad's, exhausted, and bruised from my topple down the steps. I sat in my room and drafted a text to Detective Brimley, informing him I had a witness who could clear my name. I asked him to meet me at a neutral location. I didn't reveal Ernest's name. If I did, Brimley would swoop him up before I extracted the information I needed to prove my innocence. Also, if arrested in front of Mrs. Depew, Ernest would clam up. I wanted to bring Ernest to Brimley myself. Ernest could serve a dual purpose. He could clear my name if Detective Brimley was on the up and up. If Brimley meant to frame me, he'd see I had strong evidence of my innocence. He wouldn't be able to set me up. The bonus was, if Ernest was the real killer, Brimley could protect me. I was still unsure of Ernest's character, but I would let Brimley sort it out.

As I sent the text, Dad knocked on my door.

I opened it to find him scowling, arms crossed. *Oh boy.* I put on my cheeriest smile and said, "What's up, Dad?"

"How was your first day of work?"

I had forgotten about the Nubbin Nut job. Hoping against hope I said, "Swell. I loved it. Thanks for the referral. You're the best, Dad." I started to close the door, but Dad pushed it wide open and stepped in.

He said, "Start packing. My friend called this morning and said you never turned up at the factory. You made me look like a fool and I used up a favor for nothing." He started to leave, but turned back and said, "Nothing."

NINETEEN

My world spun faster than I could handle. Up, down, up, down, my emotions rollercoastered. Charles had said to call him if I needed him. I had nowhere else to turn. I pulled out my cell phone and searched for his number. I scrolled up, then down, then up again. No Charles Charles. I went through my contacts one by one. He wasn't there. *Now what?*

I laid my phone on the bed and started packing my stuff. I had no idea where Murphy and I would go. We'd be like orphans, living in backyards, eating berries off the trees. In my distress, I almost missed the soft purr of my cell. I grabbed it and said, "Charles?"

Malik said, "Charles?"

Gulp. "Hi, Malik. I'm glad to hear from you."

"Are you sure? You seem to be expecting another call. I'll clear the line for him."

I said, "No. Please don't hang up. How have you been?"

Malik said, "We don't need small talk between us." The tenderness of his voice surprised me. "I called to apologize. I have no right to tell you who you can see. After all, we're just friends. Right?"

"Yes." The, now familiar, lump returned to my throat.

Malik said, "That's what I thought. I can't desert my friend when she needs me. If you want to, we can still work together."

I said, "Malik, I'm so happy to hear you say that. I do need you." *More than you know.* I took a deep breath. "Can I please stay with you?" I held my breath in the long silence that followed.

Malik said, "Things not working out with your father?"

"No."

"And you have nowhere else to go?"

He's going to make me work for this. "I can't return to Paradise. I need a place to stay or I'm out in the streets."

After another long silence, Malik said, "Okay."

An hour later I arrived at Malik's. He met me at the curb and took the duffel bag while I carried Murphy to the guest room. Murphy settled in on the soft comforter and I sat next to him. He let me stroke his thick fur and confer with him.

I said, "I need a moment before I can face Malik. He's already pissed and he's not going to like what I have to do."

Murphy nudged my arm.

I said, "You're right. Better to get it over with."

I left Murphy napping and joined Malik on the couch. Before Malik could say a word, I laid his brown envelope on the coffee table.

Malik shoved it back toward me. "No."

I picked up the envelope and laid it on his thigh. Malik opened his mouth, and I raised my hand in protest. "I can't take this from you. No arguments. You need this money more than I do. You may not think so, but I care about you too."

Malik said, "This money was a gift. I can't take it back. You're my friend and you need help."

I laid my hand on his and said, "And now you need help. Let's find a way to support each other."

He wiped his misty eyes, put the envelope in his pocket and turned away. We sat in quiet, each in our own thoughts.

Malik cleared his throat and broke the silence. "To keep you safe, you cannot let people know you're living here. You cannot bring other people here." At that statement, he glared into my eyes until I acquiesced.

I knew that by 'other people' he meant Charles. I would never bring Charles there anyway. It would be too weird. Besides I didn't even know how to contact him. I made a mental note to put my phone on vibrate in case Charles called me.

Malik said, "By the way, I did more research on Brimley and found something interesting." He handed me a printout of an old newspaper article. "You were right about Brimley being the lead on the Depew theft. Your friend omitted some information. Mrs. Depew accused Brimley of using excessive force during an interrogation. He tried to coerce her to confess to fraud."

My weariness dropped away, replaced by adrenaline.

Malik said, "Brimley's superiors charged him with failure to properly collect evidence. Also, with the unlawful searching of property. Apparently, he entered the same abandoned house you did, but without a warrant. Brimley received a warning on his file and a temporary suspension. If he makes any more mistakes, they could fire him." Malik cocked his head. His raised eyebrows said, "Interesting, right?"

I said, "No wonder he's pursuing me so hard. He can't afford to lose again. But you'd think he would go after Mrs. Depew. He knows she's dirty."

Malik splayed his hands. "If he goes after her, he could get charged with harassment. You've seen movies where the cop hunts an innocent man like in The Fugitive."

I said, "But in this case, I'm the innocent fugitive and it doesn't feel good."

Malik shrugged. "He has to get somebody to clear this case. You're an easier target."

Malik cooked dinner again. This time we had juice instead of wine and fluorescent kitchen lighting in place of candles.

I did the dishes. When I finished, I squirted a dot of lotion from the dispenser on the windowsill and rubbed it into my hands. Something nagged at my memory, and I stopped mid-rub. I stared at my fingers. A vision of Mrs. Depew wringing her hands flashed through my mind. Mrs. Depew wore no ring.

I've known women who put their rings away after their husbands passed, but not so soon. Mr. Depew died a short time ago. Also, Mrs. Depew came from an age when women wore their wedding rings for years after being widowed. Then again, maybe she sold it to pay bills. I didn't know the significance of the missing ring, if any. I needed Malik's insight.

I entered the living room to find Malik asleep on the couch with CNN playing in the background. I sat in a chair by the window and watched his muscular chest expand with each breath. His tattoos flexed with each move as he stretched and turned over. My eyes ran down his back to his full buttocks, wrapped in tight jeans. Meow.

I didn't understand why I chose Charles over Malik. They both excited me. Maybe Malik was too safe while Charles oozed mystery. I turned and gazed out the window. When I turned back, Malik's eyes were on me. I couldn't hide my desires if I tried.

Malik rose and approached me. He put his strong hands on my shoulders and pulled me from my seat. Our lips were inches apart.

I opened my mouth to receive his tongue and my cell vibrated in my jeans pocket. I flinched and pulled away. Malik put his hand on my pocket and said, "Which vibration means more?"

I stepped back. My heart pounded and I panted. I turned away from Malik and went to my room in silence. The call had been from a blocked number, untraceable. I tossed and turned in bed, squeezing my damp thighs together. Malik's essence beckoned me. I barely slept that night.

The next morning, I arose to find Malik at the kitchen table sipping coffee and eating a bagel. He pushed an aromatic paper bag toward me and said, "I bought breakfast."

I stuffed a bagel into my mouth to keep me from saying anything stupid, since that's all I seemed capable of doing.

Malik said, "Aunt Lusty called me with a job. Are you up for it?"

I recalled my last conversation with Lusty. No wonder she called Malik instead of me. It surprised me she called at all, given my rotten attitude.

I said, "What's the job?"

Malik said, "Aunt Lusty says someone needs us to transport some special paper."

I said, "What's special about paper?"

Malik shrugged. "Stores sell lots of specialty paper. There are papers used for art, origami, and stationery. They sell tissue paper, wrapping paper, card stock, handmade papers..."

I raised my hand and said, "I get it." I wasn't gonna argue with him and he didn't seem in the mood for a discussion.

We finished our bagels and went to pick up the paper. Malik backed the Escalade up to the warehouse. A muscular guy on a pallet truck loaded a pallet of shrink-wrapped paper into Malik's trunk. We walked around the back of the car to check it out. I was curious to see what was so special about this paper. We both gaped as we saw a pile of money shrink-wrapped on top of a pallet. Neat bundles of $100 bills stacked in a three-foot-high block that filled Malik's cargo area.

I put my hand to my heart and said, "How much money is this? It doesn't make sense to transport cash like this. Don't you need an armored truck?"

The loading guy laughed and said, "It looks real, doesn't it?"

I didn't realize I had stopped breathing. I swooped in some air and said, "This is fake money?"

The guy said, "Yeah. All the guys are freaking out about it."

Malik closed the hatch and we headed to a party store in downtown Newark.

I longed to explain my conflicted feelings about both Malik and Charles. I didn't understand them myself, so I sat in tortured silence. Some women would say keep them both, but I've always been a one-man woman. Malik was sexy in a gentle way, kind, and reliable. He trusted me with his intimate feelings. He was the kind of man I could cuddle into for the rest of my life. Charles, on the other hand, brought out my sexy side. I lusted after him. He swept me off my feet in romantic ways I couldn't resist. The problem was, other than those encounters, I knew nothing about Charles. Reaching no conclusion, I switched gears.

I said, "Did you notice Mrs. Depew wears Air Jordans?"

Malik shrugged. "So? She needs something on her feet."

I said, "She doesn't walk anywhere."

Malik said, "Have you ever visited an old folk's home? People in wheelchairs wear shoes. Foot protection is good for everyone. You're fixated on shoes. You should get help for that."

Still, Mrs. Depew's sneakered feet danced in my thoughts. I tried to distract myself by watching the dense traffic.

Central Ave was a tangle of backed up traffic. We were only a few blocks from the party store but moving at a crawl. Then screech, bang, bang! Traffic halted in a series of car crashes. Malik narrowly avoided hitting the car in front of us. A second later someone slammed the Escalade in the rear. People emerged from their cars, hands on hips, arms waving, and yelling. I had no idea where the crash started but it was a mess now. In moments, police arrived on the scene.

The crashed cars lined the length of the block. The police methodically went from car to car taking statements and checking vehicles. Malik and I went to the back of the Escalade to check the damage. The back door was bent, and the fender crushed. Malik wrestled the hatch until it creaked open. We both breathed a sigh of relief when we saw our cargo untouched. But the pile of money attracted attention. As we scrutinized the shipment, a crowd had gathered pointing at the pallet of cash. We didn't notice them until they pushed against us. Their voices rose above the other confusion. We tried to close the hatch, but we were too late.

Two policemen noticed the crush of people surrounding us and rushed over. They angled their way through the crowd and froze at the sight of the cash. One officer tried to hold the spectators back and the other talked to us.

"Is this your money? Can you prove it? Why are you driving around the city with a pallet of money?"

When Malik reached for the bill of lading, the officer slapped his hand on his holstered gun. He said, "Don't move. Keep your hands where I can see them." My stomach tensed and I couldn't breathe. Behind me, the ruckus grew louder. I craned my neck to see the horde closing in on the other cop. The officer flailed his arms but failed to keep the agitators back.

A chant rose from the crowd. "We want money! We want money!" The onlookers pushed in, and the cops went down in a heap. They pushed Malik and me aside as they scrambled to get inside the Escalade. Malik and I watched in horror as people climbed over each other. We could hear them ripping the shrink-wrap off the fake bills. The Escalade rocked and $100 bills floated into the air as the crowd fought for their piece of the pie. In a matter of seconds, the crowd morphed into a mob and fists began to fly. It only took one punch to start the brouhaha. Before we knew it the people were rolling on the ground punching each other, money forgotten.

Malik took the opportunity to slam the hatch closed as best he could. We jumped into the Escalade. Malik sped onto the sidewalk, down the block and careened around the corner. The cops were caught up in mob control and we made good our escape. I crawled into the back of the car and restacked the bills the best I could. I used duct tape to re-seal the shrink-wrap. It looked almost presentable. We delivered the load to a sleepy-eyed kid who reeked of marijuana. He signed off on the delivery barely glancing at the pallet.

As exhausted as I was, I couldn't rest as we returned home. I had to meet Ernest within the hour. "Malik, can't you go any faster? I have an appointment to keep."

Malik said, "An appointment? Do you mean a date?"

I rolled my eyes. "I mean an appointment and I can't be late."

Malik said, "That's okay. I have a date tonight too."

I said, "You do?"

"Yes. Valerie set me up with her friend. She's cute."

If she looks anything like Valerie, she's gorgeous. I pouted and said, "Well, I hope you enjoy yourself." *Could I be any more juvenile? I have to make the most important meetings of my life and all I can think of is Malik's date.*

Malik dropped me at my car, and I sped to Ferdinand's Pharmacy. I remembered the "Help Wanted" sign in their window. I had no retail experience, but I hoped to charm my way into the job. I had become desperate to pay my mortgage, even if I had to interact with the public to do it.

Ferdinand's appearance erased the image of the suave bullfighter I'd expected. He was round with a ruddy complexion, graying hair and a mustache. He met me at the door and thrust an application in my hand, no pen, no seat. With a thick Spanish accent, he said, "Don't block the door. Fill this out." He disappeared behind some shelves leaving behind a thick odor of cigarettes.

I dug a Hello Kitty pen out of my bag, found an empty shelf and filled out the scant information. I wrote Lusty's name in references and knew she'd back me up, if necessary. I found Ferdinand throwing packs of onion soup mix onto an already cluttered shelf.

He took the application without reading it and said, "You start first thing tomorrow morning." He hustled his way down the aisle, leaving me alone.

I left assuming I had taken a minimum wage job. So what? I had reached a point where I had to make money any way I could. The pharmacy could supplement my Rocky Recovery income and who knew? Maybe I could work my way up to manager or something.

Bright and early the next morning, Ferdinand unlocked the front door, and I strolled in, ready to work.

Ferdinand quick-walked me around the small store, waving at various household items. Whoever shelved the merchandise had no semblance of order. They displayed fake poop next to chocolate candy. Dollar gas masks sat near cheese scented candles. Another aisle held a pile of dusty plastic cutlery mixed with dog chew toys. Nothing here I would buy. There were two entrances, one at the front and one at the back with registers near each.

Ferdinand positioned me behind the rear door register. He pointed at some buttons while speaking rapid-fire Spanglish and left me on my own.

I assumed I'd get on-the-job training. From what I could see from the register, the place resembled a messy dollar store with a tiny pharmacy on one side. The shelves were either half-empty or piled high with junk. It even made me want to straighten up and I'm no Susie Homemaker.

The front door dinged, announcing our first customer of the day. I checked my curls in the cash register reflection and smiled a welcoming smile. I would be the best employee Ferdinand ever had.

The customer, a tall man, went straight to the pharmacy. I could see the top of his head over the shelves. I heard someone ring up the purchase and felt letdown that I hadn't been able to use my register yet. The customer strolled my way. He turned into my aisle.

Ernest approached me with shock in his eyes. He scanned the area to ensure we were alone. He said, "What are you doing here?"

I said, "I've been worried sick about you."

He laid his bag on the counter and leaned in. "So, you took a job here to spy on me? How did you know I fill Aunt Lilac's prescription here?"

I glanced at the bag labeled Benzodiazepine. I said, "I didn't know Mrs. Depew needed medicine."

Ernest said, "She's only had the prescription a couple of months." He looked at his feet. "One more chore for me to do. She told her doctor she had trouble sleeping. I've never seen her take them, but I assume she does."

I leaned in close. "Ernest, the police raided my ex's junkyard."

Ernest's tall frame sunk into itself. He released a low moan and said, "She made me leave the trunk there. I'm sorry for the trouble we've caused you."

I said, "I know you're not to blame, but you've put yourself in a mess. The cops took the surveillance video from the junkyard cameras. They'll see you put the trunk there."

Ernest shook his head. "I'm caught in a web, my aunt, the police. Everyone is pointing at me. I don't know what to do."

I touched his rough hand. "Don't worry. We'll clear everything up together." At least I hoped so.

He glanced at his watch and grabbed the prescription bag. "I've got to go. Aunt Lilac is keeping a tight leash on me. She knows how long I should be out." He turned to leave. He looked over his shoulder and said, "I'll keep our promise."

Ferdinand marched up to my register. "You're fired."

I stared at him and blinked; sure, I misunderstood his words.

He pointed to the door and said, "Get out."

I stomped around the counter and stood an inch from Ferdinand's face. "Fired for what? I haven't done anything yet."

He said, "That's right. You stood around and chatted with a customer for fifteen minutes. You didn't sell him anything. You are here to sell, sell, sell."

I said, "Maybe I would have if you had quality merchandise. All I see is piles of junk." I walked past Ferdinand and picked up a handful of tighty-whities mixed with dish cloths. I said, "This doesn't even make sense. People couldn't find what they wanted in this store with a magnifying glass. It's a mess. Where do you get this junk anyway?"

Ferdinand said, "I buy wherever I can. I have to fill all these shelves or people won't shop here."

I scanned the area. No customers.

He stomped over to a bin of crystal glasses. He held one up and said, "I get great deals like this from Freddy."

The cut glass hid a myriad of cracks. As he waved the glass in front of my face, chips flew off in every direction.

I said, "Do you mean Freddy the Fence? That explains a lot." It occurred to me I might have bought stolen statues. I decided to drop the subject.

Ferdinand's face turned red. "How do you think I pay for these things?" He swept his hand around the store. "I pay people to work before I pay myself. And what about my overhead for this luxurious store?"

I grimaced at the dirty floors and flickering light bulbs. "Are you kidding me? First, I don't see any employees except myself. Are you even licensed to run a pharmacy? You rang up the one customer we had today, right?"

Ferdinand stomped and raised a fist. "You mind your business. I'm under a lot of pressure. I have to do what I have to do to make money. I need cash to run this place and if you don't sell, I don't need you." Ferdinand went behind the counter and returned with an orange machine gun.

I laughed and pointed. "You expect to scare me with a plastic gun?"

He squeezed the trigger. A sticky popcorn ball smacked my forehead and stuck.

I peeled it off and said, "Hey, that's assault."

He shot off another round and popcorn tangled in my curls.

I ran to the door, swatting away another popcorn onslaught. In the safety of my car, I pulled the ball out of my hair, leaving bits of sticky caramel corn. My venture into retail had closed in spectacular fashion.

After picking evidence of my morning fiasco out of my hair, I headed to my next task. I had to make my first blackmail payment to Hartness. I parked in the bank lot and sat with my hands on the wheel. Taking deep breaths, I considered what I was about to do.

In the chaos created while transporting the phony money, Shitty Kitty had whispered in my ear. She urged me to pocket a handful of fake hundreds. Today, I sandwiched those bills between two real ones from my emergency funds. I clipped them together with a jumbo paper clip and slipped the cash into a plain white envelope.

I fingered the envelope and thought about possible consequences. I said, "Hartness deals with money all day long. He might spot the phony bills right away."

Kitty said, "He's so over-confident, he'll assume you obeyed his command."

I said, "What will happen later when he tries to spend the money?"

Kitty laughed. "Don't worry about it. He'll probably throw that money in a safe or mix it with money from his other saps. He won't know it came from you."

I frowned. "Other people?"

Kitty said, "You can't be the only one he's blackmailing. Now, get out of the car."

I walked in at closing time and headed straight to Heartless Hartness' desk.

He eyed me up and down with a smug smile and put out his hand.

I slapped the envelope into it, turned on my heel and stalked out. I couldn't bear for him to see my humiliation. Even though I had given him fake money, I felt like I had given my body to someone I disliked. I had given in to his pressure. I didn't have time to dwell on the event. I had more important things to do.

I arrived at my third appointment for the day five minutes early. This meeting would change my life immeasurably. If all went well, I could stop the circus that had become my existence. No more running. No more hiding. I would become an everyday citizen again.

I parked on the street and tried to shake off the adrenaline that tensed my body. I pointed to the heavens and gave thanks that my troubles would end here.

I darted into the dark alley behind the bodega and tripped headlong onto a pile of wet clothes. But the clothes weren't wet, they were bloody. Ernest's lifeless body lay face down in a pool of blood.

I pushed myself up onto my knees just as Detective Brimley entered the alley.

My mind couldn't reconcile what I'd seen.

Brimley pulled me to my feet. He said, "What happened here?" He patted my shoulders and arms.

I said, "I'm okay. Please help Ernest."

Brimley eyed Ernest's body but didn't touch him. He said, "You expect me to help him after what you've done?"

I shook my head in an attempt to clear it. "I haven't done anything. I just got here."

Brimley whipped out a pair of zip tie handcuffs and tied my wrists together.

I raised my hands and said, "What's this? On TV they use metal cuffs." I knew I was speaking gibberish but so was he.

Brimley looked at me like I was a drooling idiot. "Would you prefer metal cuffs? How about a straitjacket with matching earrings?"

I said, "You don't have to be sarcastic. I was just making an observation."

Brimley pushed me into the back seat of his car. He leaned in and smiled. "You have no idea how happy you've made me. I'll be able to wrap up this case and present it to my superiors with a bow on top. I have strong evidence and the perpetrator in custody." He jabbed his finger toward me. Brimley slammed the door shut and engaged the door locks.

Within minutes, police filled the alley highlighted by red and blue flashes. They cordoned off the area with crime scene tape. The photographer's camera lit Ernest's bloody body in frightening flashes. An officer placed numbered markers in various areas.

Bodega Man stood at his back door pointing at me. He told an officer, "I knew she was a murderer! I called you guys on her before. Do I get a reward?"

Brimley peacocked around the scene conferring with other detectives. Then, he returned to the car and settled in.

The back of Brimley's car smelled of cigars and sweat. I sat on the worn springs and chewed at my restraints like a hamster chomping a nut.

He glanced into his rear-view mirror and said, "I see you. Believe me that won't work, but you enjoy yourself."

Alarms ping-ponged in my mind as we drove to the station. I had seen too many prison pictures. I could already feel sweat rolling down my back from hot interrogation lights. Brimley would beat a confession out of me with a phone book. Then, they'd throw me in a jail cell with Looney Lena where she'd sell me for a pack of Marlboros. Visions of filthy, bed bug covered mattresses and cold steel toilets filled my brain. My anger overtook my fear. I fumed at the indignity of it all.

I was innocent. But how many innocent people broke down and confessed to acts they had not committed. Blameless people went to prison all the time. I didn't have money for a good lawyer and wouldn't know who to call if I did. Malik and Lusty would have to visit weekly and wave at me through dirty glass partitions. Brimley was punishing me for trying to solve a murder that entangled me through no fault of my own.

Brimley hauled my ass through the station and into an interview room. I sat alone, in the locked room, handcuffed. I blinked back tears as I surveyed the gray walls and cement floor. A dank odor seeped into my runny nostrils. A constant flow of traffic filled the halls with muffled chatter. I jumped each time the door rattled. Deep breathing failed to calm my nerves. I wanted to appear confident when Brimley returned.

As my breathing returned to normal, my eyes blurred with tears. A vivid flash of Ernest laying in a pool of blood flooded my mind. I shivered uncontrollably. I wanted to strip off my bloody jeans and take a scalding shower. I stood and paced the room, searching for an exit. I craved the ability to climb walls or walk through them. The damp room felt steamy and small. The walls closed in on me.

I had done the unforgivable. I had pushed Ernest beyond his capabilities and gotten him killed. My mind couldn't settle on who killed Ernest. Mrs. Depew spent her life in a wheelchair. Even if she could kill him, she would have had to murder Ernest in her home. Did she have an accomplice? I'd only seen her with Ernest.

Then there was Detective Brimley. He had prior knowledge of the meeting. He could have arrived early, killed Ernest and then, circled back to arrest me. Now, he has me where he wants me. Brimley has the power to lock me up and cover his tracks.

And Charles. I don't know enough about him to know what he would do. How stupid I've been to unlock my emotions for him. I've kept my heart safe for some time. Then, I gave myself to a man who comes and goes at a moment's notice. He disappears and reappears at the oddest times. Also, he knows things. He has access to information and police procedures. Why did I trust him?

Round and round my thoughts merged into one immeasurable nightmare. I beat my fists against the cold, gray walls. The plastic cuffs bit into my flesh. This is what life is like when no one believes in you. I sank back into the hard, wooden chair and wept.

I cried for seeming eons. The tears relieved my stress and tired me out. I felt like myself and nothing at the same time. That wave of grief had passed. It might return but my sadness had morphed into anger. I didn't deserve to be here.

The doorknob turned and Brimley entered. He repeated my rights which he had read to me upon arrest and had me sign them. Once he completed that ceremony, he got down to business.

Brimley's words stung me like bullets or how I imagined bullets would hurt. He said, "Now you're connected to two murders."

"I haven't killed anybody." My voice squeaked, reminding me of Ernest.

Brimley said, "We know you murdered Mr. Depew by the way he was killed."

"You mean his cane?"

Brimley's eyebrows rose. "Yes. The cane you used."

"That was his cane. How would I take a cane from a big man like that?"

Brimley smiled. "How would you even know about the cane?"

Oh no. This is how people get caught on Law and Order. They just spill their guts. What do I say now? Do I tell him about Charles? Charles is the one who told me everything. How did Charles know? Suppose Charles is innocent like me? I can't go to the slammer. I can't end up as Big Betty's bitch passed around for a pack of Luckys.

Brimley said, "Well?"

"I'm not saying anything until I get a lawyer." *That's what I yell at people on television when they're arrested. I'd better take my own advice.*

Brimley slapped his hand on the metal table, making a resounding echo in the room. "Fine. Don't talk, just listen. We know you used the cane because of the angle of the blows to Mr. Depew's head. They came from someone of your height."

I opened my mouth to speak.

Brimley held up a finger and said, "Either wait for your lawyer or waive your rights."

I snapped my lips shut.

Brimley said, "I have a witness who can put you in an abandoned house where we found the cane. I have a witness statement from Bodega Man. He saw a small woman hit Ernest in the back of his head with a long object." Brimley looked me over. "You're petite."

I said, "You can't believe him. The alley was dark. Anyway, he hates me. He's setting me up."

Brimley said, "You've irritated lots of people. That doesn't mean they would lie about you, especially to the police. Bodega Man also said you flashed a fake badge at him. I'm adding impersonating an officer to your growing list of charges. We know you and Ernest moved Mr. Depew's body to your ex-husband's junkyard. I'm sure you still have access to the property. Both of your prints are on the trunk that held his bones. Then you killed Ernest to cover your trail. The coroner's preliminary exam shows that Ernest was hit on the back of the head just like Mr. Depew. You love to crack heads, don't you?"

I bit my lip to keep my sarcasm to myself.

Brimley stood to leave. "One more thing. We found a small sneaker print in Ernest's blood."

I could no longer hold my tongue. I said, "Aha! I don't wear sneakers. I told you; you have the wrong person."

Brimley said, "You could have worn sneakers as a disguise to kill Ernest. Then, you changed and returned in new clothing. Murderers conceal their identities all the time. We're searching the alley for discarded clothing now."

I couldn't help myself. I said, "This is circumstantial bullshit. You can't have real evidence like DNA, because I didn't do anything."

Brimley smiled and peeped under the table. He left, still smiling.

I looked down. My jeans were covered in Ernest's blood.

TWENTY

Alone, I shivered from both the interrogation and the cold. What was next? Fingerprints? Orange jumpsuit? Brimley had run one metal handcuff through my plastic ones and fastened the other one to a hole in the table. I got the metal cuffs I'd asked for, but I wasn't counting on two sets of cuffs. The gray walls and cement floor reflected my drab future. *I'm not going to cry. There are probably cameras in here. I'm not going to give Brimley the satisfaction. I've got no one to call. I've burned all my bridges, Dad, Malik, Holy.*

The door opened and a uniformed officer entered, head down, holding a clipboard in front of his face. *This is it.* I tightened my mouth to stop my quivering lip.

The officer lowered the clipboard. Charles Charles smiled at me and shook his head. He pulled out a silver jackknife and opened it slowly. Looming over me, he said, "Well, you're in a fix this time. Aren't you?" The knife glistened in the fluorescent lights. My chest tightened and cut off my breath. Again, I thought, *what do I know about him?*

Charles said, "I told you not to get mixed up in this. I tried to keep you safe, but you've made a mistake. You trusted the wrong person and now look at you." He stepped closer.

I jerked the cuffs, but only succeeded in hurting my already sore wrists.

Charles leaned over and kissed my forehead and then my lips. I jerked away. He smiled and said, "Don't struggle. This will go quicker, if you don't struggle."

I opened my mouth to scream as he swung the blade and cut my plastic cuffs free from my wrists. My mouth hung open in a silent shriek. He grabbed my hand and pulled me to my feet. He said, "Now, let's get out of here."

Charles said, "Put your hands behind your back and keep your head down. I'm going to walk you out of here."

I said, "I have blood on my pants. The cops will see that and stop you."

Charles chuckled. "In a police station? This is everyday stuff." Charles grabbed the back of my collar and pushed me forward.

Cops bustled around us in a frenzy of activity. Sounds of crying, yelling, and pleading assaulted my ears as we walked past open doors. Do I scream for help or leave with my mystery man? If I cried for help, would anyone notice?

As we walked, I hatched a plan. I needed to escape both the police and Charles. After all, I didn't know where he was taking me. I'll use him to get me out of here, then I'll run. To where, I don't know. It was a shitty plan, but I needed to get somewhere safe where I could think. Before I could decide, we exited out the back door where Charles' BMW waited.

He gripped my arm and shoved me into the car.

I ducked down in Charles' Beamer. "Where are you taking me? Are you kidnapping me?"

Charles rolled his eyes and said, "I'm saving you. What did you think?"

"I don't know what to think about you. I don't know anything about you. How did you know where I was? And how did you get into the police station?"

He swept his hand over his clothing. "As you can see, I'm wearing a uniform. It's a busy station. I just walked in."

I stood firm. "That doesn't explain how you knew Brimley arrested me. How did you find me?"

Charles exhaled and stared at his shoes. In a quiet voice he said, "I needed a way to keep you secure. You're so stubborn. You won't let me protect you, so I put a tracker on your phone."

My mouth dropped open and I stared in stunned silence for a moment. "When did you do that?"

Charles said, "We can discuss that later."

My eyes darted about the car. I said, "My bag is still in the station." I opened the car door.

Charles reached over, slammed the door shut and clicked the childproof locks. "I promise I'll get your bag later. I'm taking you to a safe place."

I said, "I'm not letting you take me to some hideaway."

Charles sighed and rubbed his temples. "Then where would you like to go?"

My eyes widened. I said, "You'll take me wherever I want to go?"

"Of course. What did you think? I just have to know you're protected." He took my hands and massaged my reddened wrists. "Don't you know I care about you?"

It took me a second to absorb his words and slow my heartbeat. Then I gave him instructions.

Charles and I sat in his BMW in front of my next sanctuary. He glanced up at the building and said, "I'm not sure about this."

I rubbed his arm. "Don't worry. I'm a big girl and I'm in no danger here. I'll have anonymity and security."

Charles said, "Remember, you can't trust everyone. You'd be safer with me."

I shook my head. "I need some familiarity right now. I need time to breathe and think."

Charles said, "You never really know someone. All people have secrets. Haven't you ever been betrayed?"

I cocked an eyebrow at Charles and grinned.

Charles chuckled. He leaned back and said, "You win but please be careful."

I opened the car door.

Charles said, "And remember you're my girl."

I rang Malik's bell as I watched Charles drive off.

Brimley hadn't questioned Malik, so I assumed he wouldn't know to find me there.

As soon as I entered, Malik said, "Where the hell have you been? I've been back for hours. I thought something happened to you. What the..." His eyes widened as he spied my bloody jeans.

"I got arrested."

After some wrangling, Malik calmed enough to allow me shower and change.

Hot water streamed over my body without relieving my tension. My cramped muscles didn't release. My mind wove through every mistake I'd ever made, culminating in Ernest's murder. I must have cried aloud because Malik pounded on the door.

He said, "Are you alright?"

My sobs drowned out my words.

Malik rushed in and found me curled in the tub wailing under the pounding water. He turned off the water and pulled me out. He pulled his heavy robe from the back of the bathroom door and wrapped me like a baby. Like the protector I'd dreamed of, Malik carried me to the guest room. He sat with me on the bed and held me until my tears subsided.

A half hour later, I had dressed and met Malik in the living room. He handed me a mug of soothing chamomile tea. We sat on the couch, and I recounted the day's saga beginning with my disastrous day at the pharmacy.

Malik's eyebrows rose. "Your appointment last night was to apply for a retail job? If you'd been upfront with me, I could have saved you some time. Ferdinand keeps that 'Help Wanted' sign in the window all year round. He's a son of a bitch and people quit on him all the time."

I said, "I can see why. But something strange happened." I explained Ernest's visit to the pharmacy. I said, "Maybe Mrs. Depew can't sleep because she murdered her husband."

Malik said, "More likely, she used the Benzo to kill him." Malik went to his desk and pulled his laptop open. He pointed to the screen. "Benzodiazepine can kill if mixed with alcohol, like if Mr. Depew had a few drinks. I doubt we'll ever know the truth." He closed his laptop and stood. He said, "Are you feeling better?"

I put my empty mug on the table. The chamomile had done its job. I said, "Yes, thanks for the tea."

Malik said, "We have an important matter to discuss." Malik paced the living room. "I thought we were working this thing together. I can't believe you met Ernest without me. You put yourself in danger without thinking. Even if you didn't want me there, I could have watched to be sure you were safe."

I said, "Everybody's watching me. I can't cross the street without someone trying to protect me. I'm smothering."

Malik stopped walking. "Who else is looking out for you? Charles?"

I said, "You, Charles, Lusty, my dad. Then Detective Brimley is hovering over my shoulder. It's a lot. I need to breathe."

Malik said, "Well you're breathing my air now." He gestured around the living room. "As partners in this situation, you will keep me in the loop. Agreed?"

We sat on the couch, and I let him hold me. I needed a lot of comforting these days. Murphy helped by jumping on my lap and licking my face.

Malik asked, "Was that Charles who dropped you off in that BMW?"

What could I say? I was too tired to lie. "Yes. He helped me get away."

"You called him instead of me?"

I said, "No. He just showed up and rescued me."

Malik said, "Why do you trust him? How much do you know about this guy? What does he do for a living? Is he rich?"

I shrugged. "I guess so. He bought $300,000 of statuettes from the Depews."

Malik frowned. "The picture's getting clearer now."

I crossed my arms over my chest. "What does that mean? Are you calling me a gold digger?"

"No. You're not like that." Malik turned away. "You're a nice girl."

I started to whimper. I was too weak for this back and forth. "Please, Malik."

Malik sighed and held me closer. He said, "I don't want you to leave this apartment for any reason. Not because of him, but to keep you out of trouble. Do you understand?" He treated me with tenderness or maybe pity. "Now get some rest."

The doorbell buzzed. Malik pushed his intercom button. "Yes?"

A raspy voice responded. "Malik Grainger? This is the police. We'd like to ask you a few questions. May we come up?"

Malik said, "The buzzer's broken. I'll come down and let you in."

We didn't have to speak. I grabbed my duffel bag. I hustled out the door and up to the next landing. I could hear Brimley's gruff voice as they entered Malik's apartment. As soon as they shut the door, I ran downstairs and out of the building. Now what? I had left my handbag at the police station. I had no money and no phone. How far could I get before they found me. I couldn't even go to my own house. They were bound to be watching it. Then it came to me.

I had run through many back yards lately. What was one more? I threw my duffel over the back fence that bordered the apartment parking lot. Then I scrambled over. I sprinted across the adjoining yard to the next street. No way could I run all the way to Lusty's house. My trusty Corolla remained near the bodega since my arrest.

I scanned the street for a friendly face. At the corner, I spied an adolescent boy peering into his cell phone. I sauntered over to him and smiled. I said, "Hi there."

The boy looked over his shoulder and back at me. "Are you talking to me?" His eyes widened and he took a step back. He patted the curly twists atop his head and said, "What do you want?"

I said, "Could I please make a phone call? I'm in a tough spot." I reached for his phone.

He snatched his hand back and shook his head. "You're trying steal my phone. Leave me alone."

I bit my lip to hold my frustration. People kept accusing me of crimes. Did I have a felon's face? Also, I couldn't afford to scare him off and I had nothing in my pockets to offer in return for this much-needed call.

After fifteen minutes of cajoling, he agreed to dial Lusty's number for me. He held tight to his phone and put her on speaker.

Lusty sent an Uber to pick me up and take me to my car.

In minutes, I was knocking at Lusty's back door.

Lusty accepted my apology for the tirade I had unleashed on her in our last conversation. I would have fallen to my knees if she had asked. An hour later, Lusty and I sat in her living room, popping bonbons and drinking pink champagne.

Lusty said, "Malik called before you got here. He said Holy told the police he had seen you ride off in an Escalade and gave them Malik's plate number. That's how they found him. Your ex is a pinhead."

I asked, "Is Malik okay? He's not in trouble, is he?"

Lusty said, "No. The police were only interested in you, but you can't go back there. They'll be watching for you."

I sank into the pink tufted sofa. I said, "My life is a mess. How did you make such a comfortable life for yourself?"

Lusty said, "Disappointments, mistakes and hard knocks shaped my life. I learned to cut out things and people that had caused me grief. Then I created a life based on my values and desires. Now I'm living the dream." She spread her arms like a butterfly about to take flight.

I said, "What about love?"

Lusty said, "I may have intimate love one day. I believe when you build your life around your desires, a good man is the cherry on top. But when you make a man your whole world, he holds all the power. You have to decide what kind of life you want."

I said, "But what if I've already fallen in love."

Lusty grinned. "I'm happy you've found a good man, someone who's steady and reliable. Someone you can lean into and can count on."

That didn't describe Charles at all. In fact, I didn't know from one day to the next when I would see him. He popped up, then disappeared. He made promises and broke them.

Lusty said, "Malik's always been dependable and trustworthy."

I said, "What?"

Lusty said, "He's the kind of man who makes you feel secure and protected. Right?"

"Sure." She described Malik to a tee. My intellect agreed with Lusty; my heart did not.

Lusty said, "You two could build a beautiful life together. Malik will be sure to support your dreams and help you make the kind of life you want."

I said, "You have a big heart. I see your affection for Malik. How are you connected to him?"

Lusty smiled. "Malik's father used to call my sex line, but he was different than the others. He didn't need me to talk. He wanted someone to listen. He poured out his heart for hours about his wife's gambling problem. He cried over how she abandoned their son to run off to the casinos. We developed a real friendship and eventually, met in person. He'd take me to lunch and treated me well. No man had ever been that kind to me. One day he brought Malik with him. I could see the pride in his eyes when he introduced us. Malik was just a kid then. After that day, he brought Malik around all the time. We had so much fun. One day, Malik's father stopped calling. I never spoke with him again. I was heartbroken. Not like losing a sweetheart, but I lost a true friend. It hurts the same."

I said, "How did you reconnect with Malik?"

"He turned up at my door one day. He told me he left his mother and was on his own. I let him stay with me until he found his own place. We've been close ever since."

Exhaustion overcame me. "Can I lay down somewhere? I can't keep my eyes open."

Lusty led me upstairs to the guest room where she made up a daybed for me. The room was large and held a desk, a computer, a file cabinet and five pink telephones. Each phone was a different style, antique, retro, princess and even one shaped like huge pink lips. Instead of a desk chair, sat an overstuffed settee covered in pink velvet and trimmed in gold.

I eyed the desk and said, "Why so many phones? How many people can you talk to at once?"

Lusty smiled and said, "You'd be surprised, Honey. And each phone puts me in a different mood."

I had to give it to her. Lusty lived her life with unique style. Before I crawled under the covers, I said, "Lusty, will you teach me your skill? I want to get someone's attention and you can show me how."

Lusty laughed. "Sure, Honey. Besides, you may need a new career."

I tossed and turned, never closing my eyes. The day had exhausted my body, but not my mind. Maybe I could sleep later if I worked off my tension. I threw off the covers, redressed and sat up until daybreak.

I left Lusty a note that I had to run an errand. Ten minutes later, I'd arrived at Ferdinand's Pharmacy.

I couldn't believe, of all the places in the world, I chose to come here. My short work experience at Ferdinand's had raised the bar on frustration. Still, something else nagged at me. I had to confront Ferdinand for his mistreatment of me. I also wanted to prove to myself that I could successfully work a normal job.

Again, I entered through the back entrance. I found Ferdinand dumping packages of bubble gum from a crate into a bin of plastic dinosaurs.

He dropped the crate when he saw me. "What the hell do you want? I'm not paying you for the hour you worked."

I stalked up to him, kicking the crate out the way. I said, "I'm here for two things. First, I want you to apologize."

Ferdinand stood open-mouthed, staring. "Are you crazy? You didn't even sell anything. All you did was talk, talk, talk."

I said, "Look around. There's no one here to buy your stuff. Was I supposed to sell to ghosts? And it was my first day. You never told me what to do. You stuck me behind a register and left." Waves of stress left my body as I yelled at Ferdinand. This was the best therapy ever.

Ferdinand dropped onto the crate. He covered his face and released a sob.

The shock of seeing his gruff exterior dissolve evaporated the last of my tension. In fact, his collapse made me want to comfort him. This was not the confrontation I had expected.

As I reached out to pat him on the shoulder, he rose and wiped his eyes. He said, "Lo lamento. I'm sorry." He turned to leave.

I said, "One more thing."

He stood with his back to me.

I said, "I want to work here."

He turned and eyed me. "Why would you want to work for me and in this place?" He spread his arms.

I said, "I need some normalcy in my life. Also, you really need help. I have one condition."

Ferdinand nodded.

I inhaled for strength. "I want to be a manager, not just a clerk. I'll help you straighten out this store and make it a place people want to shop. What do you say?"

Ferdinand said, "Sure, but the pay stays the same. It's all I can afford."

Somehow, I didn't care about the salary. I needed to get some control in my life and here, I could escape the circus that had become my existence.

Ferdinand stuck out his hand.

We shook on the deal.

Ferdinand said, "I don't usually get emotional, but my friend died last night."

The normalcy I experienced over the last few minutes disappeared. A foggy grief filled my brain. I said, "I'm sorry for your loss. I lost a friend too." I steadied myself by grabbing the edge of a shelf. I didn't want to see the sadness in Ferdinand's eyes.

He said, "We weren't close. He was a customer who treated me nice. Most people only speak to me when they want to return something or can't find something. They're nasty. Ernest spoke to me with respect. He was kind."

My head snapped back at Ernest's name. I said, "Ernest Depew?"

Ferdinand regarded me with questioning eyes. "You know Ernest? That's why you talked to him for so long? Now I understand."

I said, "How did you know he passed away?" The euphemism didn't fit the violence of his death.

Ferdinand said, "It happened behind the bodega. I know the owner."

I squeezed my eyes shut at the thought of Bodega Man. Then, another thought intruded. Had Bodega Man mentioned my name? Probably not. In fact, I didn't think he knew my name, just my face. The last thing I wanted was for him to poison Ferdinand's mind against me. I changed the subject.

I said, "Thanks so much for the job. I've got some ideas for the store."

Over the next few hours, we organized aisles to make sense. We dedicated one aisle to children's items, one to decorative items, one to clothing, and down the line. Another part-timer arrived and continued the process while I decluttered the display window. I removed yellowed posters and ugly merchandise, then cleaned the window.

As noon approached, my lack of sleep caught up to me. I pulled Ferdinand aside to beg off for the afternoon. I said, "I want to thank you again for this job. I really need the money." Thoughts of Heartless Hartness took the last of my strength. I sniffed once, then again. Before I could stop, a stream of tears ran down my face as I explained the blackmail situation.

Ferdinand ran to Aisle 2 and returned with a dusty packet of tissues. He presented them to me in a gentle gesture of kindness that made me cry harder. He said, "Come with me."

We went into a dusty storeroom I'd never seen.

Ferdinand pulled out two folding chairs and we sat. He opened a case of water bottles and handed me one.

I drank the warm liquid and my sniffling slowed.

Ferdinand said, "I will help you get this guy. He sounds mean and you're a nice girl."

I said, "I don't know how to stop him. He has all the power."

Ferdinand said, "What do you know about him? Can we get some dirt on him? Then, you can blackmail him back. Make him stop."

He had a point. I'd been on defense this whole time. Switching to offense might make the difference. I said, "I don't know anything about him."

Ferdinand said, "Let's dig into his life. Everybody has something to hide." So true.

Within an hour, we had a plan.

TWENTY-ONE

I returned to find Lusty whipping up pancakes and humming the Pink Panther theme song. I grabbed a mug and poured some coffee. Between the aromas of pancakes and sausage, I could barely keep the drool in my mouth.

Lusty ate a huge stack of pancakes and five sausages. As hungry as I was, I could not keep up with her. After a wordless half hour, we sipped the last of the coffee and sat back in contentment. I didn't have to broach the subject. Lusty was ready for me.

She said, "Okay, Honey, let's get started."

We went to my makeshift bedroom and sat by the phones.

My breath tightened as I reached for the receiver. I pulled back and said, "How did you get started in this business?"

Lusty crossed her arms across her ample chest. "Are you trying to get out of this?"

I said, "No. I'm just trying to understand how you got started. You have to admit this is an unusual line of work."

Lusty looked away, sighed, and then sat down. After a moment of silence, she said, "When I was a girl, I was bullied for my size. Boys treated me like a leper and the girls would outright laugh at me. I had no friends and no dates. The prettiest girls were particularly cruel. A group of them, led by a redhead, would go out of their way to tease me. They'd stand around pointing at me and laughing. The girls would circle me and flounce around in their cute little outfits. 'Look at that. Ain't she fat?' They'd follow me down the hall, ignoring my tears. I couldn't get away from them. I don't know why words from so long ago still hurt.

"In my senior year of high school, I passed a huddle of boys in the hall. One of them said, 'There goes Elustria the Elephant.' I had taken that crap all my school years, but it still stung. Then one of his friends said, 'She may be big, but I could listen to her sexy voice all day long.' They high fived each other. For the first time in my life, I had received a compliment and a little confidence. That boost also gave me an unexpected bonus.

That night I went to a phone booth and called the redhead's boyfriend. Without giving my name, I talked dirty to him. He begged to meet me. I arranged to meet him near the lake in the park. I watched from the other side of the lake as he stood around for hours waiting for me. That's when I knew I had a gift. I quit school the next day. The teasing and bullying made learning impossible for me anyway. So, I have little education. I needed a way to make a living and retail wasn't cutting it. Once I was out on my own, I started this business and I've flourished ever since. I learned a big life lesson - that natural skills can outshine formal education."

I gleamed at Lusty.

Then she said, "Now no more delays. Let's get started."

I said, "I don't want to do this for real. I just want to know how."

Lusty grinned. "I know, Honey. I unplugged this phone for you to practice on. She pushed the lip-shaped phone to me."

I wiped my hands on my jeans and reached for the phone. I glanced sideways at Lusty and pulled my hand back. I inhaled and snatched up the receiver.

Lusty said, "Now first, you must speak in a breathy voice. You know, like Marilyn Monroe or Kathleen Turner. That gets them every time."

I giggled so much; I couldn't make full sentences.

Lusty took me by the shoulders. "Change your mindset. Think about your goal, that man you want in your life. Think about Malik."

I was thinking about Charles, but I didn't have the courage to tell Lusty. We got back to work.

"Close your eyes and think of your man. Think of turning him into a frenzied, sex-craved animal."

My thighs dampened. I crossed my legs. She was good.

"Now put your image in his mind, what you're wearing, where you're laying, what you're doing to yourself. Give him a sweet little nickname. Like I have one guy who loves when I call him Spicy."

I started to breathe hard. I couldn't do this in front of Lusty. I said, "Can I practice by myself?"

Lusty smiled, "Now that's what I'm talking about. You sound breathy. Good girl." She reached into her house dress pocket and pulled out a small device.

I said, "What's that?" I thought she was giving me a sex toy.

"It's a recorder. You can practice anytime, anywhere. Play it back to check your progress. I'll leave you to practice in private. I'll check back with you later."

An hour later Lusty returned to check on my headway. I was way too embarrassed to demonstrate my fledgling skills for her. She understood. She handed me a throwaway cell phone.

"Thanks, Lusty."

Lusty smiled, "Now that you've started your lessons, I thought you might want to practice on you know who. His number's programmed in." She gave me a sly smile and closed the door behind her.

I punched a few buttons and, lo and behold, Malik's number popped up. *What should I do? Why am I so conflicted?* If I knew Charles' number, the choice would have been harder. With this phone, I had no option.

A minute later, Malik answered the phone.

In a rush of breath, I said, "Hello Malik."

Malik said, "Who's this?"

"It's me, Raquel." I thought my real name sounded way sexier than Rocky.

"Rocky, is that you?"

"Yes."

Malik lowered his voice and said, "Why are you whispering? Are you in trouble?"

"No," I shouted. "I'm being sexy."

He laughed so loud and long that I almost hung up.

Malik quieted down and said, "Sorry. I didn't understand."

I could still hear the mirth in his voice. *How deflating.* I said, "How was your date?"

Malik said, "Of course, I had to cancel since I was being interrogated. You couldn't have planned that better." He chuckled.

I was about to tell Malik where to stick it when I changed my mind.

I said, "Would you mind if I stopped by?"

Malik said, "You want to try your sexy voice in person?"

I said, "Maybe, later." My heart thumped like a drum by the time we disconnected. I wanted to run to him, but I had big plans.

I met Ferdinand in the back lot of the pharmacy at closing time. We decided to use his car in case Hartness knew mine. We slid into Ferdinand's immaculate silver Honda Accord.

I hoped Ferdinand didn't see the shock on my face. His car contrasted his disorganized, dirty store. I guessed it was a man thing where they treat their cars better than they treat their women. A lemon scent filled the interior as Ferdinand switched on the air conditioning.

I sunk into the soft seat and enjoyed the ride.

We pulled into a far corner of the bank's parking lot and waited.

Hartness left the bank and hopped into a black BMW.

We tailed him at a respectable distance. We ended our pursuit on a quiet street in Maplewood.

Hartness parked and strolled to a house half a block from his car.

I said, "Why did he park so far from his house? There are lots of closer spots."

Ferdinand smiled. He said, "You don't think like a man. He's not supposed to be here."

I still didn't understand.

We exited the car and walked up the street hoping to be inconspicuous. Ferdinand's dusty tee shirt and vest might stand out in this flawless neighborhood. We walked past the house but couldn't see inside as the building was about a mile from the sidewalk. However, we found one clue, a mailbox at the foot of the path. In shiny black script, the name on the mailbox read Banner.

We crossed the street and returned to the car.

I said, "Who's Banner? I thought this was Hartness' house."

Ferdinand pulled out his phone. He said, "I have an idea." After a few taps, he said, "This is the bank president's house."

I lost all hope. I said, "If he's in good with the president of the bank, we don't stand a chance of stopping him. I'll be on the hook forever."

Ferdinand smiled and shook his head. "You're wrong. As I said before, you don't think like a man."

We moved the car to the other side of the street for a clear view of the front door. We sat in the car for two hours. Ferdinand dozed a bit.

I fidgeted, nervous that someone would call the cops. In this neighborhood, people reported strangers surveilling houses. Ferdinand and I qualified as strange.

The front door opened and Hartness emerged with his jacket flung over his shoulder and no tie. A woman in a floral kimono stepped onto the porch and kissed him with a fervor only seen in movies.

My mouth hung open.

Ferdinand said, "I told you he wasn't supposed to be here. That's got to be the bank president's wife." He whipped out his phone and took several pictures.

We drove away before she let Hartness go.

Back at my car, Ferdinand forwarded the incriminating pictures to me.

As I scrolled through them, I said, "Tomorrow, I'll show these pics to Heartless. He'll have to stop harassing me then. I can threaten to out him to the president."

Ferdinand leaned back and eyed me for a second. He said, "Do you want to be a blackmailer like Hartness?"

The thought startled and confused me. I said, "Well, why have we been doing this? I thought the whole idea was to stop Hartness."

Ferdinand said, "Also, if you threaten Hartness face to face, he'll have no choice but to come after you hard. If you don't think of another way to stop him, you'll regret it." He left me at my car and drove off.

I sat in the Corolla and let Ferdinand's remarks seep into my mind. What other way could I use these pictures?

Shitty Kitty nudged me. "Plaster the pictures all over the bank. He'll get fired. Voila! No more blackmail."

Kitty's plan seemed to erase Ferdinand's objections, so I went for it. I drove to an Internet cafe and printed several copies of the pictures. I figured I could tape them to the front and back doors of the bank. That should do the job.

I pulled into the bank lot panting with anticipation. I patted the manila envelope that held my precious freedom. Since the bank was closed, I expected no parked cars, but one car remained. A gold Porsche sat in the space next to the back bank entrance. I scanned the area but saw no one. I'd have to be quick. I grabbed the duct tape, which was now a staple in my car, and the envelope. I started toward the back door of the bank, making sure the Porsche was unoccupied. As I neared the car, I gasped. A sign marked the parking spot as 'Reserved for Bank President'.

I heard the angels sing. This had to be fate. I didn't have to reveal Hartness' deceit to everyone. Posting pictures for all to see would also shame the bank president, and he had done no wrong. Hartness was cheating with the bank president's wife. The conflict should remain between the two of them. Leaving the envelope on the car would be kinder to Mr. Banner.

I pulled a marker from my glove compartment and wrote "Mr. Banner, Bank President" on the envelope. I laid the envelope on the Porsche windshield and popped the wiper down to secure it.

I couldn't drop the pictures and run. I needed to see the bank president's reaction to the photos. Although I felt sorry for Mr. Banner, I needed to know he'd be mad enough to take revenge on Hartness. I had only one issue. I couldn't stay in the lot. Banner would surely see me as the only other vehicle there.

An Italian restaurant stood next to the bank, separated by a chicken wire fence. I drove to the restaurant and parked in the lot. I had a clear view of the Porsche through the fence. I sat in my steamy hot car waiting for victory. A stinging bead of sweat rolled into my eye. I pulled a tissue from the dusty pack Ferdinand had given me and wiped my eyelids.

Doubts began to surface. What if the bank president wasn't in the bank? Mr. Banner could have left his Porsche in the lot and traveled another way. What if that wasn't his car, but some random vehicle?

I left my car, ran around the fence, and crept back to the Porsche. I could have climbed the fence but couldn't chance attracting attention. I peeked into the car. In the back seat, lay a copy of Fortune Magazine. The mailing label was the address where Hartness had his tryst. Satisfied, I returned to my car.

Seconds after I reached the Corolla, the rear door of the bank opened. Out stepped a handsome, suave, gray-haired man. He tossed his gray suit jacket onto his back seat and slid into the driver's seat. His head jerked when he saw the envelope. Mr. Banner exited the car and snagged the envelope. I ducked down when he scanned the area for the culprit. He leaned on the car and pulled out the photos.

I braced myself for an emotional outburst.

Mr. Banner flipped through each photo. Then, in a clear loud voice, he laughed.

At first, I thought he was crying. I squinted my eyes for a better look.

The bank president held his stomach and guffawed. He wiped his eyes and took another peek at the pictures. He held them up one by one, then bent over with laughter. When he was able to catch his breath, he tossed the pictures onto his back seat and got back into the car. He drove off, grinning.

My misadventure had absorbed my day. I called Malik hoping to try my new sexy voice skills face to face but he texted back to postpone. He had to attend to school business. I returned to Lusty's and settled in for the evening.

I laid back on Lusty's daybed in the guest room. Intermittent waves of exhaustion rolled over me. I had never conquered the skill of quiet time. Some people meditate to center themselves. For me, silence opened a cavernous door allowing demons of my past to invade.

I couldn't understand the bank president's reaction to the pictures. Did the shock of seeing Hartness and his wife make him hysterical? And how could I confirm the consequences of my actions?

I called Ferdinand and filled him in.

Ferdinand said, "That is strange. Maybe Banner wanted some dirt on his wife, and you gave it to him. You never know what's in people's heads. Maybe the guy is loco. Wait and see what happens. That's all you can do."

I finally slipped into a deep sleep and awakened to sun streaming through the curtains. Today promised to be another scorcher. I had fallen asleep in my clothes and needed a shower. As I undressed, my cell purred. I stared as my bank's number glowed on the screen. A moment of triumph raced through my body as I accepted the call. "Hello?"

At first, no one responded. Then, I heard heavy breathing. Finally, he said, "Hartness here."

My breath caught in my throat. Didn't Banner fire him? Why was he calling from the bank? I said, "Yes?" Better to let him control the conversation. I didn't want to give anything away.

He said, "I know you did it. Banner called me in first thing this morning. He showed me the pictures. He even gave me a set. Thanks for printing multiples. We had a good laugh."

He spoke English but I couldn't grasp what he was saying. I said, "I don't know what you're talking about."

Hartness said, "I checked our surveillance cameras. There you were, hiding in plain sight in your crappy Corolla in our parking lot. I saw you put the envelope on Banner's Porsche."

I slapped my forehead. Of course, a bank would have security cameras. I should have worn a disguise. I said, "Why aren't you fired?"

Hartness said, "I'll let you in on a secret. Banner and I have had an arrangement for years. I keep his wife occupied so he can spend time with his mistress."

My legs gave out and I plopped onto the bed.

Hartness said, "How's that for job security?"

I said, "What kind of bank is this?"

Hartness said, "It's the kind of bank that takes your house. As of now, my side payment has doubled. If you want to keep your house, you'll pay me $2,000 on top of your mortgage."

I sucked in a big gust of air. "I can't pay that, and you know it."

Hartness laughed. "Now you're catching on. It's only a matter of time before the bank owns your house. You're done."

I said, "Suppose I go to the police or the newspapers?"

"Oh, please." Hartness said. "With what proof? Reporters and police need hard evidence. Why do you think I talk with you one on one? Our conversations have all been private."

I said, "The police can trace phone calls between us."

Hartness said, "Proving what? That you're behind on your mortgage payments? They'll say you're taking revenge on the bank. Let me stop you right here. I've heard these threats before from other people. Nothing ever happens. You might as well start packing." He hung up before I could reply.

I had nothing to say anyway. I peeled off my clothes and took a hot shower. I leaned against the wet tile, grateful the beating water masked my sobs. My situation couldn't get worse, and I had nowhere to turn. Hartness dominated me, yet another man in control.

The next morning, I took a chance and walked to Malik's apartment to let the warm breeze clear my thinking. I had tired of ducking and hiding like an animal. I needed to feel human again. Also, I had to choose between

Malik and Charles, or I was going to Hell. How could two such different men make my heart flutter. Men didn't seem to have this problem. They could happily date multiple women with no sense of commitment to any of them. Maybe that was my conflict. I needed commitment. I wanted to pledge true love with someone. Hopping from one bed to another made me feel like a bad person. That's why I flirted with both men but took the romances no further. *Was I making a mistake now?*

I rang Malik's bell, and he buzzed me in.

We sat near each other on Malik's comfy couch.

Malik leaned close and whispered in my ear. "So, you were saying?"

I opened my mouth to say something sexy.

Malik's doorbell buzzed.

He said, "Hold that thought." Through the intercom, I heard the unmistakable voice of Detective Brimley.

Malik motioned for me to hide.

I hid in the kitchen pantry and peeked through the cracked door into the living room.

Brimley strode through the door with two uniformed officers. "Mr. Grainger, I need you to come to the station with me."

Malik said, "Why? Can't you ask your questions here? And why all the backup?"

Brimley said, "Malik Grainger, I'm placing you under arrest for aiding and abetting a fugitive. These officers are here to search your apartment. Here's the warrant for your arrest and for the search."

I heard Malik say, "I'm not aiding anybody. Rocky is only a fugitive because you think she committed murder. If you knew her well, you'd know she's a gentle soul. There's no way she killed anyone."

Brimley snickered. "You think you know her so well? I have evidence tying her to the murder weapon and the location where we found Mr. Depew's remains. I caught her with a second victim murdered in a similar way."

Malik said, "If you have Mr. Depew's murder weapon, how was it used again on another person?"

Brimley paused.

Malik laughed. "See? You think you have the case all tied up, but there are holes."

Brimley said, "You're talking yourself into a conspiracy charge. You should be careful of protecting Rocky. She's not as helpless and sweet as you think. If you want to save yourself, you better wipe that love dust out of your eyes. You seem to think she needs your protection, but does she want it? How many times has she gone off on her own and done things she's hidden from you?"

It was Malik's turn to be silent.

Brimley kept talking. "You better open your eyes, Buddy. That girl doesn't need you or anyone else. If we find evidence that Rocky has been staying here, we'll add the charge of harboring a fugitive. Put your hands behind your back."

Malik said, "When will I get back here? I have obligations."

Brimley said, "You're in serious trouble. You won't see the light of day until Rocky turns herself in or we capture her. Turn around and put your hands behind your back."

Malik said, "Oh brother."

I stepped out of the pantry. "Leave him alone. I'm here." I offered my wrists to be handcuffed.

Malik hung his head. "No, Rocky. Why did you do that?"

"Because you're worth saving."

Brimley looked from me to Malik and back again. "I'm not surprised."

The two uniforms stepped toward me, but Brimley held up a hand. "She's mine."

I dragged toward my fate as slowly as possible while my mind raced. I had no words of explanation, no sarcasm, no fight. I had failed. Not only would I go to jail, a killer would go free.

Brimley wrapped my wrists in zip tie handcuffs and pulled them tight. He gripped my arm and said, "Let's go fellas."

One of the uniforms took Malik's arm.

I said, "Wait. You said you'd let Malik go if I gave up."

Brimley grinned. "I can say anything I want. You're both going in. We'll sort everything out at the station."

I stomped my foot. "That's not fair. You lied."

Brimley said, "I lied? You're the one who escaped jail. You're the one we found hiding in your boyfriend's kitchen. You're the one getting booked for murder and whatever else I can throw at you. Which one of us is the criminal here?"

Malik said, "Rocky, don't make things worse."

We marched to the cars in a motley parade, gawkers pointing at us.

I watched Malik's hunched shoulders as they pushed him into the squad car. Inside, his chin dropped to his chest, and he turned away.

I shut my eyes and lowered my head as the officer slammed Malik's car door shut. I hated to admit it, but Brimley was right on the nose. I had run out on Malik in more ways than one. He had stood steadfast with me, and it got him nothing but trouble.

Malik never raised his head as the car disappeared down the street. My deeds had broken his spirit.

My eyes roved the street for an escape.

Brimley gripped my arm and jerked me toward his car, making me stumble.

A tiny object fell from my jean pocket, rolled in a circle, and settled in the grass.

With effort, Brimley bent and picked up the ivory ring. He examined it with squinty eyes, then looked skyward retrieving a memory. He said, "You just added a nail to your coffin."

I said, "What do you mean? Give that back to me. That was a gift."

Brimley nodded. "Sure, it was. Mrs. Depew reported her wedding ring missing at the same time her husband disappeared. You just locked yourself in tight."

I leaned against Brimley's filthy car as he fumbled for the keys. My jaws clenched so hard I thought my teeth would crack. What had Holy done to me? He must have tucked the ring into my jeans while I slept. The car locks beeped as they unlocked, making me jump.

Brimley cracked the door open and smiled.

That smile ignited a fire in me. I shoved the door hard.

Brimley fell on his ass and rolled to the curb.

I took off at top speed. Running with cuffed hands proved difficult. I had never realized how much pumping arms propelled you. I ran behind

Malik's building and attempted to climb the fence bordering his parking lot. Between my stilettos and the cuffs, I couldn't make it over. I spied a narrow gap between the fence and the next property and squeezed through.

I darted through the adjacent yard, across the street and around the corner. I slowed to a normal pace and walked quiet, back streets to Lusty's house. The walk back to Lusty's filled me with angst. My stomach churned at the impending confrontation. Back in Paradise, I scanned my street for patrol cars as I quickstepped to Lusty's. I ran around back and banged on her kitchen door.

After ages, she opened the door and I fell inside.

Lusty helped me up and stared, wide-eyed, at my flushed face and handcuffs. She sat me down at the table. Without a word, she cut off the cuffs with a kitchen knife.

I sat in place for twenty minutes before I could face Lusty. How in the world would I tell her Brimley had arrested Malik? I ran scenarios through my mind, none ending with success.

Lusty stood by patiently waiting. She broke the silence. "What happened?"

I explained what had happened in rapid chatter so as not to lose my courage.

With each word, Lusty's face reddened until it was indistinguishable from her hair. Her eyes bored into mine and her girth expanded as she rose and moved to within inches of my face. Her pancake breath blew my wiry curls back from my forehead.

She spoke in a decidedly unsexy voice. "If that boy gets in trouble because of your shenanigans, I'll wring your neck."

Tears filled my eyes. "I don't know what I can do short of turning myself in."

Lusty tilted her head and said, "Well?"

I said, "I'll call Brimley and have him pick me up at my house." I started up the steps to gather my things.

Lusty said, "Wait. I'll make some calls." She plodded up the stairs to my makeshift bedroom and closed the door. I imagined Lusty had any number of police she could contact, right up to the chief.

She returned a half hour later. She said, "We'll have to wait and see if I did him any good." She glared at me. "You better hope I did."

I opened my mouth, but before I could respond, Lusty's doorbell rang. *What now?*

I stiffened and sought a hiding place in the pink palace. Hiding had become my life. I ducked behind the tufted sofa and pulled a coral throw pillow over my head.

Lusty opened the door.

A familiar voice said, "Is Rocky here?"

Lusty said, "Who?"

"I want to return her bag. She left it at the station."

"I'm sorry, you have the wrong house."

The man said, "I know she's here. Tell her it's Charles."

At the sound of his name, I jumped up and bumped my head hard against the wall. "It's okay, Lusty." I ran to the door.

There he stood in all his chocolate glory holding my bag. He was back in civilian clothes. We smiled at each other in the lustful way of new lovers. My heart pumped with joy until I saw the scowl on Lusty's face. "I can explain."

Charles interrupted me. "She left her bag at the station when she was interrogated. I retrieved it for her."

I asked, "How did you know where to find me?"

He tapped a finger to his temple, "I have my ways. May I come in? I don't want to attract attention." He gestured toward the street.

We settled in the living room, Lusty keeping a watchful eye on us.

As we talked, Charles' eyes wandered around the room. I could only surmise he had never seen a pink palace before.

Again, I asked, "How did you find me?" This time I crossed my arms and waited for a suitable response.

He leaned in close and asked, "Is it possible for us to speak in private?"

Lusty stood and put her fists on her meaty hips. "No need to whisper, Mister. I get the message." She flounced out of the room.

I held a finger to my lips. When Lusty started banging dishes in the kitchen, I beckoned Charles to speak.

Charles stood and turned in a circle taking in the decor. He said, "So, this is trustworthy Lusty."

I said, "Did you come here to start an argument?"

Charles shook his head. "I brought your bag to Malik's apartment just in time to see you run out of his building. I followed you here. I hoped to get you alone, but your neighbor never left the house. I didn't want to leave it on your porch. I had no choice but to ring the bell."

I said, "How did you know I live next door?"

Charles said, "You gave me your business card."

I made a mental note to burn those cards and buy new ones as soon as I could afford them.

Charles shuffled his feet and then said, "You deserve to know I work for the government."

I said, "Sure, you do. If you're going to lie to me, you can leave now." I stood.

He took my arm in one warm palm and pulled me down to the sofa beside him.

I must admit, I put up no resistance.

He took my hand and gazed into my eyes. "I work undercover for the Federal Trade Commission. I'm investigating the Depews for consumer fraud."

The words didn't compute at first because I was caught up in his light eyes, cologne, and warm touch. When the fog cleared, I pulled away and said, "Prove it."

Charles slipped his identification from his inside pocket. It looked official, not that I would know the difference. It featured a scales of justice emblem and an eagle below it. Still, I scrutinized it like I was an expert. I said, "You could have faked that."

Charles sighed. "You are one stubborn woman. Let me explain."

I leaned back and crossed my arms and legs.

Charles said, "We've received numerous complaints about the Depews. They sell rare items on the Internet, collect the money and keep the goods. In fact, they may have posted pictures of merchandise they never owned. They sell the same items to multiple people. We still don't know everything. I am part of a sting operation. The first phase was easy. I ordered ivory statuettes from Mr. Depew and paid him $300,000. I contacted him several times about delivery of the statuettes. He kept putting me off. I couldn't get my money back. It was wired to his account. I was closing in on him when he disappeared. Now he's dead."

I asked, "Doesn't that end your case?"

"No. I suspect Mrs. Depew launders the money. She's the key to this investigation. In fact, I think she's the brains of the operation."

I said, "It makes sense. I don't know what's going on in that house, but something's off. Mrs. Depew's kind of scary and she controlled Ernest."

"So, you believe me?"

I said, "I believe what you're telling me now. It explains your actions."

Charles said, "Then why are you grinding your teeth?"

Before I knew what was happening, I reached over and slapped his face. The crack resonated in the room. Activity in the kitchen paused for a beat, then continued.

Charles rubbed his reddening face and said, "Why did you do that?"

I said, "All this time I was completely honest with you. You got to read the open book of Rocky while keeping me in the dark. You used me for information."

Charles splayed his hands. "I gave you information too. I've protected you. I rescued you from jail."

"Yes, you shared information with me, but you didn't share yourself. That's not how you treat someone you care about."

Charles opened his mouth to speak.

I raised my hand in front of his face. "Don't bother with an explanation. I wouldn't know whether to believe you or not. Let's stick to information about the case." I ignored Charles' hurt expression. "So, Brimley knows you're an agent?"

Charles looked at his feet and spoke. "No. The FTC isn't sharing information with the local police. Until we are sure who is in on this operation, I can't reveal my assignment to him. As far as Brimley is concerned, I'm a slighted customer of Mr. Depew's."

"Doesn't that make you a suspect in his murder?"

Charles shrugged. "It does, but I'm not worried about myself. I'm concerned about you." He pulled me close.

I could feel his breath on my face.

He said, "I don't know how this happened."

"What?" That perfect husky tone imparted from my lips naturally.
"You were such a pain in the ass in the beginning of this case, but now..."
I turned my face and fought the urge to give in.
Bam, bam, bam! The front door resonated.
Lusty creaked her way to the door and peeked out.
Charles said, "Run."
I didn't need coaxing.

TWENTY-TWO

I grabbed my bag and raced out of Lusty's back door. I should've hopped the fence and run out to the other side of the block as per my usual M.O., but curiosity overtook me. I peeked around the side of the house and saw Detective Brimley's car. I knelt behind Lusty's pink rhododendrons and waited. I hoped Brimley would leave once he knew I wasn't there.

I spied around the side of the house in time to see Brimley leading Charles to his car in handcuffs. I gasped, then slapped my hand over my mouth and ducked back behind the bushes. *What have I done to the men in my life?* A moment later I heard the car drive off. I peeked out and saw Brimley had gone. I trudged back into the house where Lusty awaited me with squinty eyes and hands on hips.

She beckoned me with one meaty finger. We sat on opposite sides of her kitchen table. Lusty gripped the dish towel she had been using.

I shifted in my seat and bit my lip, not knowing what to say. Where could I start? I couldn't express my feelings for Charles, although she had surely surmised them by now.

Lusty said, "Well?"

I asked, "Why was Charles arrested? He didn't do anything."

Lusty's eyes widened, and her voice rose an octave. "For aiding and abetting you. Do you want to explain about this Charles guy?"

I didn't want to, but I had no choice. I licked my lips and rubbed my sweaty palms together. "I think I love him, Lusty." Those were the hardest words I ever had to speak.

Lusty slapped the dish towel on the table, cracking the quiet. "What about Malik? I thought he meant something to you. I know he's fond of you." Her words sliced through me like cold steel.

I couldn't look Lusty in the eye as I spoke. "I care about Malik, but not the same as Charles. I mean I thought I loved Malik until I met Charles. I mean I care about them both. I mean..."

Lusty put up her hand to stop my rambling.

I said, "Please let me explain. Malik means a lot to me. He's a good friend and I do find him attractive. But Charles and I clicked instantly. We have a chemistry I can't define."

Lusty said, "True friendship is important in a relationship. When the hot sex is over, you want someone to talk to, to lean on. You need a mate you can count on. That's real intimacy. Is this Charles guy there for you like that?"

I looked away.

Lusty said, "That's what I thought. I've never had a man of my own, but I've talked with enough men to tell the good ones from the bad ones." She pushed herself up and lumbered toward me. She leaned over me. "I got a call back from the police. Malik's charges are too serious for them to release him. I'm getting him a lawyer."

I said, "How about Harry Sunshine? I heard he's good."

Lusty grimaced and waved me off. "That creep that advertises on bus shelters? He preys on poor people. Why do you think he puts his posters there? Malik will be arraigned in the morning. If I can't free him, he'll go to a real prison. Malik's not made for that. He's a good boy." Lusty wiped her eyes with the dish towel. "I didn't protect Malik for a decade to have you undo his life with one stupid action."

I could have reminded Lusty that she referred me to the family that involved me in murder. I could have begged for Lusty's forgiveness. I could have made a myriad of excuses for falling in love with the other guy. In the end, I couldn't utter a word.

Lusty delivered the ultimate blow. "You need to leave. I don't know what to think of you now. Malik put himself in trouble for you. Now your *other* boyfriend is going to jail. I don't plan to be the next person you use while you stay free."

I didn't feel free. Also, I'd never intentionally put anyone else in jeopardy. I could turn myself in but what purpose would that serve besides letting the real killer go free?

In my room, I packed my duffel. Since a desk and multiple phones filled most of the guest room, I had only unpacked a few clothes and toiletries. The rest of my stuff had remained packed. I pulled on an orange tee shirt and tugged it back off. I changed into comfy, black traveling clothes as my plan took shape. I slipped my feet into black stilettos and sat on the daybed to think. In the end, I had only one option which is no choice at all.

I slunk down the stairs where Lusty waited.

Lusty's lips pressed into a tight, red grimace as she held out a roll of bills. I shook my head.

Lusty said, "Go ahead, take it. You're gonna need it."

I couldn't believe how my friends stood by me no matter how I betrayed them. My hand shook as I accepted cash from my friend. Even though Lusty was throwing me out, I would forever trust her with my life. "Thank you for everything."

Lusty opened the door and stood back.

I couldn't look her way as I dragged my bag to the porch. An unseasonable cold had gripped the night making me shiver.

Lusty shut the door before I reached the steps.

While driving, my thoughts wound around one mission. I pushed my self-pity aside. To clear both Malik's and my names, I had to do Brimley's job and crack the case. I knew the real culprit but what should I do when I found her? I'd like to beat Mrs. Depew senseless for the misery she'd caused me and my friends, but that wouldn't free Malik. I could capture Mrs. Depew and drag her to the police, but she'd pull her sweet old lady routine. The officers would serve her tea and cookies, and make sure she was comfy. I needed a sure-fire way to take her down.

Route 9 was dotted with nondescript motels. I didn't know one from the other as I had never stayed in one. I pulled into the parking lot of one. In minutes, I had rented a room for the night. If my plan didn't go well, I'd extend my stay. I dumped my bags on the threadbare bedspread and checked my cell for messages. My dad had called ten times since my arrest. I'd have to listen to him in the car.

I stuck my cell to my dashboard and headed to Mrs. Depew's. My dad's first message was filled with incoherent language and heavy breathing. I had to listen to it twice to understand what he said. Police had searched his house looking for me. Brimley had called Dad to advise him of my arrest for murder. I was going to strangle Brimley when I next saw him.

The next messages followed suit in the panic I heard in my father's voice. My hands gripped the cold steering wheel so hard I thought it might crack. I had never heard my dad cry until tonight. His tears broke my heart. I would have called him to ease his mind, but I would have to lie to calm him. I have told so many lies. I wanted to run to him like a loving daughter should, but I didn't know how this would end. Better to play out the night and have something real to tell him.

Next, I dialed Holy. I took deep breaths while his phone rang. I had to lower my heart rate to give me any chance of speaking calmly.

Holy answered on the second ring.

Before he could say something aggravating, I said, "Where did you get that ivory ring?"

Holy said, "Are you wearing it? I knew you'd love it."

I said, "Answer me. Where did you find that ring?"

Holy said, "Somebody left it in the junkyard."

I sped up and said, "And you just happened to see a little ring laying in the dirt in the junkyard?"

Holy said, "It was sitting on top of a trunk somebody dumped in the yard. In fact, I think it was the trunk the cops stole. The police owe me. I bet I could have gotten good money for that trunk."

I swerved, pumped the brake, and slowed down. "The ring was laying on the trunk? Did you open the trunk?"

Holy said, "No. I never got around to it. You were coming home. I had to prepare the house for you. Then the cops took it."

I beat my hand on the wheel. "And you didn't think to tell me about this? Did you mention the ring to the cops?"

"Of course not. They would have wanted it back."

A wave of relief mixed with frustration washed over me. I would have told him how much trouble he had caused me, but Holy was just being Holy. He remained the same man I had married in my naivety. Rather than raise my already high blood pressure, I disconnected.

TWENTY-THREE

The clock was ticking. I had to fix everything before Malik's morning arraignment. The sky had darkened to a cloudy midnight blue by the time I reached Mrs. Depew's house. I parked around the corner and crept through her neighbors' back yards with the expertise of a spy. I stood at the bottom of her back stairs, listening for movement. I tiptoed up the steps to the back door. The solid steps didn't creak a bit. *Maybe this is my lucky night.*

I stopped at the back door and listened. No sound. No lights shone from the windows. No light emitted from the cloud-covered moon. I blended into the darkness in my Catwoman suit. Unfortunately, the night camouflaged everything else too. I fingered my tool belt until I found my lock picks. I needed both hands to work them so I couldn't hold a flashlight. I held the picks in my teeth as I felt the door frame for the lock. The metal lock pricked my fingers with its icy cold, making me gasp. The lock picks clattered to the porch, echoing in the night. I froze, straining to hear any motion. Leaves rustling in the cold wind accented the silence.

I grasped the doorknob for leverage as I knelt to search the wooden porch. The knob twisted and the door swung open to a dark, silent kitchen. I walked in on the tips of my Christian Louboutins. *I'm getting good at this detective stuff.*

I stretched an arm in front of me, feeling for objects. I didn't want a kicked chair or fallen pot to alert Mrs. Depew to my presence. Tiny, hesitant steps led me to a table. I felt my way around the perimeter.

As I reached mid-kitchen, the door slammed behind me. A bright overhead light nearly blinded me. I swung around to see Mrs. Depew standing by the back door.

She said, "Close your mouth, Dear. You look like a dead fish."

I swept the confusion from my brain. I pointed at her petite feet encased in Air Jordans. "You can walk."

"Observant, aren't you?"

I said, "That's what's been bugging me about your sneakers. I wondered how your sneakers got gritty on the bottom since you didn't walk. Later, I wondered why you needed to wash your Jordans. They couldn't get much use...so I thought."

"You're the only one who knows that, and you'll take that secret to your grave."

"What makes you think that?" I whipped out my cell phone.

"Because I'm going to kill you. It'll be easy." She pulled a small gun with an ivory handle from her sweater pocket and leveled it on me. "You see, I heard an intruder in my house. I got scared and protected myself."

I had to admit, it sounded plausible. With my recent record, Brimley would close this case, shove my body in a pine box and move on. I said, "I can see now that you were able to kill Mr. Depew and Ernest, but how did you do it?"

"Perry didn't know I could walk, and Ernest was too scared to tell. One day Perry fell asleep on a chair in the sitting room. Well, I must admit I added some crushed benzos in his sherry. I couldn't leave anything to chance. Then, I simply rolled up behind him and hit him with his cane. That memory makes the sitting room my favorite room." She smiled.

I cringed to think I had been in another murder scene. I said, "You killed him while you were both sitting. That's why the angle of the wound worked as if you both stood."

She said, "That's smart dear. Then I had Ernest pack him in a trunk and stash him in the basement. Once I hired you, Ernest moved him to the abandoned house on the invoice. I knew you'd find the trunk. Transporting that trunk made you an accessory to murder and put you under my control. I didn't count on you being so stubborn."

As long as I kept her talking, I'd stay alive. I said, "How did you mask the smell of a dead body?"

Mrs. Depew waved a hand at me. "Oh Honey, the Internet offers so many products that mask dead body smells, I had trouble choosing."

"I didn't think you were computer literate. You don't have a cell phone."

Mrs. Depew laughed. "You're so gullible. Like most people, you accepted my little old lady act. Young people see older people as ignorant, slow-walking technophobes. In truth, most of us are sharp as you. We have experience in areas you have yet to conquer. When you underestimate me, it plays to my advantage."

"How did you hide your ability to walk from Mr. Depew? You lived in the same house. What did he think was wrong with you?"

"A few years back I tripped down the stairs and broke my ankle. I healed remarkably well for a mature woman, but that's when my plan hatched."

"You've been planning this for years?" My heart quickened. Mrs. Depew was more cold-blooded than I had anticipated. "Why?"

Mrs. Depew smiled. "You're a young woman, Dear. You wouldn't understand how one can tire of a man, of a marriage, over time."

You bet your butt, I can.

"This was my opportunity to get rid of his overbearing ass."

Even knowing how evil she was, hearing this little old lady curse still made me flinch.

"After my accident, I simply stayed in my wheelchair. He accepted my explanation that I would never heal, and he didn't care enough to pursue health care options. You see, his love had faded too."

"You could have divorced him Why did you have to kill him?"

"He was a ruthless man. I wouldn't have gotten a penny. Perry controlled everything. He watched every cent and dictated how I lived. He traveled the world collecting valuable artifacts. I rotted away in this house living on a stingy allowance. You think I live in luxury, but everything was in his name. Killing him gave me control of the money and property. I've gained my freedom."

I said, "Why didn't you leave him?"

"Are you deaf? I had no money. Why should I give up my comfort for that pig? Where was I going to go? To a seedy old folk's home? No way. With his death, I can live out my days in comfort."

I flinched as she swept the room with her gun as if to emphasize the luxury of her life.

"Agent Charles was closing in on us. He told Perry we were going to jail for fraud."

I said, "You knew about the investigation?"

Mrs. Depew sneered. "Of course, we knew. Agent Charles made no bones about it." Giggle. "We plotted ways to get rid of him, but Perry had worn down. He even considered turning himself in. Imagine, after all these years, he goes soft. Then I figured out a way to cure all my problems. I'd get rid of Perry."

I couldn't breathe. If she could kill her husband, she'd surely kill me.

Mrs. Depew continued. "With Perry dead, I'd inherit everything and be rid of him."

"I suppose you had Ernest dump your husband in the junkyard?"

"Of course, Dear."

"And the ivory ring?"

Mrs. Depew grinned. "That was a nice touch, don't you think? Even if the ring implicated your ex-husband, it made another link to you. Lots of little links made one long chain to you."

"Why frame me?"

Mrs. Depew shrugged. "Because you fit the plan so well. After Perry's death, Agent Charles persisted. I needed a fall guy and that was you." Giggle. "I made a detailed plan. I knew about your connection to the junkyard long before I hired you."

I sucked in my breath so sharply I thought my lungs would explode. "How?"

"Lusty, of course. She was a friend of my husband's."

I rolled my eyes so violently, I thought they would pop out.

Mrs. Depew said, "That's also how I knew the junkyard cameras were fakes." She smirked at me. "When Ernest told me about being seen on surveillance, I laughed in his face. Nice try. Again, Lusty is a wealth of information. She had rattled on about how cheap your ex was and said he put up fake cameras. That sealed the deal for me to hire you."

Lusty and Holy had sealed my fate.

Mrs. Depew's smile vanished. "Ernest's concern about the junkyard told me I couldn't keep him under my thumb much longer. It also told me he trusted you. All this time, I've been able to keep Ernest isolated. No friends. His mother under my control. No hope for escape."

I said, "You're the cruelest person I know. Ernest was sweet and you used that against him."

Mrs. Depew said, "Ernest's lack of a support system made him vulnerable. People need other people. Then you entered the picture. You encouraged Ernest to rebel. You were his downfall."

My eyes watered. I blinked the tears away. No way would I let this bitch see me cry.

Mrs. Depew said, "You, on the other hand, have good friends. But even well-meaning allies can betray you. Lusty had been searching for jobs for you for weeks but you know how she talks. It took one call to get your life's story. I knew all about how you were down on your luck, your ties to the junk yard, everything. That was the final piece for me. I had a perfect way to pin the murder on you. Once you accepted the job, you were done. The job connected you to this family. Your junkyard was a bonus." Mrs. Depew grinned.

I said, "But I have no motive."

Mrs. Depew shrugged. "Do you know how many people go to prison on circumstantial evidence? Once the police believe you did the crime, they'll find a way to convict you."

I had to agree with her there. I put my hands on my hips to fake some bravado. "You've forgotten one thing. The police could trace the murder weapon to you. After all, you handled it."

Mrs. Depew waved the gun. "Hah. Of course, I touched it. It was in my house. The cops are so stupid. They'll never think I could commit such a crime.

I had to keep talking while I thought of how to escape. This was especially hard since I could barely walk and breathe at the same time. "Why did you kill Ernest? He was loyal to you."

"Don't lie to me. I saw your text to Ernest. I know he met you in the park and planned to meet you again. It would have only been a matter of time before you convinced Ernest to go to the police. I had to kill him before he had the chance. I followed him right to that alley. That gave me the perfect opportunity to trap you." Giggle. "You should have seen the look on your face when the detective got you."

"You were there?"

"I hid behind some crates trying to hold back my laughter. It was like watching an episode of Cops. What a hoot." She slapped a skinny knee with her empty hand. "You came into the alley right after Ernest died."

"You mean *you* killed him. How did you do it anyway?"

Mrs. Depew grinned. "I snuck up behind him while he watched the street for you. I hit him with a piece of rebar I had Ernest take from your husband's junkyard the night he dumped Mr. Depew. You see, Dear, I plan thoroughly."

"How did you get away? You must have been covered in blood."

"I just wrapped my shawl around me and walked away. Nobody pays attention to old people. It's like we're invisible."

My eyes darted about searching for a way to flee. I reminded myself to breathe.

"Forget about escaping." Mrs. Depew waved her gun at me. "Give me that phone."

I glanced at my cell.

She straightened her puny arm and aimed at my head. "Now."

I pushed the button on the bottom of the phone and the touch screen lit up.

Ms. Depew stepped closer. "What did I say?"

I offered her the phone.

Mrs. Depew reached for it with her free hand. Zzzzzt! She slumped to the floor in an electrified heap. Her gun slammed to the floor, a bullet whizzed past my leg and blasted into the wall. I hit the floor like a gangster in a B movie.

I think I screamed and then screamed again when the kitchen door banged open. Detective Brimley rushed in, pistol raised.

He stopped short of tripping over Depew's comatose body and stood gawking at her and me.

I raised a shaky hand and Brimley pulled me to my feet.

He said, "Are you alright?"

"Do I look okay?" My body vibrated with adrenaline.

Brimley knelt and touched two fingers to Depew's neck. "What did you do to her?"

"I used my handy stun gun cell phone. It was a gift from my ex."

"Well, it certainly did the job. She's out cold, but she'll be fine." He called for an ambulance.

I said, "Where did you come from? Did you follow me here?" For once, I was grateful for his perseverance.

Brimley said, "I was coming to check on Mrs. Depew. I've been keeping an eye on her since Ernest's murder. I spotted your car on my way here. That meant trouble. I didn't know you'd be the one who needed saving."

My eyebrows raised to within an inch of my scalp. "Saving? You call that saving? I knocked her out before you rescued me."

"You don't have to be sarcastic. She could have shot you."

I said, "Yeah. Then you could have called the coroner from your hiding place on the porch. Am I under arrest again?"

Brimley shook his head. "But I still need you to come in with me. I heard Depew's confession through the door."

"You were out there while she was holding a gun on me? What kind of cop are you?"

Brimley shrugged. "I came in when I heard the shot."

"Oh yeah, that was right on time." I rolled my eyes.

"It's over now. It will only take a few hours to clear your charges."

DePew walked into the station on her own spindly legs. The EMTs had deemed her healthy and remarkably strong for a woman her age. The police took her right to jail.

I was annoyed that they hadn't subjected Mrs. Depew to handcuffs, plastic or otherwise. In light of the fact that she had tried to kill me, they should have hogtied her. Instead, the cops treated Depew as if she were a kindly grandmother who spent her days baking cookies.

Brimley and I met in an interrogation room to expedite my release and clear my charges. I would have to testify, of course.

Brimley sat his girth in one of the hard chairs. "Let's get this report done. If there's one thing I hate, it's reports." He opened a laptop.

My mouth gaped open. "Is that all you have to say to me?"

"Don't you want to get out of here?" He concentrated on the screen in front of him.

"You hunted me down, handcuffed me, arrested me, humiliated me..."

"And now I'm releasing you."

I crossed my arms with such strength I almost cut off my breath. "You owe me an apology. I was innocent and you treated me like I was Public Enemy Number One. If it wasn't for me, you would never have caught Mrs. Depew."

Brimley rolled his eyes.

I said, "Are you sure you have enough evidence to prosecute her? I know you heard her confession, but what else do you have?"

Brimley studied me for a moment. He leaned back, folded his hands and said, "We have the Depew cane with DNA evidence. Both victims were hit by a petite person of Mrs. Depew's height. We found Ernest's blood on Mrs. Depew's sneakers and the soles matched the print we found in Ernest's blood. Do we have enough Sherlock?"

"You don't have to be sarcastic." I said, "At least, I solved the murder."

Brimley closed the laptop and folded his hands on top. "If you had shared information with me, I would have solved the murder quickly. Instead, you confused the case. I spent time pursuing you instead of the real killer."

I splayed my hands. "How did I know you weren't the killer?"

Brimley shook his head in disbelief. "Where would you get a cockamamie idea like that?"

I said, "First, you handled the theft of the statuettes. Then, you oversaw the murder case. You could have easily stolen the merchandise and covered yourself by getting rid of Mr. Depew."

Brimley rested his chin on one meaty fist and stared at me in silence for a few seconds. Then, he said, "Where would you get the information about the theft case?"

Uh oh. Did I talk myself into a corner? Do I tell him about Charles? I said, "Police reports are public records."

Brimley nodded. "True. Some are. But think. Maybe I got the assignment because I already had a connection with the family. Do you think that's possible?"

The foolish look on my face said it all and marked the end of the topic.

Brimley locked eyes with me. In a cool, steady voice he said, "I did my job. I go where the evidence leads me. Did you move a trunk for Mrs. Depew?"

"Yes."

"Was Mr. Depew's body found in a location associated with you?"

"Yeah."

"Did you escape police custody, thus making *yourself* a fugitive?"

"I guess."

Brimley waved a finger in my face. "Did Mrs. Depew's ring fall from your pocket?"

I said, "Yes." A detailed answer would have thrown suspicion on Holy.

"Did I find you leaning over the dead body of Ernest Depew?"

I didn't bother to answer that one. I was beginning to see his point. Besides, if I kept talking, I'd end up going to jail on a charge of stupidity. "Okay, I get it."

Brimley leaned back. "Now would you like to apologize to me for all the trouble you caused? Your escape almost cost me my job."

"I think we're at a standoff." I couldn't hold my tongue. "You're a terrible cop. You have no bedside manner."

Brimley stared at me like I was a simpleton. "Bedside manners are for doctors, not police." He had me there.

I persisted. "You should have been a lawyer or a used car salesman. You need a profession where you can treat people like crap and get away with it."

Brimley said, "I get away with it now."

"Why did you join the force anyway?"

Brimley's face softened. He turned away. "In my twenties, I lived an unfocused life but my beautiful niece, Diane changed that. I never had kids of my own. I poured my love of children into Diane. She was a naïve, happy girl. She befriended everyone whether they were worthy of her trust or not."

Suddenly, I had no desire to hear his story.

Brimley said, "One day, Diane didn't return from school. My sister called me to help find her. We searched and called everywhere. We were too late. The police found Diane in a park a half mile from home. They never found her killer." Brimley swiped his eye. "I'd never felt such emptiness. I went into a depression and couldn't work for months. We had such dreams for her. Her death erased all our aspirations, leaving the future bleak. I couldn't sleep. I wandered the streets at night. One night I saw a light pole littered with missing persons flyers, including my niece. A lightning bolt of purpose hit me. I turned my grief into resolve. I applied to the Newark Police." He looked into my eyes. "Since then, I vowed to protect naïve girls who believe they're safe wherever they go."

I turned away. "Oh."

He returned to his laptop, and I shut my mouth.

After a few minutes of uncomfortable silence, I said, "I'm sorry I accused you of being a killer."

Brimley gazed at me. "Is that all?"

"And I apologize for any trouble I caused you."

Brimley grinned. "And?"

I screwed my eyebrows together and thought. "I didn't mean to interfere in your investigation, but you were going to put me in jail."

Brimley said, "Anything else?"

I huffed. "That's all I've got. Are you going to accept this apology or what?" I leaned back and crossed my arms.

Brimley laughed. "I knew it was only a matter of time before your real attitude showed itself." He turned back to his laptop.

I said, "What about Malik? He's innocent too."

Brimley said, "Don't worry. I called ahead. He's being released as we speak." He stopped typing. "I hope you realize you've got a good man there. He stood up for you under the worst circumstances."

I looked away. "He's a great guy."

Brimley teepeed his fingers. "In the short time I've known you, you've been self-centered and stubborn. I can take that behavior, but not everyone can."

I clamped my lips shut for the remainder of the time.

With all loose ends tied up, Brimley released me with a handshake. "You're done."

I stumbled to the door and turned back. I said, "Maybe you could help me with one more thing."

I reconvened with Malik outside the police station. We hugged in celebration of our freedom, then we Ubered to his apartment. Against Malik's wishes, I collected Murphy and he drove me to my car parked near the Depew house.

We hugged again, this time like long lost lovers, relieved and exhausted.

Malik smiled at me. "We'll talk in the morning?"

I said, "Maybe afternoon. We both need sleep."

We parted ways with a new bond.

TWENTY-FOUR

Two hours later I arrived home, exhausted, and hungry. I had retrieved my duffel bag from the motel. All I wanted was a hot shower, some greasy comfort food, and a cuddle with Murphy. I put my key in the lock, and it jammed.

I looked up to see a large notice posted to my front door. There for all the world to see was an eviction notice. Hartness had stapled one of the fake hundred-dollar bills to the front of the notice. The lock had been changed and so had my life. I snatched the cursed bill, tore it into tiny pieces and threw it into the yard. The green bits floated to earth, blending into the grass.

I twisted and shook the doorknob, then beat on the door until my tears wet my tee shirt. The last vestige of strength left my body. I lay in a fetal position on my wicker loveseat, closed my eyes and waited to die. All my efforts had led to this humiliating moment. I had almost been jailed for life trying to save my home. Now, coming full circle, it was all for naught. Heartless Hartness had won.

I don't know how long I lay there before someone shook my shoulder. I opened my bloodshot eyes to see Holy. This is how we met. I was a weak, weeping woman and he came to my rescue.

I had first seen Holy through a blur of tears. School had just closed, and I wanted to hide out until the school property cleared, so I could walk home in peace. I had hidden behind the high school, crying, because some mean girls had taunted me about my curly afro. I hid behind a dumpster at the rear of the building. I had found the place I belonged.

Holy pulled up in an old, gray truck and started picking through the junk in the dumpster.

That should have been my first clue, but being a naive, sad girl, I missed the warning.

He came around the side of the dented, smelly dumpster and stared at me. He knelt down and said, "Are you okay? Can I help you?" Even over the garbage stench, I could smell the funk of his Aqua Velva and sweat combo. He reached into his back pocket and offered me a white handkerchief with a black smudge on it. That one act of kindness had started our relationship.

Today, I would much rather have opened my eyes to Malik or Charles, but at this point, I'd better take what I could get.

Holy said, "Are you alright?"

I started to blubber. "I'm evicted. I can't get into my house and I'm pretty sure Murphy needs to be fed."

Holy wrapped a chubby arm around my shoulders. "You look like you need to eat too."

"What's that supposed to mean?" I was beginning to get my nerve back.

He removed his arm. "Nothing. I'm just concerned about you."

"If you're so concerned, then get me into my house."

"Don't worry, Honey. I can open our door."

"*My* door." I was starting to grind my teeth.

Without another word, Holy pulled a set of lock picks from his pocket and set about unlocking my door. Brimley had confiscated my picks as burglary tools.

I said, "You just happen to be traveling with those?"

"I saw the eviction notice earlier and thought you might need my help."

I sighed. I was too tired to fight, even with Holy.

In two seconds, we were inside.

Murphy pattered to the kitchen and sat in front of the refrigerator. He glanced at me, then leapt up and slapped the handle. The fridge popped open.

I scooped him up and gave him a big kiss. Nothing he did could anger me now. We were home.

Holy said, "What about me? I let you in."

With all the patience I could muster, I said, "I need food. I'm too weak and too broke to get any."

Holy called the bodega and ordered a slew of hot, cheesy sandwiches, fries, pastries, and drinks. He rolled off to pick them up.

I climbed the stairs and pulled off my clothes to take a hot shower. As I reached for the faucet, a hand grabbed my arm. I screamed and jerked away. I turned to see Charles Charles.

He was staring at my naked body, like a wolf eying a tasty carcass.

I yanked the shower curtain in front of me. "What are you doing here and where the hell have you been?"

"What kind of greeting is that for your man?"

"It's the kind of greeting I give people who desert me when I'm in danger. I thought you were going to protect me."

He smiled. "You want me to be your bodyguard? I could arrange that."

"I don't need a bodyguard now. How did Brimley find you?"

"He was looking for you. When he saw me, he recognized me from surveillance video from when I rescued you from jail, so he took me in."

Forgetting my nakedness I said, "How did you get out?"

"I had to break my cover. Once Brimley knew I was undercover, he let me go." Charles reached for the shower curtain.

I held tight and said, "Go downstairs and wait for me there."

"Are you sure you don't need me to watch the bathroom door?"

I glared at him. How I could want him and be pissed at him the same time, I didn't know.

I came downstairs all clean and fresh, to find Charles and Holy munching on my sandwiches and fries. "Hey! That's my food. I haven't eaten all day."

They stopped chewing, considered me for two seconds, then resumed their meals.

What could I do? I sat down and joined them. Holy had bought enough food for an army anyway.

After I had satisfied my voracious hunger, my mind returned to the matter at hand, my house. I didn't want to discuss my finances with Holy. After all, he's the reason I had no finances. I didn't want to talk to Charles about it either, although he must have seen the eviction notice on the door. He'd never want a relationship with someone with financial problems. I know I wouldn't. My pride prevented me from asking for help from either man.

What were my other possibilities? My father? God forbid. Malik had been arrested on my account. Lusty blamed me for Malik's arrest. *Wow, I'm like the kiss of death to friendship.* Still, I had to keep my home.

Someone rapped on the front door. *I haven't had this many visitors in a year.*

Lusty entered without waiting for my reply. She looked at each of us and then at the food. "Mmm, smells good. What's the celebration?"

I said, "This isn't a party. I haven't eaten all day so Holy brought me some food. Help yourself."

Both men grabbed extra fries and sandwiches before Lusty could reach the table.

Lusty smothered my loveseat with her ample butt and took a sandwich. Between bites she said, "Malik was asking about you. He's home now if you'd like to call him." Then her eyes settled on Charles. "What are you doing here?"

I almost gagged on my diet Slurpee. "He just dropped by to see if I was okay."

Lusty turned to me. "And are you?"

All eyes bore into me.

Holy spoke up. "She's evicted." Then he popped some fries into his big mouth.

My chin dropped to my chest.

Lusty said, "Don't be ashamed, Honey. I saw them put the notice on the door. I'll help you out."

Charles nodded. "I'll take care of it."

Lusty frowned. "As her friend, I will handle this matter."

Charles looked surprised. "I'm her friend too."

Lusty glared at him. "And just how close a friend are you?"

I stood up. "Alright. Party over. I'm really tired." I stretched and yawned. "Thank you for coming. I'll be in touch soon." I ushered everyone out the door, placed the remaining food in the fridge and went to bed.

The next morning, I wiped the crust out of my eyes and tried to roll over, but Murphy's fat back was adhered to my butt. My only option was to get out of bed. I shuffled to the bathroom and stared in the mirror. As the night's fog lifted from my brain, I remembered that I was standing in a house that no longer belonged to me.

My criminal career had been expunged, leaving me homeless, poor, and tired. After a shower, I fed Murphy and then opened the fridge to see what was left for breakfast. A forlorn half of a ham sandwich, some fries and a melted diet cherry Slurpee sat on the top shelf. What the Hell? Such is my life.

A ROCKY RECOVERY

As I chewed my sandwich, I tried to work out my next steps. I looked around. I'd sold everything I didn't need long ago, except my shoes, of course. I trudged upstairs to my closet and stared at my stilettos. I must have stood at the closet door for twenty minutes when I heard my doorbell.

I opened the door to see Malik.

"Can I come in?" He had my eviction notice in his hand. "I didn't think you'd want this on the door."

We settled in the living room. Throw pillows and cushions were still displaced from last night's gathering.

I said, "Malik, I'm so sorry about your arrest and all the other trouble I've caused you."

Malik shrugged. "I offered to help you and I'm good with that. Brimley expunged the arrest. It won't affect my academic record."

"Why are you here?"

"Aunt Lusty called me. I wanted to know if I could help in some way."

"How? You're as broke as I am."

"I can offer you a place to live." His eyes were gentle and kind. He laid his muscular arm around my shoulders, and I sank into his warmth.

Malik offered the safety and protection I'd needed for eons. I could have stayed there forever if the doorbell hadn't rung again. I stayed one more luxurious moment and then opened the door.

Lusty stood, hands on meaty hips. "Hey, Sweetie, can I come in?" She spotted Malik and burst out in a big grin. "Well, things are looking up." She waddled across the room and hugged Malik before settling into my loveseat. "I want to help, Rocky."

I said, "I can take care of this myself."

Lusty held up a bejeweled hand. "As one independent woman to another, let me tell you I have been in some tough situations. I know what it's like to be fiercely independent."

"It's not that..."

"Yes, it is. Don't let your pride get in the way of your future."

She was right. I needed help and for all my bravado, I was about to be homeless.

Malik said, "Aunt Lusty's right."

"Now you're double-teaming me. Did you two plan this overnight?"

Before they could answer, the doorbell rang again. Malik let Holy in.

Holy had two armfuls of real breakfast food and coffee. My mouth watered at the smell of greasy, cheesy egg sandwiches.

All conversation stopped as we eyed the bags. Holy plopped down on the couch between me and Malik. In two minutes, food was being consumed like we'd never eaten before.

Between bites, Holy said, "Let me help you. I know you don't want me in your life, but you need help now."

I said, "What is this, an intervention?"

Holy wiped his mouth with the back of his hand. "I'm serious. I care about you. I'll pay your back mortgage so you can get back on your feet."

I opened my mouth to respond, and a loud rap rattled the front door.

Holy jumped up. "I'll get it."

"What the hell are you doing here?" My father glared at Holy. Then he surveyed the breakfast club in the living room with an expression that said, "What the hell?" When he'd taken it all in, he said, "Where have you been, Raquel? I've been calling you for two days." He strode over to me and hugged me to his chest.

When he released me, I looked into his red-rimmed eyes. "I'm fine, Dad."

"What's this I hear about you being arrested and mixed up in murders? I've been worried sick. And why are all these people here so early in the morning?"

Everyone stopped eating and stared at him. I shot them a warning glance. My dad was the last person I wanted to know about my situation.

Another spirit entered the house. Charles Charles stood serenely in the foyer.

I broke out in a genuine grin.

Lusty scowled.

Malik stood.

Charles said, "I want to help."

Did someone send out an all-points bulletin?

Dad said, "Help what?"

While Dad faced Charles, I shook my head and waved my hands.

Charles caught my frantic signal and said, "Help with breakfast." He sat down and grabbed a bear claw.

Dad stood in the middle of the living room and scratched his head.

One more voice at the door. "Hello?" Brimley filled the room.

Could my life get any more complicated? I said, "Good morning, Detective."

Brimley said, "I received a notice that you were evicted. You don't look evicted to me."

Dad said, "That's it. You're moving back with me. I come over here to find you, just released from jail and partying in a house you no longer own." He glanced around the room. "You've surrounded yourself with this cast of characters. Girl, you've gotten way out of control."

"Dad, I'm good, really. These are my friends. They care about me, and I'll be fine."

Everyone stopped and gazed at me. I thought I saw a tear in Lusty's eye."

She said, "That's right Mr. Rhodes. We love Rocky."

At that Holy, Malik and Charles all stood and said, "Yeah." Then they eyed each other in a way I couldn't interpret but felt uncomfortable just the same.

Lusty pushed her girth out of her seat, took Dad's arm and led him into the foyer. Our eyes followed them in astonished silence. Lusty peeped over her shoulder and said, "Carry on."

We resumed our chatter, but I tried to eavesdrop. I inched closer to the foyer and listened.

Lusty said, "Mr. Rhodes, you're treating Rocky like a child. She is a capable, self-reliant woman and getting stronger every day."

Dad said, "You call getting arrested and evicted capable? She needs me to take care of her."

Lusty took Dad's hand. "Look around. Rocky has a strong support system. She is loved. And trust me, this experience has matured her more than returning home with you ever would. Rocky will never be a little girl again, but she can be a loving daughter, if you let her come to you."

Dad's expression softened. He said, "My friend tells me I can be a little spicy at times."

I sucked in a breath and scooted back into the group.

Dad and Lusty continued to talk. Dad's demeanor went from aggressive to soft in two minutes. His shoulders sagged and he glanced my way.

Brimley pulled a large envelope from his pocket and handed it to me. "What's this?"

"It's the reward paperwork." Brimley grinned.

"I get money?"

Brimley said, "As you so aptly stated, you led us to the real killer. And Mrs. Depew is still responsible for paying the reward regardless of her incarceration. And you'll be happy to know that Mr. Depew's will left provisions for Ernest's mother. She can stay in her nursing home."

I let out a giggle and did a little jig in the middle of the room.

Brimley pointed to the envelope and said, "If I were you, I'd fill that out asap before she remembers to rescind it."

"I'll bring it to you this afternoon."

When Brimley left, I explained the $10,000 reward to my dad, leaving him no excuse to attempt to rescue me. "Dad, I'm sorry I worried you. I'll do my best to be a good daughter. In fact, I think we should have dinner together more often, maybe even monthly. What do you think?" I had to shove those words out of my mouth. I hoped I could keep that promise.

Dad smiled and nodded. He surprised me with a kiss on the cheek and left.

I watched from the window as Dad sat in his car, holding the steering wheel and taking deep breaths. After a few minutes, he wiped his eyes and drove off.

I pulled Lusty aside and said, "What did you say to my dad? I've never seen him calm down so fast. What's your secret?"

Lusty shrugged. "I know how to talk to men. I just explained you're a grown, independent woman and he needs to respect that." She gave me an enigmatic smile.

I didn't believe a word she said but I accepted her help with gratitude.

Lusty had *work* to do and toddled home.

That left Holy, Malik and Charles. Each was wedged in his seat, refusing to leave me alone with the others. They stared each other down in total silence. *This was going to be interesting.*

I called Holy to the door. He gave the other guys a haughty smile, wiped his mouth, straightened his collar, and strode to the door. He wrapped his arm around my waist and kissed me on the cheek, leaving a bit of bacon.

We strolled out to the porch. I said, "Goodbye, Holy. Thanks for the food, and for the friendship."

His mouth dropped open. "What? What about those guys? Don't they have to go too?"

"Don't worry. They will."

With slumped shoulders, he got in his truck and left.

I glanced into the living room. Malik was glaring at Charles. Charles sat there with a smug smile. They sat opposite each other, each sprawled in a power position taking up as much space as possible. At that moment, I loved them both.

Malik was the sweetest, most protective guy I knew. I could stay in his arms forever. Charles was a sexy, mysterious stranger who I lusted after with a ferocity I hadn't felt in years. *What do you say, God? Can I have them both?* I didn't think his answer would be 'yes.' I let my selfish side win me over.

I entered the room and said, "Okay guys. You should go now. I have paperwork to fill out."

They hesitated.

"Now, please. I will be in touch."

Malik said, "I know you will." He beamed a glistening smile. "We have work to do...together." He gave Charles a triumphant look.

Charles rose, took my arm, and led me to the porch. He said, "Just so you know, the FTC will be trying Mrs. Depew for Internet fraud once her murder trials are over. She'll never get out of jail."

I released a deep breath.

Charles smiled and pulled me close. "I keep telling you, I've got your back." He cocked his head toward Malik. "He is just a friend, right?"

I said, "Do you doubt me?" I hoped I sounded convincing.

He brushed my ear with a kiss that made me tingly all over. "I'll call you." I said, "When?"

"As soon as I'm back from my next assignment. You'll never know when I'll pop up so behave yourself." He looked toward the living room and back at me. Then he slid into his BMW and drove off.

Malik strolled out onto the porch, grinning and waved at Charles as he left. He turned to me and said, "I've got good news. My uncles reached out to me. They found out what my mother did and restored my money. They want to reconnect even if I never talk to my mother again. They understand. I really miss them. I felt the love right through the phone. I have family again."

Malik's eyes misted and so did mine.

I stepped back from Malik and said, "Thank you for everything, Malik."

"You really want me to go?" He pulled me close and kissed me with a softness, I melted into.

I didn't want him to leave, but I needed to think. It took all my strength to send him away. "I'll call you tomorrow."

"Okay Sugar."

The Escalade disappeared. I stood on the porch and daydreamed about the kisses I received from two very different men. I desired both. I fantasized for five minutes. Then I remembered I would get ten grand for filling out a few papers.

TWENTY-FIVE

Weeks later, the sun streamed through my kitchen windows. My coffee steamed a satisfying aroma, and my egg sandwich was perfectly cheesy. Murphy smacked as he chomped on gourmet cat food, a treat made possible from the reward money.

I couldn't remember the last time I lived in such peace. My mortgage was paid up to date. I actually had food in my fridge, even if it was take-out. I had new business cards, minus my home address. Best of all, I had plans to go shoe shopping today. Life was good in Paradise.

I grinned as I recalled the look on Hartness' face when I handed him full payment for my back mortgage. I could have paid online but Shitty Kitty convinced me I needed to see his face. I slapped a cashier's check on Hartness' desk, as he threatened another citizen on the phone.

He slammed the receiver down and released the tormented soul. Then, he examined the check closely. He glared at me.

I said, "All paid up. Also, I invite you to check my bank account."

Hartness tapped a few keys and his smug demeanor vanished.

I leaned on his desk. "As you can see, I have enough funds to pay my mortgage for some time. No more blackmail for you."

Hartness regained his composure. He leaned back in his swivel chair and eyed me. He said, "I'm not worried. People like you never stay flush long. You'll get behind again and this time, I won't stop your conviction no matter how much you pay me on the side. I won't offer you a way out."

I said, "Won't you miss the extra pocket money?"

Hartness grimaced and shook his head. "I've got lots of people on the hook. They'll pay anything I ask to keep their homes. Like I told you, my pockets will always be lined with cash." He picked up the cashier's check and said, "Get out."

Detective Brimley and I passed each other at the door.

We nodded and smiled.

Through the large front windows, I watched Brimley stride up to Hartness and flash his badge. I ducked into a black van around the corner.

There, a uniformed officer removed the microphone from my shirt. This time Kitty had the right idea.

Later that evening, Brimley called with an update. He said, "As soon as we brought Hartness in, he called his lawyer, Harry Sunshine."

I said, "It makes sense. They have the same morals. I didn't realize they knew each other."

Brimley said, "More than that. They've preyed on people together for years. Hartness blackmails poor people and puts them into foreclosure. He passes his victims' names to Sunshine. Then, Sunshine swoops in and offers to stop the proceedings for a fee. Between them, they bleed people dry. Their clients borrow from friends and family until they run out of options. In the end, they lose everything. I've contacted the district attorney. She'll prosecute both Hartness and Sunshine."

I grinned so hard my cheeks hurt. "That's great!"

Brimley said, "You know, you weren't the first person to contact us about Hartness."

I said, "Really? Who?"

Brimley said, "A businessman named Ferdinand. Hartness and Sunshine pulled their act on him. Then, Hartness threatened to take ownership of the guy's business. Ferdinand wouldn't stand for it. He refused to give up a business he'd built for years. We couldn't prosecute because Ferdinand didn't have hard evidence we could present."

No need to tell Brimley about my connection to Ferdinand. Why complicate matters? My relationship with Ferdinand had morphed from conflict to gratitude to friendship. I still had questions though.

I now know why he pushed his clerks to sell his crappy merchandise. Hartness had been squeezing him. Also, I now understood why Ferdinand tried to help me take Hartness down. I don't know if he had sympathy for me or just wanted his own revenge. Either way, I was grateful for his support when my back was against the wall.

Ferdinand's Pharmacy had started making money. The merchandise was still shoddy, but people could find what they wanted.

I convinced Ferdinand to stop buying stolen merchandise from Freddy the Fence.

He agreed he needed no more trouble in his life. Ferdinand replaced the light bulbs and mopped the floors. He was able to hire a full-time clerk with retail experience.

The pharmacist quit so Ferdinand closed the pharmacy. He expanded the area to hold all the snacks and food items. No more chocolate mixed in with fake poop. He hung a banner over the area that said Ferdinand's Food Emporium. I wouldn't eat there, but it looked inviting.

I resigned my position at the pharmacy. Retail didn't suit my personality. I had a few squabbles with crabby customers and trouble navigating the register. I offered to stop in from time to time with organizational tips and product suggestions. We both liked that arrangement.

I said, "What's going to happen to Mrs. Depew now?"

Brimley said, "She's been arraigned on murder charges for both her husband and Ernest. Of course, Mrs. Depew pled not guilty. We exhumed Mr. Depew. The medical examiner found a large dose of Benzodiazepine in his system. Apparently, Mrs. Depew had stockpiled her pills for the occasion."

I said, "Can she get bail?" The thought of Mrs. Depew freely roaming through Newark would keep me up nights.

Brimley said, "She tried but we froze her assets. The FTC is charging her with fraud. She killed the only people who could have helped her. The judge had no choice but to keep her in jail until her trial."

I released a deep breath.

Brimley said, "And get this. Mrs. Depew tried to hire Harry Sunshine to defend her."

I laughed. "He won't help her. He's all about the cash and now she doesn't have any."

Brimley said, "That's right. Besides Sunshine has his own troubles now. Don't worry. With all the evidence we have against her, Mrs. Depew will live her life out behind bars." Brimley hung up with a promise to keep me apprised of the trial date.

My phone purred again, and I picked up Holy's call. Yes, I changed his fire alarm ringtone to match my friends'. As aggravating as Holy could be, he had stuck with me even under threat of arrest. After all, we could have both ended up in jail. I don't think he had any idea of the danger surrounding us. Holy ambled through life, grinning while slings and arrows barely missed him.

Holy said, "I called to see if you needed anything. Food, company?"

"No but thank you. You've called every day for weeks with the same question. I keep telling you I'm fine, better than fine. I'm happy."

Holy said, "I read persistence pays off in romance."

For a brief second, I considered resetting his alarm ringtone. I said, "Holy, we will never have romance again, but you will always be my friend." Before he could reply, I said, "Goodbye." I knew he wouldn't get the message. His mind didn't work that way. He saw us as a couple forever.

A knock and a "Woohoo" at the door interrupted my thoughts.

Lusty flounced into my kitchen, poured a cup of coffee and grabbed a donut hole out of my box of fifty. "You sure smile a lot these days."

I took another steamy gulp. "Everything's going my way for a change. I couldn't be happier."

"Oh, couldn't you?"

"What do you mean?"

Lusty set her mug on the table. "Well, you could add romance to your life." She grinned and raised her eyebrows. "I know someone who's perfect for you."

I didn't know what to say. After all, Malik was a comfortable fit and who knew when I'd see Charles again. He had probably jetted off to another secret mission. I finished my sandwich without comment.

Lusty lowered her gaze. "In truth, I'm happy for you. You have two men loving you. I've never had such a yummy choice. You're a lucky girl and I care enough about you to wish you happiness with whomever you choose."

I sat in stunned silence for a moment. Then I said, "Thank you, Lusty. I love you too."

Lusty changed the subject in the awkward silence. "Now, how about some work? You know that reward money won't last forever. I don't have any referrals right now."

I leaned back and rubbed my full tummy. "I've been spreading my cards around and had some posters made. Bodega Man even let me put one up in his store. I'm sure to get some hits soon."

"Well, if you don't want my help, I understand." Lusty dropped a half a donut hole onto her napkin and brushed the powdered sugar off her hands.

"I'll still need you. After all, you give the best referrals. I'll give you a percentage of my jobs. How would you like to be a part of my team?"

"Oh, you don't have to do that."

"This should mean more money for Malik too."

Lusty brightened and popped the rest of the donut into her mouth.

The doorbell rang and I answered it to find the next love of my life smiling down at me. I leaned into his bear hug and let his kiss warm my nether regions.

Lusty called from the kitchen, "Who's at the door?"

Everything fell into place when, in the background, my phone rang.

Lusty answered, "Rocky Recoveries."